The
Monks Hood
Murders

Karen Baugh
MENUHIN

Front cover: An old Monastery courtyard garden,
with flowers, statue and fountain. / Old Monastery
Garden Courtyard By Larry Jacobsen

First paperback and ebook edition August 2020

ISBN: 978-1-9162947-4-5

To Philip & Trudi Palin
With love.

CHAPTER 1

April 1922

'I must inform you, sir, there is a ghost in the garden.'

'No, there isn't.' I didn't look up from the magazine I was reading.

'I have the word of Cook that there is, sir.' Greggs' tone deepened to better stress the seriousness of the situation. 'She is withholding the tea tray until the matter has been investigated.'

I sighed. I was sitting with my feet up in my library, having spent most of the morning in the attic chasing a bat. Spring had arrived, and with it, spring cleaning. The maids, who came twice a week, had decided to start at the top of the house. Normally, I would be outdoors during their incursions, but a clammy mist had descended on the day and driven me and my little dog, Mr Fogg, back inside. Having spent a fruitless hour hunting said bat, I'd come down empty-handed and sneezing from the dust. I'd been looking forward to tea and cake by the fireside and perusing the latest news on field sports and fishing.

'Where's Tommy Jenkins?' I asked. Young Tommy was our boot boy and perfectly capable of searching the gardens for imaginary spectres.

'You sent him to the village, sir, to pay the charge on the letter.'

'Ah, yes.' That gave me pause. The postman had left information that a letter 'stuck all over with foreign stamps' was being held at the post office. Apparently there was duty to pay on exotic missives. I didn't see why the postman couldn't have brought it to my home so I could pay the Government-sponsored extortion myself. 'Hasn't he returned yet?'

'I'm afraid not, sir.' He cleared his throat. 'Cook has baked a Simnel cake.'

'Oh?' I eyed him.

'The cake is becoming cold, sir.' He gazed upwards, chins wobbling above his stiff collar, hands held together over his butlering waistcoat. A sure sign of perturbation in my old retainer, who, no doubt, had been deprived of his tea and cake, too.

I tossed the magazine aside. 'Where exactly is this ghost supposed to be?'

'Cook told me she saw it glide past the kitchen window,' he intoned.

'Are you sure it wasn't the gardener?'

'It is his day off, sir.'

'Someone with a sheet, playing the fool, then?'

'She said it was black, sir. Like Death without his scythe.'

'Right.' I stood up. 'Tell her I'm going outside and the tea and cake had better be here when I get back.' That was a bit of bluster actually, because Cook would do precisely as she saw fit.

I shrugged my shooting jacket over my tweeds and walked out into the murk alone. Foggy had refused to join me, having already experienced the damp chill swathing my old house, The Manor at Ashton Steeple. There was nothing to see, of course – not that I could see anything more than a couple of feet in front of me. I strolled around with hands in pockets, wondering why Cook, the most common-sensical person I'd ever met, had suddenly started spotting ghosts. Perhaps she was going gaga, which would cause all sorts of problems. Not least the lack of excellence in the kitchen.

Winter had been lengthy, freezing and frequently blanketed with snow. Spring had struggled to leap into bloom and remained soggy and wet for the most part. I wandered past magnolia trees and cherry blossom drooping under the weight of silver-hued droplets. The grass lay sodden beneath my feet, beads of moisture clung to glistening cobwebs, and a trailing rose-briar brushed my hair to comb it with dew. Mist had rendered the garden ghostly, trees and arbours reduced to pale traceries stitched in shades of gossamer grey.

My mind was far from the fog, it was on the letter held by the damned post office. The news had given my heart a lift. It must be from my girlfriend, Persi Carruthers. Actually… she might not be my girlfriend. I'd last seen her in the sun-drenched city of Damascus where she'd been torn between me and her idiot ex-fiancé. But, she'd decided on me – well I was pretty certain she had. She'd told me she would write, and I'd been waiting for weeks and weeks, and now I was wondering if she'd changed her mind or…

A wraith glided across the path ahead of me.

That stopped me in my footsteps. It was a shadow, dark and indistinct, it passed through the trellis archway and into the walled garden beyond. The hairs rose on the back of my neck. I took my hands out of my pockets and broke into a run.

The spectre, or whatever it was, had vanished into the mist, but I knew the old gate at the other end of the walled garden was jammed shut and he'd have the devil of a job getting through it. I raced down the path, past raised beds of berry bushes and bare earth to find nothing at all at the end. I turned, looking this way and that, when a voice called softly from behind a gnarled crab-apple tree.

'Good day.'

'What?' I froze.

'I wish you good day.' He came slowly towards me, a drifting shade, muted and blurred.

'I…erm, greetings. What are you doing in…in.' I stuttered to a halt as he approached.

'Major Heathcliff Lennox?' The apparition spoke quietly. His shape took form, he wore a sort of coat, or cloak…actually Cook was right, he did look awfully like Death without a scythe.

4

'Oh, right, well that's me. Why... I mean... who are you?'

He came closer and suddenly emerged from the fog, garbed in black cassock and cowl. He was a monk!

'I'm Father Ambrose.' He pushed his hood back and smiled gently. 'I'm the Abbot of Monks Hood Abbey.'

'Ah, um, well. Excellent. Would you um...care for some tea?' I stuttered.

He nodded, so I led him back to the house, wondering why an Abbot had taken to lurking in my garden.

Fogg greeted us with a woof as Greggs opened the front door. The little dog kept his wits better than my butler, who stood open-mouthed in the hallway, letting the damp air into the place.

'Refreshments,' I hissed to him.

'Sir?'

'For our guest.'

'Yes, sir.' He dithered, gaped again and then tottered off in the direction of the kitchen.

I settled the unexpected visitor into a wing chair in the library, it being cosy and warm from the blazing fire. The Abbot's thick cassock steamed gently in the heat, adding to the comfortable fug in the oak panelled room.

He looked around appreciatively. 'How delightful. I do feel quite at home surrounded by books,' he said, his voice warm with enthusiasm.

'I haven't read them all,' I confessed.

He smiled and confided, 'I haven't read all of mine, either.'

Greggs entered carrying a tray laden with silver teapot, jug, cups, sugar bowl and the cake.

'Tea?' I offered.

'Thank you, dear boy.' Father Ambrose smiled. He had the look of an elderly professor; round cheeks, a fuzz of white hair, faded brown-eyes and an air of innocence.

'And cake?' I asked.

Greggs was poised with a knife over the Simnel cake. I'd noted all the usual goodies; cherries, sultanas, spices and a thick marzipan topping.

'Oh…' His face lit up before he hesitated. 'But I must not. I eat with the Brothers and we have rules, you see.'

'Ah, right. Well, I'll forgo too,' I said out of good manners, although it was a wrench. I suppose monks must do a lot of abstaining.

'You must wonder why I am here.' He lifted his cup with both hands.

'Umm, yes,' I admitted.

'My wife advised me to seek you out,' he said, as though this were entirely normal.

Greggs and I exchanged glances across the length of hearth-rug, his hangdog eyes growing rounder. We waited for further revelations, but the monk sipped his tea, pausing now and then to glance about at my ancient desk, threadbare chairs and dingy old paintings. Greggs fidgeted with napkins and whatnots, but as nothing more was said he had to go off without a hint. No doubt he would speculate the strange events with Cook and the maids around the kitchen table.

'I didn't think monks had wives, actually,' I said, breaking the silence.

'You are quite correct.' He spoke shyly. 'When I thought to enter the monastic life, my wife agreed to lay aside our wedlock. We were very young at the time.'

'Oh,' there wasn't much I could say to that. 'But why did she advise you to come to me? And who is she?'

'Lady Maitland,' he replied. 'I believe you met her in...'

'Damascus. Good Lord!' That made me sit up. Lady Maitland had made a very distinct impression, and none of us who'd been with her in Damascus would ever forget it. 'So...erm, you're Lord Maitland?'

'I *was* Lord Maitland. Oh! I suppose I still am!' He chuckled as if surprised. 'I think of myself as Father Ambrose now, Abbot of Monks Hood Abbey. It is in Calderstone, in Yorkshire, have you been there?' His face lit up at mention of the place.

'No, I'm afraid not.' I glanced at the Simnel cake on the table where Greggs had left it. Fogg's gaze followed mine.

'Ah, well, it is rather remote. Actually, I think that was why they gave it to me.' He explained. 'But I have surprised them. Brother Paul and I have transformed the Abbey. We've rebuilt it! They didn't expect that.'

'Jolly good.' I'd rather taken a liking to the old fellow.

'But now...well, dear boy, I have a terrible predicament... My wife said you may... you may...' His words puttered out.

'I may... what?' I tried prompting him.

His mouth opened and closed before he managed to reply. 'You may be able to save us, all of us, and the Abbey. It could bring utter ruination, but you mustn't mention it, not a word. It's imperative it remains a secret.'

'Ruination?' I repeated, thinking that it all sounded rather dramatic. 'How?'

'It was... it was. Oh, I am in a fluster. I had to seek peace in your garden, you see. I haven't left the Abbey in such a long time and the train was such a hustle and bustle, and after the events of the past two weeks. Well, it really was too much.'

'I see,' I said, although I didn't see at all. 'You came here because something is going to bring ruination, but it's a secret?'

'Yes, indeed.' His voice quavered. 'And to ask for your help.'

'Perhaps you could enlighten me?'

'Of course, dear boy, I am trying. It began with the death of our benefactor, Sir Clarence Calderstone. He had a dreadful accident and I attended him. As he lay dying on his bed, he made his confession. Shocking, quite, quite shocking.' His hands began to tremble.

I took the cup and saucer from him to place on the tray and waited, but he seemed to have lapsed into a daze. Tubbs, my rotund black cat, had been asleep among the leather-bound tomes on top of the highest book case. He woke, hopped down the oaken shelves on silent paws and crept across the carpet, as cats do, before finally making a leap for the knots on the end of Father Ambrose's cincture.

That snapped the Abbot out of his trance. He smiled as he caught hold of the little cat and held him up to stare him in the face.

'You naughty creature,' he remonstrated gently, Tubbs gazed back, entirely unrepentant as usual.

'Mister Tubbs,' I informed him. 'He's a bit of a reprobate, I'm afraid.'

'I am most fond of cats. Such fragile little souls, yet they brave the world with fortitude and curiosity.' He placed Tubbs on his lap, who began to knead the thick woven fabric of the Abbot's black cassock.

'You were going to tell me…' I tried again but was interrupted by the loud clang of the doorbell.

Greggs entered, rather flustered. 'Sir, it's Chief Inspector Swift…I mean, ex-Chief…'

'Lennox?' I heard a voice call out.

'Swift! What on earth are you doing here?'

He walked in as I leapt to my feet. Foggy jumped about, barking with excitement.

'We have to go to Yorkshire,' Swift ordered, brushing moisture from his trench coat. 'Lady Maitland rang me. She demanded that I go to see her in London. I arrived at her office, saw her for five damn minutes, she said something about Monks Hood Abbey then ordered me straight here. She really is the limit! Absolutely infuriating…' He came to an abrupt halt as he spotted our visitor.

'Swift!' I had been trying to shut him up, but he was his usual hasty self. 'This is Father Ambrose, the Abbot of Monks Hood Abbey in Calderstone. Lady Maitland is his wife.'

Swift looked from one to the other of us. 'Lady Maitland? What? You mean... I thought monks didn't...'

'Indeed, in general, that is the case.' Father Ambrose rose to his feet while cradling a sleepy Tubbs. 'How delightful to meet you, Chief Inspector.'

'But...' Swift spluttered then pulled himself together. He offered a neat bow of the head. 'I'm very pleased to meet you, Father Ambrose and I, um, I apologise for my language.'

'Swift,' I told him. 'Sit down, will you.'

'I'm doing it, Lennox.' He went to fetch a chair from beside my desk and tugged up the crease of his brown trousers before settling down before the fire.

'Greggs, we need more tea.' I turned to my butler.

'Indeed, sir.' He lowered his voice. 'Would a drop of whiskey in the pot be appropriate?'

'Excellent idea!' I brightened then glanced at our visitor. 'Um, no, better not. Save it for later, there's a good chap.'

He gathered the tray and left, probably to have a quick dram himself; the old soldier had a fondness for good Irish whiskey.

Swift was still bearish. 'Lady Maitland ordered me to come and fetch you, Lennox. She said some appalling event had occurred and we had to go to the aid of Father Ambrose...' He turned toward the Abbot. 'But you are here already, sir, and I don't quite understand...'

Father Ambrose's cheeks flushed pink. 'Oh dear, it is quite my fault. I had written to her, you see, when it happened. I asked for her advice and she replied that I should seek you out. I wrote in return, reminding her that I could not leave the Abbey and...' He paused, struggling for words before continuing. 'But then... after... well, I simply had to come. We sent a telegram to my wife straight away, but it appears it was too late.'

'Right. Well there you are then, Swift,' I said, pleased we'd cleared that up.

'Lady Maitland mentioned Sir Clarence Calderstone.' Swift fixed me with his sharp gaze.

'He's dead,' I told him.

He didn't bat an eyelid. 'Murdered?'

'No, he confessed his sins. Apparently it could mean the end of everything.'

Swift turned to Father Ambrose. 'The end of what, sir?'

'The Abbey, our work... all of it,' his voice faltered again.

'But it's a secret,' I added, by way of clarification.

'What is?'

'No idea,' I replied. 'But we're not to tell anyone.'

'That shouldn't be difficult,' Swift remarked dryly.

'I'm so sorry, dear boys,' Father Ambrose flustered. 'Do let me try to explain...'

CHAPTER 2

The Abbot raised his eyes toward the thin rays of light coming in from the window, or possibly Heaven, and began his tale.

'We live in the light of Christ by the Rule of Saint Benedict.' He intoned the words almost as if in prayer. 'Our days are devoted to serving the Lord. *Pax, ora et labora;* the sacred duty of our hours and hearts.' He clasped his hands together, his eyes lowered.

Greggs came in almost on tiptoe. He put down the tray and waited in solemn silence.

The Abbot spied him. 'More tea?'

'Indeed, sir.' Greggs bowed.

'How marvellous.' A smile hovered on the monk's lips, he seemed to have found comfort in his recitation.

Greggs poured a cup and reverentially handed it over. He'd found my late mother's best china, dusted it off and now offered a delicate floral platter, carefully arranged with slices of cake.

Father Ambrose vacillated. 'Oh, the temptation.'

'It is Lenten Simnel cake, sir,' Greggs coaxed.

'Ah, well, perhaps just this once…' he indicated a slender slice. Greggs carefully manoeuvred it onto a plate and deposited it, along with a polished silver fork and pristine white napkin, on the table at the Abbot's elbow.

Swift and I were given even thinner slices, in deference to our guest. Greggs went off while we all ate in silence. I dropped a titbit to Foggy at our feet and saw Swift do the same.

Father Ambrose started again. 'When I arrived at the Abbey… oh, it must be twenty five years ago now… the walls were tumbled and the Brothers were few.' He shook his head at the memory.

'How did Sir Clarence Calderstone fit into this?' Swift had pulled out his notebook.

'Oh these explanations are rather difficult. The Brethren had done what they could before my arrival, but they were without resources.' He paused, his lips moving silently as though searching for words. 'Then Sir Clarence Calderstone came to me, saying he was willing to offer support. His family had been patrons of the Abbey in the past and he explained he wanted to continue the old tradition. I admit, I was most surprised,' he leaned forward and lowered his voice, 'he had been considered quite the Casanova. The Calderstones were always regarded as an intemperate family, but Clarence swore to me that he had given up his *adventures* and wanted to reaffirm his faith, and I believed him.'

'He was your financial saviour,' I stated.

'He was, his donations made our repairs possible and our small community grew. Our elder brethren once again taught their skills to the novices.' He paused and attempted another smile. 'You see, we uphold the Benedictine traditions; we illustrate manuscripts and tend our physic gardens, just as our Brothers have done for centuries before us.'

Swift tried again to bring him to the point. 'But what did Clarence do to cause you anguish, sir?'

'He…he…' He puttered out of words again.

I frowned at Swift for his hastiness. 'Father Ambrose, perhaps you could tell us what happened to Clarence?'

'Yes, I do believe I could.' His voice gathered strength. 'He was injured on the hunting field. He had only just returned from, now let me see, I think it was Switzerland, but it may have been Italy.' Wrinkles formed on his forehead. 'This past winter has been hard, even harder than usual, but, we had a break from the frost and snow and the Hunt decided to make a day of it. Clarence had barely arrived, but he declared he would borrow a horse and join them.'

'Oh, it was such a sight…' His tone wistful. 'Well, off they went under a bright sky; it was the perfect day for a gallop. Some time later, a commotion was heard at our gates. The hunt-master had arrived with a group of riders calling my name. Clarence had been thrown from his horse and was asking for me, they said it was serious. Of course I went immediately to Calderstone Hall. Doctor Wexford was ministering to him and Clarence

14

was still conscious, but I could see he was near to death. He pleaded to make his confession and that was when he admitted his terrible sin...'

We waited for him to compose himself. Foggy had fallen asleep by the warmth of the fire and snored in the silence.

'Are you able to tell us what Clarence confessed?' I prompted.

'I cannot, no, no, it is not permitted. You see, Clarence was a Catholic and he feared what was to come. After he made his confession, he expected the grant of absolution. I tried to explain that atonement is a state of mind, not the washing away of sins, and that he had caused us such distress. His confession was a shock, a terrible...' He paused to pull himself together. 'Clarence clutched my hand and said there was a book, it was of great value and the worth would come to the Abbey, it was his act of reparation.' He shook his head, the light catching his halo of white hair. 'I refused him again but he pleaded with me, saying the book would save lives, it was a Codex – an ancient book of herbal medicines. He said he'd brought it for us and he pressed a key into my hands, it was the key to his strongbox. He begged me to save his soul and grant him absolution.' He lowered his head and let out a long sigh. 'And so I gave him his wish.'

'He wasn't the first who thought he could buy his way into Heaven,' Swift commented.

'No,' the Abbot raised his eyes from Tubbs on his lap. 'I almost withheld absolution because his sin was so grave but that was wrong of me...' His voice trailed away again.

I wondered what Clarence had done, my mind skipped across a few ideas.

Swift asked, 'Did he say anything else before he died?'

'He was agitated, he mumbled "he will come" and "she must not have it". He was gasping for breath and barely coherent.'

'Who must not have it?' I asked.

'I'm afraid I do not know.' Weariness creased the old man's face.

'What of the book, was it in the strongbox?' Swift was chasing facts.

'It was.' He nodded. 'We found it, just as he had said. A medieval Codex of medicinal herbs. Brother Paul was with me, he said some of the recipes may be quite unknown to us today.'

'You took it to the monastery?' Swift was jotting a series of short notes.

'I'm afraid I did not.' His eyes closed momentarily. 'I realise now that it was quite silly of me, but after Clarence's appalling revelations I was utterly unnerved. I did not wish to bring the book into the Abbey and we thought it would be perfectly safe in the strong box. But then...'

Swift looked up and eyed him as closely as I did.

'Then...?' I asked.

'The complications began. You see, the Calderstones were the local landowners and Clarence was the last of them.'

'Is the Codex part of the Calderstone inheritance?' I asked, realising there was likely to be a battle brewing over the estate.

'I'm unsure…it's possible.' He stroked Tubbs again. 'I received a note from Mr Stephen Fenshaw. He works for Clarence's old solicitor, Humphrey Lawson, Fenshaw's actually his nephew. Well, Fenshaw informed me a letter had arrived from a gentleman in Switzerland. This Swiss stated that he had a legal interest in Clarence's estate.'

'What was it?' I asked, slightly confused over the plethora of solicitors.

'It wasn't explained,' Father Ambrose replied. 'He merely stated he had a claim.'

'And has this Swiss arrived?' Swift asked.

'No, but his was not the only foreign intervention. An Italian appeared for Clarence's funeral, she was… well, she was quite striking. There is a village next to the Abbey, the village of Calderstone, and all the villagers attended the service – it was at the Calderstone's own Chapel,' he added in explanation. 'This lady marched through the congregation to the very front of the church without a word. She looked as a bird-of-paradise would among sparrows.' He shook his head at the memory. 'Well, she remained until the coffin was carried out and then followed with head held high on teetering shoes. As you can imagine, there was much speculation as to who she was. After the interment she declared to Fenshaw and Lawson that she was Clarence's lawful wife. Everybody heard her, it caused such talk.'

'Good Lord,' I uttered. 'And nobody knew she existed?'

'No.' He shook his head. 'Clarence had never mentioned a word. It was extraordinary, although when I think of the…' He stuttered again to a halt.

'He didn't live in Calderstone then?' I tried to jolly him along.

'He spent almost all of his time on the Continent, he only returned once or twice a year. I had never given it a thought before now.'

'What's the lady's name?' Swift returned to the topic.

'The Contessa Mirabella Ferranti.' Father Ambrose pronounced it carefully. 'She insisted that she was entitled to her husband's estate and had come to claim it.'

'The entire estate?' I asked.

'Indeed.' Father Ambrose sighed. 'Lawson's wits are wandering and young Fenshaw now stands in his stead. Fenshaw told her she must follow the correct legal process. Then old Lawson interrupted and ordered her to prove it, which I thought very brave of him. She became quite impassioned and declared that she would return with her own lawyer.' His shoulders sagged. 'We watched with relief as she drove away, but then it occurred to me that she might try to take control of Calderstone Hall and I had left the Codex there. So Brother Paul and I went to retrieve it,' he looked up with consternation in his eyes. 'When we unlocked the strong box, the book was gone.'

'What! You mean stolen?' I exclaimed.

He sounded near to tears. 'Yes, it was so foolish of me, and now I realise it is the key to everything.' He tried to pull himself together. 'My wife thinks you are the men who can find it and I do hope you will, because... because... all may be lost.' He ended on a breathless note.

'Ah,' I uttered, thankful that he'd finally got to the point. 'Well, we'll do our best.'

Swift looked up from his writing, a frown to his forehead.

'Thank you.' The Abbot wobbled to his feet. 'Oh dear, I am quite fatigued. May I beg of you a quiet room in which to rest for a short while?'

'Of course,' I crossed to my desk and shook the bell.

Greggs arrived instantly, he can't have been much further away than the key hole.

'I have the guest room ready, sir.'

'How did you know that was why I rang?'

'I...um... Intuition, sir.' He didn't bat an eyelid, just turned to usher Father Ambrose towards the door.

'Greggs,' I called.

'Sir?'

'Packing required, old chap.'

He sighed. 'Very well, sir.'

CHAPTER 3

I tossed more logs onto the fire, then picked up the plate of remaining Simnel cake and offered a helping of the goodies to Swift. Fogg woke up and watched us with bright spaniel eyes.

'So, mysterious sins which must not be spoken,' I mused.

Swift pushed his notebook into his pocket. 'None of it makes sense. Why should the Codex be the key to everything?'

'The Abbot said all could be lost; 'utter ruination' or some such words.' I tried to decipher Father Ambrose's rambling account.

'He wants us to find the Codex to prevent disaster falling on the Abbey,' Swift stated. 'But he doesn't explain what the disaster is.'

'He can't. It's part of a confession.'

'Is it?' He sounded sceptical.

'Yes, he said so.'

Swift wasn't convinced. 'He's barely given us half the story.'

'What did Lady Maitland tell you?' I changed tack.

'Nothing,' he replied through bites of cake. 'I saw her at the crack of dawn this morning before I'd even had breakfast. All she did was order me to come and get you, then go to Monks Hood Abbey and report to the Abbot. I had to take the overnight train from Braeburn to London and now I've come here and you could have gone yourself. The Cotswolds is almost on the doorstep to London and I've been dragged from the Highlands to...'

'Nobody asked me to go to London,' I objected. 'I didn't know a thing about it until Father Ambrose arrived a bare hour ago. And you could just have easily said no.'

'What, to Lady Maitland?' He suddenly gave a wry smile.

I laughed and stretched my legs in front of the fire. Swift was ever a 'man on a mission', even when the mission made no sense. I thought he looked drawn, the angles of his face lean and sharp.

'How's Florence?' I asked. 'I thought she was due any minute.'

Lady Florence was Swift's wife and the cause of his new life at Braeburn Castle in the Scottish highlands.

'It's a month off yet.' A worried frown creased his brows. 'I didn't want to go anywhere before the birth, but she insisted.'

'Ah.' I polished off the cake.

'She's got it into her head that I miss being a detective. I keep telling her it's nonsense, but she can be very single-minded.' He looked askance at me. 'And that woman's come back. You remember her, the medium, Miss Fairchild.'

'Yes,' I muttered, recalling the lady from our adventures at Braeburn Castle last Halloween. 'She was rather...'

'Peculiar.' Swift was blunt. 'Anyway, she and Florence are great friends and now they're knitting together. So, I'm here, and we'd better get moving Lennox, because I don't want to be away from Braeburn for long.'

'We can't go until Father Ambrose is ready,' I reminded him.

'I didn't mean...' He was cut off.

'Sir! I've got it, I've got the letter!' Tommy Jenkins bounced in, waving a grubby looking envelope. Actually he was looking particularly grubby himself, with mud on his knees, a graze to his forehead and dark hair even more dishevelled than usual.

'What happened to you?' Swift asked as I took the proffered letter.

It was indeed 'covered all over with foreign stamps', some of them had camels on, which gave my heart a lurch. I rubbed my thumb over the imprinted seal then shoved it in my pocket for a spot of solitary reading later.

'Fell off me bike and had to walk home.' Tommy grinned. Despite being orphaned, he was a cheerful boy, given to scruffiness and escapades. He lived here at The Manor, with his aunt – my cook. I'd designated him boot boy to keep him occupied and put some pennies in his pocket. 'It's dead foggy out there, but it's liftin' in the village now. It was spooky goin' by the woods.'

'How did you fall off your bike,' I questioned, as the boy rattled on.

His face fell. 'Hit the kerb with a bang, sir.'

'Damage?' I asked taking a closer look at him.

'The chain come off, an' the tyre went flat. Mudguard's got bent as well, but it's nothin' as can't be fixed, sir.' He pushed his fringe back from his face with a grubby hand.

'Never mind the bike, are you all right?' Swift cut in.

'Aye, right as rain.' His grin reappeared. 'Aunty told me there's a monk here. She thought 'e was a ghost, but that's tommy-rot, there ain't no ghosts around or I'd have seen 'em.'

'Yes, but why did you hit the kerb, Tommy?' I asked again because I could see he was avoiding the question.

A blush spread across his freckles. 'Sally Hastings put her tongue out at me, sir. Right by the post office.'

'Ah,' I nodded. So young Tommy had noticed *girls*.

He perked up. 'Aunty says you're going off to Yorkshire to do some detecting. Can I come, sir? Can I? Please?' He was almost hopping. 'There's bound to be dead bodies, you're always finding them!'

'No,' I told him firmly. 'You have to go to school. And anyway, there aren't any bodies.'

'You mean there aren't any bodies – yet.' Swift added, then cracked a smile. 'Come on, young man. Let's go and mend this bike of yours.' He ruffled Tommy's hair and the lad skipped out of the room on the heels of the ex-Inspector.

I headed for the calm of my bedroom to pore over the letter in my pocket.

'Dear Heathcliff, or must I call you Lennox? I had hoped for a reply, but, so be it. If you would rather not continue as friends, or more, I do understand – well, I don't really, but I'm trying to.

We're leaving the Levant to travel to Egypt. The whole team has been invited to a dig in the Valley of Kings, it's all rather speculative, but quite fascinating. We will journey by boat to Alexandria before continuing by caravan to Cairo. From there, it is a trip down the Nile to Luxor.

This means I'll be incommunicado for a couple of weeks, but should you wish to contact me, and I hope you do, please write to me via the British Embassy in Cairo.

I remain your friend, with love, Persi. xxx'

What the devil...? I read her letter again. It was written with a neat hand in dark ink on blue paper, but I couldn't make head nor tail of it. Then it occurred to me that she must have already written, and the first letter hadn't made it. I read it once again, word by word, trying to decipher the message. '*...continue as friends, or more...*' she seemed to think I'd changed my mind.

Greggs entered as I knitted my brows.

'Sir, I'll complete your packing now.'

'Um, yes, but not the trunk, old chap. Too many people in the car. Carpet bag.'

He harrumphed and began unpacking the trunk, removing folded shirts and whatnots and placing them into the empty carpet bag. He seemed piqued.

'We'd better get a move on,' I reminded him. 'The Abbot's keen to leave.'

'I will not be coming, sir.'

'Greggs it's only Yorkshire, I'm hardly proposing a trip to the tropics.' He was always objecting to our excursions.

'I have prior commitments, sir.'

'What sort of commitments?' I eyed him narrowly.

'*Private* commitments, sir.'

'Oh.' I ran my fingers through my hair, assuming him to mean romantic entanglements. 'Well, can't it wait, old chap? We won't be away long.'

He pulled in his paunch and turned stuffy. 'I do not believe it can, sir.'

I have previously observed that the onset of spring can bring unlikely romances in its wake and Greggs was no exception. I hazarded a guess.

'It's not the new maid, is it?' The maids were from the village and usually consisted of two sturdy spinsters, but one had developed arthritis recently and sent a comely widow in her stead. I'd noticed Greggs had thrown a glad eye in her direction more than once.

He turned pink – I'd hit a nerve!

'She's already affianced, old chap,' I told him bluntly. 'It was mentioned in her letter of introduction.'

He deflated. 'Oh, really, sir?'

'Afraid so.' I tried to smooth the blow. 'A spot of fresh country air will do you the world of good, Greggs.'

'But, sir. I...'

'And I noticed you've let your role in the local theatre production slip recently.'

'Ah, that was a misunderstanding. The husband was really quite unreasonable and…' His vim suddenly wilted. 'But a monastery, sir?'

'It's in Yorkshire, Greggs, renowned for hearty food and excellent ale. Treat it as a sabbatical, a chance to let the heart heal, or whatever it does.'

He looked set to argue, but gave it up on a sigh and continued packing.

I returned to my desk and the missive I was trying to pen to Persi. I cudgelled my thoughts, nibbling the end of my pen. What should I say?

I read her letter again, she sounded disconsolate.

'Dear Persi, I believe your first letter didn't arrive. Of course I haven't changed my mind, have you? Write twice in case the next one gets lost too.'

I paused and read what I'd written. As love letters go it seemed lacking. I sighed, I wasn't the romantic sort, despite my ridiculous name. I added a ps. *I still love you and you can call me Heathcliff if you* must *want, xxx.*

I folded it, placed it in a thick brown envelope then stopped. Should I add more? But what? I had a signet ring, a token from our adventures in Damascus, I tugged it off my finger. Somewhere in a drawer I had some red sealing wax. It took ages to find. I lit a match and managed to melt a blob onto the envelope and push my ring into it. It made a neat impress of a galleon with a single sail and a cresting horse's head. I'd managed to drip quite a few red blobs onto the envelope too and it looked as if someone had bled all over it.

I sat back and looked at it, wondering what she would think when she read it. I'd said I'd go and find her, I promised actually. But then I remembered she was travelling, so I wouldn't be able to and she was in Egypt, which was a damn long way and... I realised I was making excuses. Was it all too fast? I'd been waiting and waiting for her reply, but now that I had it...

Greggs finished packing and turned to me. 'If you've finished the letter, sir, Tommy can run to the post office with it.'

'Um, not necessary, old chap.' I pushed it into my pocket. 'I'll send it off myself.'

'We cannot be sure there will be a post office near the monastery, sir.'

'Greggs, I'll send it when I'm ready.' I may have sounded rather sharp.

He went off downstairs in a bit of a huff.

I followed shortly after to find the hall bustling. Greggs, Swift and Tommy carried the luggage out to the car. Bags, basket, dog bowls and cat hamper, complete with cat, were ferried through the door. Father Ambrose waited beside the stairs looking anxious, his frizz of white hair almost on end.

Fogg was sitting on the bottom step watching the activity with ears cocked. I bent to scoop him up and tuck him under my arm.

'Right, come on,' I ordered and walked outside. The sun was emerging between pale clouds and a change of scenery was just the ticket.

The Bentley took a couple of cranks to fire up and she rattled and coughed as everyone climbed aboard.

Tommy ran up to me as I slipped into the driver's seat. 'Sir, was there a letter? You know, back to the one with them foreign stamps? I can go to the post office for you.'

'So you can see Sally Hastings again?' I teased him, then handed him a shilling. 'Here, have the mud guard fixed and buy Sally an ice-cream.'

'Thank you, sir!' He grinned as his cheeks blushed. 'And don't get into no trouble, will you.'

'We're hardly likely to get into trouble in a monastery!' I shouted over the noise of the engine, then dropped a gear, spun the wheel and raced the car down the drive.

The journey was excellent! I left the top down and could hear the roar of the engine all the way. I wore my flying helmet, goggles, scarf and greatcoat to keep the worst of the weather out. I didn't even notice the occasional spots of drizzle as we wound through Cotswolds lanes and up into the rugged hills and vales of Yorkshire.

Wooded valleys veiled in umber, rock-cut dales glossed in green, squat white cottages of hand-hewn stone, humpback bridges and sparkling streams. Yorkshire's palette of pastoral hues was forged by man in nature to create a rural masterpiece.

On empty, plumb-straight stretches I tipped seventy miles an hour; racing up and down hills like a roller coaster, it was almost as good as flying. There was the occasional grumble about my speed – mostly from Swift – but otherwise I think they all enjoyed it.

We drew to a halt in a slew of small stones on the crest of a high hill. I leaned out to read a moss-ridden milestone; it was carved with an arrow and the name 'Calderstone' in worn lettering.

The horizon in every direction was ringed by green hills dotted with sheep and clumps of wind-blown trees. Below us, in a hollowed dale, lay a crescent of land bound by a winding river. A village stretched across the base of the hill. Beyond, on a slight rise, the fortress-like Abbey stood enclosed by high stone walls, the river hooked around its back like a half-moon moat. It looked serene and ancient, as though we'd arrived in a time long gone.

I slipped a gear to coast down to the neat cottages gathered around a broad green, complete with a set of old stocks, a duck pond and spreading chestnut trees. The black and white edifice of the pub caught my eye, its sign proclaiming it 'The Calderstone Arms'.

We passed a general-store cum post-office with a dumpy red letter box, a school and a squat church and braked to a halt in front of the Abbey's towering gates. No-one moved so I hopped out and opened the door for Father Ambrose. He was in the back, his hands tightly clasped around the picnic hamper securing Tubbs, his eyes were closed and his knuckles were white.

He tottered a bit when he got out. I took the hamper from his grasp to lighten the load. Tubbs pushed a black paw through a gap in an attempt to escape.

I turned to Greggs.

'Bring the bags, will you old chap,' I called. I don't

think he heard because he remained immobile in his seat. Foggy jumped out and chased around the cobbled expanse, barking with excitement.

Swift had been in the front, he started grumbling the moment his feet touched the ground. 'Lennox, it wasn't the damned Monte Carlo rally!'

'You said we were in a hurry,' I reminded him, but he ignored me.

'Father!' A large monk in black cassock and clean white apron, squeezed out of a small wicket door cut into the gates. 'It's a blessing you've returned.' He spoke in a rich baritone, his voice belying his age because, despite his plump face and red cheeks, his hair was white and his skin creased – if he'd sported a beard he could have doubled for Santa Claus.

'Brother Tobias, has anything happened?' Father Ambrose asked anxiously.

'Not a thing. I'm glad to see you're safe back, that's all.' Brother Tobias grinned. 'And you've brought the cavalry with you!' He bent down to fuss Foggy, who was leaping about the monk's knees in greeting.

'Cavalry, dog and cat.' Father Ambrose looked relieved as he passed the genial monk and stepped through the gate. 'Oh, I am so pleased to be home.'

'Come along, you're all welcome.' Brother Tobias threw out his arms, cassock sleeves flapping. 'Let me help you.' He strode around to the boot, where Swift was tugging at a jumble of bags. The big monk pulled them out one by one and placed them on the ground.

'Thank you,' Swift picked up his suitcase and followed in Father Ambrose's footsteps.

'Greggs,' I called my old butler and he finally shifted himself to climb stiffly out of the car.

His nose and eyes were all that was visible between his bowler hat and tightly wrapped scarf.

'Sir, this is an automobile, not an aeroplane,' he admonished in muffled tones, then went to retrieve his own bag and stalked off.

'Greetings, I'm Major Lennox,' I informed Brother Tobias, as he took the hamper from my arms. I gathered up my own bag, Fogg's basket, blanket and whatnots.

'Welcome, Major.' Brother Tobias smiled. 'Seems your friends are a bit shook up.'

'Can't imagine why.' I grinned.

CHAPTER 4

We crunched along a gravel path between clipped hedges bordering neatly tended gardens. Brother Tobias entered a canopied doorway almost hidden below twisted branches of blue-flowering wisteria. I followed him into a stone building which proved to be a kitchen, and stopped to stare. The entire end wall was filled by a huge fireplace blazing with bright flames leaping from blackened logs. Bubbling iron cauldrons hung from chains above the heat of the fire, oozing the smell of beef stew. I caught the scent of fresh bread from a brick oven in the corner, a large copper kettle on a griddle next to it: it seems I'd arrived in culinary heaven.

The big monk placed the hamper on a long wooden table, filling the centre of the room, and opened the lid. Tubbs looked about, stretched and yawned, then jumped out and down onto the red-tiled floor. He sauntered over to the blazing hearth as if he owned the place and sat down to clean his whiskers.

Brother Tobias laughed. 'He's made himself at home.

And I can see by your face that you were expecting thin gruel and a cold cell for a billet.'

That made me grin. 'Well, I've never stayed in a monastery before.'

'You don't get a belly like mine on light rations!' He patted his ample stomach then went to a large dresser which took up another wall. It was lined with white plates and dishes and hung with pewter mugs. He picked up two bowls from a shelf and went to open up a larder beyond the dresser. 'I've got a few titbits in here for the little ones,' he said and came back holding the bowls heaped with slivers of ham. He gave one to Fogg and one to Tubbs. I watched them eat, feeling rather peckish from lack of lunch myself.

'Lennox?' A voice called from somewhere above.

I looked around. 'Swift?'

'He's up the stairs, these are our guest quarters. I'll show you the way.' The good monk went through a doorway in a far corner of the kitchen. A simple stone staircase wound upwards to open onto a blue carpeted corridor, lined with dark panelling and hung with rich tapestries. I glanced at them in passing, there were saints, angels, martyrs and the like. I preferred horses, cottages and cows myself, but I suppose religious themes were pretty much obligatory in a monastery.

Swift was standing in an open doorway. 'Lennox, you're next to me, Greggs is at the end. I'll see you shortly.'

'Fine, Swift...' I began, but he disappeared back inside his room.

'You come along with me, Major Lennox.' Brother Tobias ambled into the next room.

I dropped my bags and Fogg's basket by the unlit hearth. Heavy patterned curtains adorned an ancient four-poster bed, the walls were white, there was a sturdy oak washstand, a wardrobe, a carved coffer and a desk below a mullioned window. Elizabethan in style and probably in age, I thought.

Brother Tobias waved a hand in the direction of the hearth. 'We don't usually light bedroom fires until nightfall, but you're welcome to do as you please. And there ain't no electric, so you'll have to make do the old way.'

'It'll be just like school.' I pulled out my fob watch. 'What time is dinner?'

'You're too late for that, we had dinner at noon. Supper's at six.' He leaned forward and whispered. 'But you can get a good bite of pie down at the Calderstone Arms if you're peckish.' He laughed loudly and went off, shutting the door behind him.

There was a damp chill in the air and I regarded the unlit fire with arms folded. Should I light it? Was it bad manners? What did one do in a monastery?

'Lennox.' Swift marched in.

'What?'

'I've made a list of questions,' he waved his notebook. 'We should open the investigation by searching Calderstone Hall.'

'We know the Codex isn't there, Swift,' I objected. 'And

we haven't had lunch yet and it's almost three o'clock. We could go to the pub...'

He didn't listen to a damn word I said. 'Father Ambrose has given me the key to the house and the strongbox. We have to start somewhere and Calderstone Hall is as good as anywhere. Come on.'

He wore his trench coat over his suit, I was waiting for him to tighten his belt but he didn't, he just marched off. Perhaps Florence had finally fixed the buckle?

We headed down the unmade track leading to the village.

'I'll go and ask where Calderstone Hall is,' I offered, breathing in the enticing aroma of beer, tobacco smoke and hot pie wafting from the open doorway.

'No, I won't be a minute.' Swift beat me to it.

I was about to follow him in when Fogg spotted ducks on the pond. I chased after him as he took off.

Swift emerged just as I returned with my dog under my arm.

'Over yon hill.'

'What?'

He had already started walking and was a couple of yards ahead of me. '"Yon' – yonder, it's the local dialect.'

'I know what it means!' I countered. 'I don't need a damn translation, I need a drink. And food!'

He pretended not to hear so I followed him across the village green, the grass lush and long under the leafy chestnut trees. Then we panted up the steep hill we'd just motored down and stopped to catch our breath at the top and stare.

'There,' I said, pointing to a rambling house almost hidden by a belt of trees. It was set to face its overgrown gardens which stretched to the bank of the winding river.

'Calderstone Hall,' Swift stated the obvious.

I didn't bother to reply, just strode in its direction, still stung by the lack of lunch.

Built in fine Jacobean style, the house had tall windows formed from leaded diamond panes set in stone surrounds. The roof was a medley of pitches and valleys with crumbling pinnacles and slipped slates. We entered the iron gates, half hanging from broken stone pillars, and walked along the weed strewn drive. I noted cracked glass and peeling paint and thought it was a shame to see it rotting because it was a handsome place in pretty surroundings.

'You're sure there's no one living here?' I asked again, as Swift turned a large iron key in the rusted lock of the heavy front door.

'Certain.' He swung the door open.

'Saluto.' A husky voice stopped us in our tracks.

It was a lady. My heart skipped a beat. She had glossy black hair and deep dark eyes. She was standing on the bottom step of a sweeping staircase, one elegant hand on the bannister rail. Her long dress hugged her voluptuous body, it was slit to the knee and red and silky... and... and ... 'What?'

'I said, 'you are friends of my husband?" She sauntered towards us, her hips swaying. 'He iz dead,' she drawled, her every word infused with Italian dramatics.

I closed my mouth and tried to stop staring. Even Swift was struck dumb.

'I…erm. We thought there was no one here,' I stammered. 'We're investigating… I mean, we've been asked…'

'Police.' Swift suddenly snapped into action. 'I'm a detective and we're investigating a theft. You have to tell us who you are, madam, and why you are here.'

'If you are a detective, then you must know.' She pushed a tendril of long black hair behind her ear, her mouth a pout of disdain.

I still hadn't moved, hadn't taken my eyes off her actually. I guessed she must have at least a decade on me, but her figure, her hair and her lips… they were very red and … 'What?'

'I said, 'come to the parlour.'' She didn't wait for a reply, just sauntered off along the hall, her every movement a study in sultry seduction. We hesitated then followed. Fogg clung closely to my heels, his ears drooping, no more sure than I was about the unexpected encounter. It occurred to me that the lady was rather underdressed for a chilly day in the depths of rural Yorkshire.

The parlour proved to be a lofty room with elaborate cornices, draped in grime and cobwebs. The floor was bare boards with nothing more than a moth-eaten wolf skin for comfort; I stepped across it, not being keen to walk on the dead. The lady dropped languidly onto a gold satin throw that had been tossed over a sofa. I assumed she'd put it there earlier because it was the only thing in the place that didn't look centuries old.

'I am the Contessa Mirabella Ferranti,' she pointed a finger for us to sit in front of a smouldering fire.

We perched on rickety chairs which shed dust and stuffing in equal measure.

'So, you are purporting to be the Italian widow,' Swift stated bluntly.

She laughed huskily. 'Signor, I *am* the Italian widow.'

'You shouldn't be in this house until that is proven,' Swift continued.

'Swift,' I whispered. 'Don't you think we should...?' I was cut off mid-objection.

'It is proven.' The Contessa leaned forward, a smile playing on her lips. 'My lawyer, Danton, he has all the papers. He has gone already this morning. You are too late to do nothing, he gives papers to the lawyer who belongs to my dead husband.' she waved a dismissive hand. 'I forget his name.'

'Clarence,' I blurted out, then realised she meant his solicitor.

'His name's Fenshaw.' Swift frowned at me.

The Contessa fixed me with a direct gaze. 'You interest me – tall and handsome. I like the blond, it is a good colour with your eyes so blue. What is your name?' She leaned forward, her red silk dress straining to contain her brimming décolletage.

'I...I...' I stopped, took a breath, stood up and declared, 'Major Heathcliff Lennox.'

Swift sat unblinking for a moment then rose and made a stiff bow. 'Detective Chief Inspector Swift, retired.'

I noticed he'd begun using 'retired', I suppose he'd taken objection to being an 'ex' detective.

'*Affascinare*. You will call me Contessa Mirabella.' She leaned back against the stole, her movements carefully casual.

'When did you arrive?' Swift demanded.

'Yesterday, Danton says it is all fine and legal, and he knows all your laws. But…' She looked around with a curl to the lip. 'It is a terrible house. *Pasticcio.*' She suddenly snapped her fingers in the air.

A tall, slim woman walked into view. I hadn't noticed her before, she must have entered behind us on silent feet. She was older than Mirabella; black hair in a tight bun, olive hued with a thin roman nose and hooded, dark eyes. Her expression could have been fashioned by Medusa.

'This is Marta,' the Contessa announced. 'She will help you leave, now.'

'What?' Swift protested. 'But, but…'

'I do not have to talk to you,' Mirabella purred. 'You must see Danton, I told you, he is my lawyer man and he has all your answers.'

'You're the one who should be leaving…' Swift was stung.

'Leave or I will call the police. The real ones, not the 'retired' ones.'

'I…I…' Swift stuttered.

'And give me the key. Because it is not yours and you should not keep things that are not yours.' The purr held the hint of a growl.

Swift bristled. 'There's no proof it's yours either.'

'Ha. Danton has the will, he has everything and you…' She laughed lightly. '…have nothing.'

'What *will?*' I asked sharply.

'The will that leaves all to me. I told you Danton has the papers. Danton is barrister from London. Do not hold no doubt, *amore*, he tells me this is mine and if Danton says it is so, then be assured, it is so.' She waved a hand in the direction of the motley furniture, decrepit house and presumably whatever Clarence had owned outside. 'Now go.'

'Come on, Swift. We'll find Fenshaw,' I told him. 'He can tell us what this claim is.'

We went, almost marched out by Marta who closed the door firmly behind us.

'Blast it,' Swift complained as we began climbing the hill.

'Did you believe her?'

'About the will? Anything's possible,' he said, a note of resignation in his voice. 'Even if she isn't his real widow, you can be sure she and her London barrister will have enough documents to muddy the waters for a long time to come.'

We walked in silence each of us lost in thought.

'Swift,' I said as we reached the top of the hill. 'She'll claim the Codex.'

'Yes, I know.' He caught his breath as we began our descent.

'So even if we do find it, Father Ambrose might not get it anyway.'

'Exactly. This isn't just about finding the Codex, it's about the inheritance.'

Damn it, I thought. That had just dropped us right into the middle of the fray.

CHAPTER 5

We reached the village and headed straight into the welcoming portals of the Calderstone Arms.

'Sit yer'selves down, I'll be right with you.' The barmaid greeted us with a merry smile.

We found a table in front of a glowing fire. It was a homely pub, blackened beams pitted with hooks holding pewter mugs and polished horse brasses; tobacco-stained walls bearing old paintings of rural scenes, cows and whatnot. The seats were a collection of simple benches, stools and spindle-back chairs.

The barmaid arrived to place a pint each in front of us.

'I'm Betty,' she announced. A plump lady, with dark chestnut hair stippled with grey, she was dressed in a simple black skirt, white apron and lace blouse. 'We've shepherd's pie in the oven. You're in luck, 'tis well after dinner time, but I made extra today, so I can bring you a plate apiece.'

We nodded our enthusiasm and she bustled off.

'Swift.' I'd been thinking. 'Clarence's estate – what does it consist of?'

'I can't imagine that house is worth fighting for.' He was dismissive. 'One bad sneeze could bring it down.'

'I meant the village.'

'Oh.' He put down his beer. 'I hadn't thought of that. I forget you toffs own whole villages.'

'People who live in glass houses,' I reminded him. 'Or glass castles...'

'Braeburn isn't mine, it's the Laird's.' Swift's marriage into the Scottish aristocracy hadn't diminished his socialist tendencies, although I sensed a note of despond in his voice.

Betty returned, her round face warm and friendly.

'Here ye go.' She placed steaming plates of shepherd's pie in front of us and handed over the cutlery. 'And don't forget your doggie.' She leaned down to glance at Fogg, who peered out from under the table.

'One minute, Betty,' I began. 'Could you tell us who owns this village, and the land hereabouts?'

'Calderstones of course. It's all owned by Calderstones round here. Although there's a lot of folk who'd like to dispute that.' She winked and went off, hips swaying.

We looked around the pub where locals chatted in groups, clay pipes between teeth, pints in hands. They sported the standard country wear, flat caps, country boots and thick woollen jackets. It didn't look to be a hotbed of revolt.

I scooped a forkful of minced steak and creamy mash mixed with thick gravy. It was delicious, we cleared our plates in short order.

'Betty,' Swift called the barmaid back over as she wound her way between tables, filling up pewter mugs from stoneware jugs.

'Top up?' She grinned.

'No, thank you. A lawyer,' Swift replied.

'Ain't never been asked for one of them before.' She laughed.

'Mr Fenshaw. He's Sir Clarence's man,' I added.

'Ay, that's right, that nephew who's taken over from old Mr Lawson, poor duck. He's not up to much no more, his mind's gone seekin'.'

I imagined she meant the old man had lost his marbles, or was in the process. 'Where can we find Fenshaw?'

'Over yon hill.' She raised a jug of beer to indicate the other side of the hill we'd just come from.

'What?' Damn it, we'd just come all the way back over it.

'By Calderstone Hall?' Swift was already on his feet.

'No, that's south, the lawyers place is north. Fell House, nice spot, an' a brass plaque. You'll find it easy, my lovely. 'Specially with you being a detective an' all.'

'How do you know...?' Swift began.

'Word gets about.' She wiped a hand on her apron and held it out. 'That'll be three shilling and fourpence apiece.'

We settled it between us, including a generous tip, and began the walk back over the hill. I'd debated retrieving my Bentley from outside the Abbey, but that would have meant trailing in the opposite direction first, so we climbed the hill instead.

The sun was dropping in the sky and the temperature with it, as we reached a fine stone house set back in a glade of beech trees. A pair of wooden gates protected the raked drive and well-kept grounds, it spoke of comfort and old fashioned gentility. A name plate stated Fell House, and a brass plaque below it declared, 'Lawson and Fenshaw, Solicitors and Notaries.'

'Who be you, then?' An old man in butlering togs opened the door.

'We're here on behalf of Father Ambrose,' Swift announced. 'Is Mr Fenshaw in?'

'Aye, he's here. Come along with me.' He tottered on spindly legs.

We followed the elderly butler down a corridor into an office. It was in the usual style with a bookcase, dusty ledgers, a large desk and a window overlooking a garden coloured with bright spring flowers. I caught a flash of light from the river just beyond tall trees at the bottom of the neatly cut lawn.

A youngish chap in a sharp suit was seated behind the desk, which was covered in stacks of files and papers. He slipped a few in his drawer as we entered.

'You must be the gentlemen helping Father Ambrose? Please sit down.' He had slicked brown hair and eyes the same colour as his suit and dull furnishings. He looked coldly calculating to my mind and regarded us with ill-concealed hostility.

'Greetings,' I replied coolly.

Swift said nothing, merely eyed him narrowly.

'That dog shouldn't be in here, this is an office of business,' Fenshaw snapped.

'He's with me,' I retorted.

The lawyer looked me up and down and decided against an argument. He struck me as the sort of oily tick you find all too often in positions of petty power.

'I'm Stephen Fenshaw. My Uncle Lawson would have been dealing with the Calderstone case, but his health is failing, so I've taken over.'

Swift cut straight to the point. 'Which papers did the Contessa's lawyer deposit with you?'

Fenshaw looked taken aback. 'None. Not yet anyway.'

'What?' Swift sounded surprised.

'We were told Danton was on his way to you,' I struck up.

'When?' Fenshaw demanded.

'About an hour ago,' I replied.

Fenshaw looked at his wrist watch. 'That's strange, he…?'

Swift cut in, 'Major Lennox meant we were told an hour ago. Danton actually left the Contessa this morning.'

'What, I mean, pardon?' That took the shine off Fenshaw's slick gloss, his mouth opened and closed before he could continue. 'But, he telephoned early this morning. He said he was coming before the end of day. I… I didn't realise he'd left. I assumed he'd found some discrepancy and…'

'Would he have gone elsewhere?' Swift asked.

'No.' Fenshaw slumped in his seat, his suit creasing at his trim waist. 'Danton's a first class man. One of the top London barristers, I met him when I did my training there. He has the highest reputation, very precise… professional. I… I can't imagine where he is.' He floundered then got a grip of himself. 'I'll call the Contessa.' He stood up abruptly and left the room.

'He could have called from here.' Swift nodded toward the candlestick telephone near the window.

'Yes,' I agreed, wondering if it was worth taking a look at the neat piles of papers on the leather-topped desk.

Fenshaw returned a bit breathless. 'He must be missing. This is…' He ran fingers through his neatly combed hair, then patted it back hastily. 'I should call the police. Do you think I should call the police? Perhaps we should go and look for him?'

'I am the police.' Swift stood up and rattled out orders. 'Call the local station and set them off on a search. Tell them we'll meet them on the road. Come on Lennox.' He tightened the belt of his trench coat and marched out. It seems Florence hadn't fixed the buckle after all.

'He must have come along this road,' Swift insisted as we strode in a southerly direction.

Dusk was sending long shadows across our route from a belt of tall trees as we made our way down a stretch of patched tarmac.

'You don't know this area,' I reminded him.

'I looked at a map before I came.'

'But there will be any number of farm tracks.' I watched a barn owl sweep ahead of us, as the sun tinged the air with pink and orange.

'Look,' he stopped and pointed. 'Tyre tracks! A car pulled off the road.'

He was right, the grass had been flattened. I dug in the pocket of my tweed jacket and pulled out my torch. Swift had one too and we followed the trail into a shadowy glade. It was darker in the forest and our beams swept over fissured bark and crooked branches layered with lichen. Fronds of green bracken and budding brambles were clustered between gaps in the dense trees.

'There's a car,' he hissed.

'I'm not blind, Swift.'

He ignored me and ran over to tug open the door handle. It was a sleek blue Lagonda, classy, costly and entirely vacant.

I swept my torch around the walnut and leather interior and then at the ground surrounding it.

'Damn.' Swift made a complete circuit of the abandoned car. 'I can't make out any footprints, there are too many dead leaves.'

'Fogg.' I looked down at my dog, his tail drooped as he realised what I wanted. 'Fezzie, off you go,' I urged him. *Fezzie* being the call to go and find game, although I admit he'd never taken an interest in proper hunting. But he was a good little dog and I think he realised this was more serious than chasing birds. He put his nose to the ground, his ears low, his tail wagging and snuffled a couple of circuits, then halted for a second to raise a paw before setting off with a determined air.

'Swift,' I called and ran after Fogg.

'Lennox, are you sure?'

It was only a short distance in a straight line between the trees.

'What is it?' Swift ran his torch light across a wooden door set in a framework of brick. The humped structure was covered in grassy turf and ferns.

'Ice-house,' I said, pushing at the door. It swung open on oiled hinges to reveal a narrow entrance.

'Stay,' I told Foggy, who sat down, obedient for a change.

The smell of damp and mould hit us first, followed by a freezing draught. It cut through my tweeds as we stepped down onto worn stone steps. I cursed silently, I was beginning to form a distinct dislike to underground passages in the dark. Something skimmed my hair, I ducked.

'Cobwebs,' Swift said too loudly.

I swept my torch upwards to light on a brick-built passage, glistening with ice and frosted spider webs. I kept my head low as we reached the bottom step.

'Must belong to Calderstone Hall,' I whispered.

Swift shone his beam into the darkness, creating dancing shadows along distant walls. We were in a long, low chamber, stacked with barrels and boxes. Some were shedding straw, no doubt used to insulate whatever was inside.

'Do you think there's a tunnel from here to the Hall?'

'Unlikely,' I replied. 'Ice-houses only became fashionable in Victorian times and Calderstone Hall is a lot older than that.'

'These ice blocks are huge.' Swift reached a finger to touch a large slab of grey blue ice.

'They cut the ice with saws in the winter from lakes and rivers, and haul them on sleds,' I told him. 'I used to help at my Uncle Melrose's place when I was a child.'

I don't think he was listening. He raised the lid on a rectangular box the size of a coffin. 'Looks like lamb.'

'Um,' I agreed, glancing at the glimmer of frozen flesh in a bed of straw.

Swift shone his torch into another box. 'Beef.'

'Wait.' I aimed my beam between two tea chests at the far end of the chamber. 'There!'

'Good God!' Swift uttered.

CHAPTER 6

The body lay on a block of ice almost the length and breadth of a single bed. He was very neat, flat on his back with arms crossed and palms flat upon his navy blue jacket. The sharp creases in his dark trousers were aligned in parallel. There was still a shine on his black leather shoes, although I could see fragments of mud and dead leaves stuck to his thin soles. From his smart appearance, I assumed it was Danton.

Swift whipped out his magnifying glass and placed it under the man's nose.

'He's frozen, Swift.'

'Yes, but we should check for breath, just in case. People have been known to survive longer in cold temperatures.' He peered closely at the glass, waiting to see if any mist formed. It didn't, of course. The man was icy blue and I could see his jaw was already taut with rigor mortis. Swift was just being his usual pedantic self.

'There are crystals on his eyebrows and around his nostrils.' I aimed my torch at the corpse's aquiline nose.

Swift shifted the magnifying glass. 'Strange. I suppose they must have formed when he took his last breaths.'

'How did he die?' I mused, staring at the dead man's face. He appeared unconcerned with a look of the supercilious about his frozen lips.

Swift took out his pen and lifted sections of the victim's silver-streaked hair.

'No sign of contusions,' he said.

We examined the body again under torch light. The small crystals of ice began to melt from our proximity. I played my beam carefully around and under the jaw then down the neck to his pristine shirt collar and silk tie.

'Nothing obvious,' I concluded.

'He looks to be...' He regarded the man's face, the creases around the eyes and under his chin. '...about fifty, perhaps older. He may have been dead for hours.' He lifted an eyelid to peer into a glazed eye. 'Pinprick pupils,' he muttered.

'Is he wearing a watch?' I couldn't see a fob chain.

Swift carefully lifted the dead man's sleeve to view a gold wristwatch. 'Frosted,' he said. He wiped the glass to reveal a classy dial, it was still working and showed the time as quarter past five. I pulled out my fob watch but it had stopped. It always had been temperamental, I shook it and tucked it back into my waistcoat pocket.

'Five fifteen,' Swift said. 'Note that would you, Lennox.'

'Haven't brought my notebook.'

'What? For Heaven's sake! You knew we were going out to investigate.'

'Greggs hasn't unpacked it,' I protested.

'Lennox, if you want to detect, you have to remember the basics and not leave the leg work to me – or your butler,' he grumbled. 'Try to hold your torch steady while I search the body.'

I bit back a retort because he might have had a point, and aimed my beam. He systematically went through pockets, linings, waistcoat and whatnots.

'Nothing.' Swift straightened up. 'And no apparent blood or injury either.' He began tidying the clothes back the way we'd found him.

'He must have been laid out after he died,' I remarked.

'Yes, someone has a tidy mind.' He squatted on his haunches to scan the block of ice. 'Can't see any blood beneath him.'

'Do you think he was killed here?'

'I don't know, there's no sign of a struggle or fight.' He examined the man's hands. 'He could have been killed in the forest, or even elsewhere and brought here in his car.'

'There are leaves on the soles of his shoes.'

'It doesn't prove anything,' Swift moved to look at them. 'But, you may be right, it looks like he walked in here.' He conceded. 'He must have had a wallet and papers, they aren't on him, so he probably carried a brief-case. You search by the door, I'll start here.'

'Right-ho.' I gave up my perusal of the dead and wandered about. I thought it a waste of time – whoever had murdered the man would have to be an idiot to leave anything behind. I shone my torch into dark corners and poked in boxes, but didn't find a thing and I realised it was getting late. Brother Tobias had said supper was at six. I was about to call Swift when I heard a commotion.

'There's a dog!' A voice echoed down from above. 'Look at this little dog. 'E's a nice un, ain't he?'

I heard Foggy bark a couple of woofs.

That caused me to pause. 'He's mine,' I called up.

'Who's there? We're police and we're comin' down.'

Swift shouted, 'Hurry up.'

Lamp light flickered from the stairway followed by the sound of heavy boots. 'Stay where you are, we've got you surrounded.'

Swift frowned in the direction of the noise. 'These new moving pictures have a lot to answer for.'

A bobby appeared, holding a storm lamp above his head. 'I'm a Sergeant of the law, and I've got a truncheon.'

'So have I,' another voice behind him called out. 'And a whistle.'

'I'm from Scotland Yard,' Swift stated. 'We've found a body.'

'Ye never did?' A fresh-faced, young copper came into view, his eyes bright with excitement beneath a police-man's tall helmet. 'I'm Sergeant Beamish.' He turned to the Constable. 'Bill, did you hear that! It's a real detective of the Yard and a dead body.'

The young Sergeant was tall and thin; the Constable short and grizzled.

"Ee, you'll be able to learn some real detecting now, lad,' the Constable replied.

'I'm retired, actually,' Swift admitted.

'Aye, well, but *Scotland Yard...*' The Sergeant's voice held a note of awe.

'Where's this dead bloke, then?' The Constable came closer, he looked to be a wiry old man in an over-large uniform. His helmet fitted like a lampshade and wobbled when he moved.

'Mr Fenshaw rang the station and told us about that lawyer gone missing.' Sergeant Beamish's face was flush with the drama. 'Is it him?'

'We think so.' Swift stepped back and revealed the body of the man we'd discovered. 'Can you identify him?'

'He's no'but asleep,' the old copper exclaimed. 'Give 'im a prod.'

'We did,' I told him. 'He's dead.'

The Sergeant brought his lamp closer to the body. 'That's him! That's Danton, that is. How's he died then?' He peered at the dead man's face.

'We haven't ascertained that fact, yet.' Swift shifted into policeman mode. 'It requires a post mortem. You'll have to alert the Coroner.'

'There's one in York, but don't you worry, I'll be right on the telephone to him.' Sergeant Beamish grinned. 'We only ever have broken windows and lost dogs around here. Never had an unexplained death afore.'

'Murder,' I said.

'*Murder...* Did ye hear that, Bill? *Murder!*' It was said with some relish.

Swift frowned at me. 'Nothing has been proved yet.

And a doctor should examine the body before you move it.'

'Yes, sir, I'll tell Dr Wexford.' Sergeant Beamish suddenly snapped to attention and saluted.

Swift squared his shoulders. 'Very good, Sergeant. There are no papers or means of identification on the body, we believe he had a briefcase. Search the premises, the woodland and his car. Use fingerprint powder and wear gloves.' He mustered his troops for action.

'Right you are, sir. We've got lanterns,' Beamish held his up. 'We'll search all night if we have to.'

Swift nodded. 'Very good. As we found the body, you'll need to confirm the time of our movements with Mr Fenshaw.'

'I'll be doing that.' Beamish nodded, he turned to his short compatriot. 'Bill, are you writing this down?'

'No, I ain't. I didn't bring me glasses.' He squinted. 'But I'll remember it – got a good memory, I have.'

'You forgot your glasses,' I reminded him.

'Aye, but we weren't expecting murder, were we?'

There wasn't much to say to that.

'Come on, Swift. We'll be late.' I clapped my hands, looking forward to supper.

'Lennox, I…' He wanted to stay, I could see he was back in his element with a couple of underlings to command.

'There's nothing we can do that the coppers can't,' I reminded him.

'Aye, that's right, sir.' Sergeant Beamish was brimming with enthusiasm. 'We'll do a proper job, we will.'

Swift's shoulders drooped. 'Oh, very well.'

Foggy was still waiting outside the door of the ice-house, he woofed when he saw us. I bent down to give him a reassuring ruffle of the ears.

'What's this?' I noticed a speck of white in the muddy grass and picked it up.

'What?' Swift aimed his torch.

'Paper.' It was crumpled and crushed, as though stepped on.

'Looks like the sort used for rolling cigarettes.' Swift remarked.

'Or wrapping sweets?' I carefully straightened it out and held it on my palm. It was a blank square of almost translucent waxed paper; muddy, wet and creased.

'I'll take care of it.' Swift pulled out his wallet and laid the slip of paper carefully between the folds. 'And... um, well spotted, Lennox.'

We climbed the hill in breathless steps and entered the village just as the church bell struck six. Fogg headed toward the ducks nesting by the pond as we crossed the green. I stopped to call him to heel; just as I turned, I noticed the dark form of a monk at the far end of the road. He passed beneath a yellow street light, then into a narrow pathway between two cottages before disappearing into the shadows.

He looked awfully like Death without his scythe.

'Ah, you're too late, lads.' Brother Tobias greeted us with an apologetic smile as we entered the lamplit kitchen. 'They're gathered in the refectory and shut the doors. There's no disturbing them now. You eat on time or not at all.'

My heart sank. 'Does that mean there's no supper?'

'We can always go to the pub, Lennox.' Swift went over to the blazing fire to warm up.

'Not for a bite, ye can't. They only serve drink after dark. Folk go home for their supper. It's only dinner you'll get at the ale-house.' Brother Tobias wiped his hands on the white apron tied loosely around his black cassock. 'But, if you take a seat at yon table you might find a bowl of stew and dumplings appears before you.' He picked up a thick cloth and pulled two heaped dishes out of the bread oven. 'And don't you be tellin' no-one.'

'We found a body,' I told Brother Tobias between mouthfuls.

He was in the corner, pouring ale from the spigot of a small barrel into a large stoneware jug. 'A body?' he spun around, his ruddy face showing shock.

'Danton. The lawyer from London,' Swift added, watching the monk's reactions.

'Probably happened just after eleven this morning.' I paused with a forkful of stew.

The monk's eyes widened. 'You mean, he's dead?' He seemed to have forgotten about the beer.

'Frozen in the ice-house,' I added. 'Pretty sure he was murdered.'

He came back to the table, half-filled jug in hand – I held up a pewter mug but he didn't seem to notice.

'Murdered!' He sat down heavily on the end of the bench. 'And him a lawyer, too.'

'Well, lawyers are hardly the most popular sorts.' I tried holding up the mug again. 'The beer would be welcome...'

'But I only saw him yesterday...'

Swift reached over and took the jug from his hands before it spilled. He filled his mug and mine.

'Where did you see him?' He turned back to the monk.

'Here, in the Abbey. He came to the gate yesterday afternoon demanding to see Father Ambrose. Rang the bell with such a clatter, he did. Brother Paul went to let him in. I was in the garden picking herbs for the stew.'

'What did he want to see Father Ambrose about?' Swift continued.

'I don't know, but he had a briefcase and was holding a bundle of papers. He was shouting and it seemed to me he was itching for a bust-up. It upset Father Ambrose, he was in a rare tizzy afterwards.'

Swift and I exchanged glances.

'And then Father Ambrose set off this morning to the Major's house at Ashton Steeple,' Swift stated.

'Almost first light it was, aye. He said he'd come back with some help.' He shook his head, bemused. 'He's never been out of the district since the day he arrived twenty five years ago... and now... murder.'

Swift took another mug from the long dresser against the wall, poured beer into it and handed it to the monk, who drank it straight down.

The door opened behind us.

'Sir!' Greggs walked in, or rather swayed in.

'Greggs? Have you been drinking?'

'I may have had one or two.' He straightened up and smoothed his waistcoat. 'But I can inform you, sir, a body has been discovered.'

'Lennox and I found the body,' Swift informed him.

That made Greggs' eyes open. 'Oh, well, I remained in the Calderstone Arms to listen for clues.'

'Very noble,' I said dryly.

'What was being said?' Swift put the empty beer-jug down.

'A great deal, sir. It was an animated discussion.'

I could imagine the chatter that the discovery of a murder must have generated in a small village.

'Greggs, tell us what you heard.'

He swayed and sat down on the bench. 'Very well, sir. There was a lot of speculation, but the general sentiment was one of relief that the village had been saved from foreign hands.'

'So they know about the Contessa's claim?' Swift asked.

'Swift, this is a village,' I told him. 'Everybody knows everyone's business. And Father Ambrose told us the Contessa made a fuss at the funeral in front of everyone.'

'That's right,' Tobias nodded. 'I was there, it's been the talk of the place ever since. They all think she's after taking over where the Calderstones left off. They'll still be working to keep the rich in comfort while they can't even call their homes their own. Been right worried they have.'

'That was discussed in the pub, sir.' Greggs added. 'The

locals have heard about the will the Contessa said she had and there was considerable speculation about what it contained.'

'Danton didn't have it when we found him,' Swift said, almost to himself.

'And it could be the reason he was killed,' I added, although my suspicions rested more within the Abbey.

'Were there any policemen in the pub?' Swift aimed the question at my butler.

'Not to my observation, sir.' Greggs sobered under the Inspector's steely eye.

'You did very well, Greggs, thank you,' I told him.

'I will take my leave now, sir. Goodnight.' He gave a dignified bow and wobbled off up the stairs.

'This will affect the investigation.' Swift's face had hardened.

'How?'

'If the killer's a local they'll cover it up.'

'Not necessarily. Sergeant Beamish seemed keen,' I reminded him.

Brother Tobias joined in. 'They're good people. They'll not let a murderer go free.'

Swift responded. 'Are you sure? You heard what Greggs said, whoever did it probably just saved the whole village.'

'Not just the village,' Brother Tobias said.

We turned to look at him.

'The land the Abbey stands on is owned by the Calderstones. Whoever murdered that man most likely saved us too.'

CHAPTER 7

I went to bed with my mind churning the day's events, and thoughts of Persi. I know what the waiting was like, and the longing. What the hell was wrong with me? She was everything that meant anything to me, beautiful, intelligent, intrepid... all I had to do was to post the damn letter. And yet... Was my heart in it? Or was I still lost in the past? I spent a fitful night troubled by memories and indecision and aware that I should have been focusing on the murder and the mystery of Clarence's confession.

Morning broke to the sound of a bell tolling somewhere in the monastery.

'Sir?' Greggs placed a steaming mug of tea on my bedside table. He didn't seem to be suffering too much from his evening jaunt to the pub. 'I'm afraid there is no breakfast. It is not the custom.'

'What?'

'Nothing until noon.'

'Then it's down to you, old chap,' I informed him. 'We

need bacon, eggs and toast, sausages, mushrooms and the like.'

Fogg and Tubbs were curled up in the covers of my bed, and woke up at mention of food.

'I do not believe it would be felicitous to raid the monastery larder, sir.' He bent to place lengths of fresh kindling onto the glowing embers of the fire and waited as it flickered into flame.

'No, but I noticed the post office included a general store. Provisions will be available.'

'Indeed, sir.' He went to the curtains and pulled them aside.

Sun streamed through the mullion windows, although the room was freezing – I could see my breath in front of me.

'Good Heavens!' Greggs exclaimed loudly. 'A body, sir.'

'What?' I tossed aside the covers and instantly regretted it as the cold hit in full force. Nevertheless, I strode over. 'Another one?'

He stood aside to let me stare.

It was a mouse. Its corpse lay on the window sill in a ray of early morning light. 'Very amusing, Greggs.'

'Should I find the magnifying glass, sir?'

'No, you can interrogate the cat.' I went back to pull on my dressing gown and dig out my slippers from under the bed, then turned about and went back for a better look. 'Actually, it doesn't look very mauled, does it?'

'Pardon, sir?'

'It looks a bit contorted. I think I do need the magnifying glass.'

Greggs sighed. 'Sir, is it really necessary to investigate the murder of mice?'

'I don't think it was murdered, I think it was poisoned,' I found my magnifying glass in my bedside drawer along with my notebook, pen and my favourite pocket pistol.

'I believe poisoning is murder, sir.'

'Semantics, Greggs.' I peered at the small corpse. There weren't any tooth marks or apparent breaks in the brown fur, nor any blood. Its ears, tail, paws and claws were all intact, but its little mouth was pulled back from its chiselled teeth in something akin to a snarl. The body was twisted and curled as though it had suffered a seizure.

'It has fleas, sir,' he was peering over my shoulder.

'So I can see.' I picked the corpse up by the tail to twirl it in the sunlight. 'Could you find a jar or candle holder, or whatnot?' I asked.

He brought a simple white mug from the wash stand.

I dropped the cadaver into it. 'Poisoned! I'm certain of it.'

'Yes, sir. So the cat didn't do it?'

'No.' I looked at my little black cat on the bed, probably wondering where breakfast was. 'Mr Tubbs is innocent.'

He rolled his eyes.

'Is Swift about?'

'He is in the kitchen, sir, he appears keen to continue the investigation.'

'Yes, he wants to get back to his wife and castle.' I clapped my hands, then rubbed them together. 'Right, I'll be down shortly. See what you can do about rations,

Greggs. Nothing good comes of starting the day on an empty stomach.'

He went off, muttering under his breath.

The bathroom was at the end of the corridor. I washed and dressed in no time, compelled by the freezing cold, then collected my little dog and cat from my room. Tubbs was almost too fat to fit in my shooting jacket pocket, but he scrambled in and I tucked Foggy under my arm and headed downstairs.

The kitchen was empty of life, so I put the cup with mouse cadaver on the table. I assumed Swift must have gone in search of supplies with Greggs, so the way was clear for an outing to the monastery gardens.

Fogg snuffled ahead and Tubbs skittered about in kittenish fashion along gravelled pathways. Jasmine, wisteria, roses and honeysuckle climbed high stone walls between fanned fruit-trees and splayed berry-bushes. The scent of damp earth, greening leaves and burgeoning blossom diffused into crisp clear air.

The gardens ran in a broad ribbon between the surrounding wall and the central complex of the monastery. I wandered between grids of well-tended beds and passed a small barn brimming with sacks of potatoes, beans, carrots and whatnots of the like. The gardens had been divided between neatly hoed vegetable plots, and box-hedged squares filled with herbs.

I turned a corner and paused as I caught the sound of chanting from a short-spired chapel. It was a lilting laudation to God, the monks' choral merging with the humming bees and trilling birds to weave an earthly melody to heaven.

Tubbs had squeezed through one of the low box-hedges hemming a cultivated square. I picked him up, not wanting him to make his toilette near anything destined for the table. I didn't recognise the particular greenery, I bent down to regard the label, 'Artemisia Dracunculus' and wondered if it was one of the herbs Brother Tobias had been picking for the stew.

I paused at an ancient stone archway framing a door leading into the monastery proper. I hadn't trespassed there yet and thought that I probably shouldn't without a guide. I put Tubbs back down and he gambolled over to Fogg, who was sniffing around tangled rose bushes growing up the wall of a whitewashed building. I strolled over to join them and paused at the green painted door. It was ajar and nobody was about, so I stepped inside.

Dried herbs, flowers and even thistles hung from the beams supporting the dark slate roof. The scent of old roses laced with spices and herbs infused the air. The sun-washed window sill held a pair of brass scales, a tall glass jar of small sponges and a terracotta dish of tiny black seeds. Beneath the window, a long wooden table supported the requisites of the dispensary. A large pestle and mortar stood next to a white marble square, covered with heaps of granulated powders in shades of mustard, cream and brown. In the centre, a ledger lay open with a quill pen in a ceramic ink-pot at its top-right corner. I leaned in to read the neat calligraphy written between margins drawn in red. *'In the case of colic with ague'*. It appeared to be a recipe of sorts; the names of plants in Latin, the rest in English.

I turned to the adjacent wall, it held blue and white glazed jars lined up on carefully constructed shelves. I perused the Latin names; 'Populeum', 'Ung. Sambuc' and 'O.Liliorum' amongst many others. An apothecary cupboard took up most of the rear wall, the numerous small square drawers similarly inscribed with Latin notations. On the other wall was a high desk and two stools with low backs and worn seats. Above it, a single shelf held more ledgers. I counted six, they looked ancient, bound in dark red leather and impressed with Roman numerals in faded gold.

It was extraordinarily quiet, an ancient place of ancient ways; the past hanging on a fraying thread in a changing world.

'Good morrow.'

I spun around, snapping back to reality. 'Greetings,' I stuttered.

'You are one of the Abbot's guests.' He was a tall monk, not quite my height but much the same build, broad shoulders and chest narrowing to the hips, a man of muscle and bone. He wore a black cassock and was entirely bald; he obviously belonged to the place.

'Major Heathcliff Lennox.' I made a bow of the head.

He nodded graciously. 'Brother Paul.'

'Father Ambrose asked for our help.'

He regarded me with sharp intelligence in pale grey eyes set in a lean face. 'So I am aware.'

'We found a body.' I thought I'd be direct.

A smile ghosted his lips. 'James Danton, the London lawyer. We prayed for his soul at Matins.'

'Oh.' I hesitated, he was ahead of me. 'What time is Matins?'

'Three o'clock, the usual hour.'

'Good Lord, you mean three o'clock in the morning?'

'I do, and we have just completed Prime. These are the first prayers of the Daily Office.' The smile didn't reach his eyes. 'We do not take the Lord's name in vain.'

'Ah, yes. Um, sorry.'

'Were you seeking anything in particular? A nostrum, for instance?' He placed finger tips on the open page of the ledger.

'No, no, my dog... Mr Fogg, I was looking for him.'

He moved aside to reveal Fogg sitting watching me from the open doorway. Tubbs was next to him.

'Ah, excellent.' I was inclined to make an exit as things weren't going too well, but decided to stand my ground. 'You're the Apothecary?'

'I have responsibility for the Pharmacia and Physic gardens, yes.'

'I think someone poisoned Danton.'

He regarded me as though waiting for something comprehensible.

'Do you have any poison?' I persevered.

'All potions are poisonous, it is a question of dosage.'

I looked at him, his expression remote and uncommunicative, and decided to give up.

'Right, well, I'll be off then.' I followed the path back to the kitchen, my little duo gambolling at my heels as though it were all tremendous fun.

The smell of frying bacon, eggs and various culinary delights met me at the doorstep. Swift was already tucking into a large plate of sausage and egg with tea and toast at his elbow.

Greggs had tied an apron over his butlering togs. He brought a covered plate to the table and removed the pewter lid to reveal a plate laden with splendid breakfast.

'Thank you, old chap,' I said in appreciation.

'Father Ambrose has asked us to go and see him,' Swift told me.

'Why?' I replied through a slice of excellent black pudding.

'Something to do with the dead lawyer and the papers, I expect.'

Greggs placed a mug of tea next to my plate without a word.

'Anything wrong?' I whispered, waving my fork in the direction of my butler.

Swift leaned in. 'He's been like that since he came out of the post office – I think he took a shine to a lady in there. He's barely said a word.'

'Oh, hell, not again.' Greggs seemed determined to lose his heart. 'Did you see the mouse?'

He regarded me with dark eyes. 'Lennox, why did you leave a dead mouse in a cup on the breakfast table?'

'Poisoned.' I forked a fried tomato.

'Evidently.' He didn't seem any more impressed than Greggs had been. 'I saw Sergeant Beamish, he was waiting for me at the Abbey gates when we went out.'

'Really? What did he say?' I sliced a sausage in two.

'They couldn't find a mark on Danton's body, nor could the Doctor. There was no indication of how he died. They've arranged a post mortem to be performed in York.'

'So, no contusions to the back of the head? No ice pick, dagger, or..?'

'No,' he mumbled through fried egg.

'Did they find the papers or the briefcase?'

Swift shook his head. 'Not a thing.'

Greggs placed a plate of hot buttered toast in front of me. He was humming an operatic aria.

'Danton was from London.' I'd been musing the murder. 'How could he have known about the ice-house?'

Swift shrugged. 'He couldn't, and he's hardly likely to have arranged to meet anyone there.'

'He might, if it were in secret.' I spooned marmalade onto my toast.

'It would be freezing, why would he do that? There are plenty of other places.'

'The countryside has more eyes and ears than you'd imagine, Swift.'

'Umm,' he mumbled, apparently unconvinced.

I switched tack. 'Does Beamish have a culprit in mind?'

'No, there's no evidence, no indication of how he died and no witnesses because the villagers aren't cooperating.'

'You can't blame them, Swift, considering what's at stake.'

'I understand, but it's murder, Lennox,' he argued. 'And even if the Contessa doesn't inherit Clarence's estate, someone else is going to.'

That gave me pause because he was right and things were far more complex than I'd so far considered.

'Now then, lads.' Brother Tobias bustled in. 'I've been sent to fetch you. Father Ambrose is waiting in his library.'

'We're coming,' Swift answered for both of us as I gulped down my tea.

'It's a right feast your man has made.' The good monk stopped to breathe in the scent of breakfast and rest a hand on his ample stomach. 'I hope you've finished it all up or I'll be succumbing to temptation.' He grinned and led the way.

We left by the big double-doors out of the kitchen. I assume the width was to carry out feasts for whatever occasion monks celebrated. It led to a short corridor and into a large rectangular room of light and air. I paused for a moment to admire the tranquil simplicity. There was a broad fireplace laid with kindling and logs on one long wall. Furnishings were sparse; bleached tables set as in a horseshoe with benches backing onto plain white walls. In the farthest corner, a yew-wood lectern stood on a platform two steps up. It held a thick book, which I assumed to be a Bible, and was open about one third through. It was the roof which really caught the eye; rafters painted dove-grey spanned the room, and between each was an oval window, letting in shafts of sunlight filled with dancing dust.

'The Refectory,' Brother Tobias told us. 'You can stop and stare another day, Father Ambrose is in a pother and fretting. Come along with me.'

Our footsteps echoed as we trod up a broad staircase, Brother Tobias puffed ahead, his thick, white hair contrasting against the dark panelled passageway. It crossed my mind to wonder why he wasn't tonsured.

'Oh, at last, you are here.' Father Ambrose rose from his seat behind a large desk, it was black, like his cassock, and burnished to a fine gloss – the desk I mean, not the cassock.

A small latticed window let in filtered light, warmth radiated from a fire blazing in a stone hearth, the rest of the room was lined with crowded book cases. The scent of beeswax, musty tomes and woodsmoke reminded me of my library back home.

'I'll be leaving, Father.' Brother Tobias gave a bow in the Abbot's direction. 'There's work waiting for me, down yon.' He went off, rosy cheeked and still puffing from his endeavours.

'Oh, dear boys.' Father Ambrose waved toward two Windsor chairs in front of his desk. 'Danton is dead, it's simply dreadful.'

Well, it was for him, I thought but didn't say.

Swift pulled out his notebook and pen.

Father Ambrose's face was pink, his eyes puffy and filled with consternation. 'Murdered.'

'We know, we found him,' Swift replied, jotting down the date and time on a fresh page. 'How did you hear?'

'Brother Paul was in the village last evening, he was told.'

I recalled the monk in the dark and our conversation in the whitewashed building. 'Why wasn't he at supper, or prayer or whatever?' I asked.

'He was delivering medicine to one of the elderly folk in the village.' Father Ambrose sighed. 'There is a great deal of talk, as you can imagine. The village has been in a state of agitation since Clarence's death and everything that has followed.'

I thought it must seem like watching one of those Victorian melodramas unfold, what with the death of the local landowner, the dramatic entrance of an exotic widow and now a murdered lawyer.

'Danton came to see you, would you tell us what it was about?' Swift held his pen ready to take notes.

'Yesterday, oh, dear, no it wasn't...' Father Ambrose floundered. 'It was the day before yesterday. He came here with some papers, insisting I produce the Codex before the reading of the will. I said I didn't know where it was, but he didn't believe me. He shouted at me. He was an intimidating person.'

Danton had been a London barrister and I imagined him in court in white wig and black suit haranguing a defendant.

'So Danton did know about the Codex,' Swift stated.

'Yes, I suppose the Contessa may have told him.' Father Ambrose didn't meet our eyes.

'You didn't mention this yesterday.' I tried to soften the tone of reproach.

'Didn't I?' Father Ambrose raised fingers to his lips. 'Oh dear.'

I thought he was deliberately dissembling.

'Did Danton say the Codex had been bequeathed to the Contessa?' Swift was focused on gathering facts.

'He said she had a valid claim upon the whole estate, but I told him the Codex had been given to us by Clarence and it was gone, so…' Father Ambrose flustered. 'He became angry and threatened to reveal all.'

'Reveal all of what?' I said sharply.

'Do you mean Danton was connected to whatever disaster threatens the Abbey?' Swift leaned forward, his note-taking forgotten.

'Yes, yes.' Father Ambrose's voice dropped to a whisper.

'Is that why you came to see us?' I pressed him. 'Because Danton was threatening to expose the secret?'

'No… Yes… I had to,' Father Ambrose admitted.

'What form did this threat take?' Swift's eyes narrowed.

'The sin, Clarence had …' Father Ambrose's voice held a note of despair. 'Please do not impel me, I beg of you. The confession is sacred.'

'If Danton knew, why can't we?' Swift insisted. 'It might have led to his murder.'

Father Ambrose clasped his hands over his trembling lips, unable or unwilling to speak.

'Swift,' I warned.

'Right, right. I'm sorry.' He looked contrite, though

he was clearly frustrated, for which I could hardly blame him.

'Father Ambrose, could you tell us about the papers Danton had with him?'

'Yes, yes, I can.' He tried to pull himself together. 'He said he had a valid will. Clarence had made it some time ago and had left everything to his wife, the Contessa.'

'Did you examine the will?' Swift asked quietly.

'No.' Father Ambrose shook his head. 'He made his threats and waved papers in my face, but he refused to let me read them, then Brother Paul made him leave.'

'He was present?' I asked.

'He came in after Danton raised his voice and he can be quite determined, you know.'

That didn't surprise me. 'You mentioned something about the reading of a will?' I reminded him.

'Ah!' A weak smile glimmered. 'That's what I wanted to tell you. Lawson just sent me a note. Clarence's will shall be read this afternoon at two o'clock. He has asked me to go and I thought you should like to attend.'

'Where?' Swift asked.

'At Lawson's office.'

'Right.' Swift made a note, then looked up. 'Lawson? Not Fenshaw?'

'Oh, I'm not sure. It was on Lawson's notepaper.'

'But which will is to be read?' I questioned.

'Oh dear, he didn't say.' Father Ambrose's voice began to quaver, again.

'We'll find out when we get there, Lennox.' Swift cut

the conversation, no doubt thinking we'd upset the old man enough.

The door opened behind us. We both turned in our seats. Brother Paul stood silently impassive, his hands folded into the loose sleeves of his black cassock.

'Ah, here is Brother Paul come to show you around the monastery. So kind of him.' Father Ambrose sighed in relief.

Swift closed his notebook with a snap and we were escorted out.

CHAPTER 8

Our echoing footsteps broke the heavy silence. Brother Paul had only spoken three words to us. 'Do not speak.'

It had rather killed the conversation, but my mind was turning over what Father Ambrose had just told us; Danton was after the Codex and he knew what Clarence had confessed. He'd tried to intimidate the Abbot with the will and, when that failed, it sounded as though he was using the confessed sin to threaten the Abbot. How? Was this the 'ruination' Father Ambrose feared? I mused over the conversation and realised that whatever it was, it was sufficient to impel the Abbot to leave Monks Hood for the first time in twenty five years and seek our help.

We'd walked back to the oak staircase, but rather than turn toward the Refectory, the silent monk had continued to follow the treads down below ground. I snapped out of my musings when he opened a door that led into a lamplit tunnel. Damn it, we were underground again.

Brother Paul took an oil lantern from a niche cut into the wall and carried it above his bald head.

'Come.'

We followed, our footsteps ringing hollow behind us. Other passageways led away from the one we were travelling, some much older than others. Judging by the draught of fresh air, one of them certainly led outside. We turned through a doorway to enter a vaulted chamber supported by stubby pillars of rough-cut stone. A carved frieze was the only decoration, it was a depiction of Hell, complete with grinning devils brandishing pitchforks, a man-sized cauldron over a flaming fire and some worried looking sinners. I scanned the walls for Heaven, but it must have been elsewhere.

'The Ossuary,' Brother Paul intoned without breaking step.

We glanced about expecting old bones or tombs, but apart from some rubble in dark corners it seemed entirely vacant.

'The Crypt,' he announced as we passed through another vaulted room, also vacant.

'Roman.' He intoned as we entered the next chamber. He stopped and so did we. The place had the oppressive air of the long distant past, an atmosphere alien to that of the rest of the monastery. The vaulted ceilings and walls were constructed from smooth white limestone, almost certainly brought from elsewhere. Alcoves were formed from slender columns carved and crafted by artists of consummate skill. They were as crisp as though they'd been made in the last century, rather than the last two millennia. Each alcove held a small marble altar, quite unlike those in the churches I was used to. They looked like plinths and I imagined they'd supported busts or effigies at one time. A number were inscribed.

'Mithras,' I read, then remembered I was supposed to be silent. I sighed quietly, Persi would have loved to explore this place, and I realised how much I wanted to show it to her. Although, given that it was a monastery, that might be rather complicated.

'This is the beginning.' Brother Paul spoke in measured tone.

We turned to face him.

'The sacred well.' He walked into a dark alcove and shone his lantern toward the ground. It was a pool of water, the stones containing it were level with the floor and it was shaped into a perfect circle, black as night and mirror flat. 'This site was worshiped by the pagans living here before the Romans came. When they invaded this place, they subdued the natives and took their sacred site. They built a temple here, this vault is all that remains,' he recited in a monotone. 'Then the Christians built a church where the temple had stood, it was a simple wooden structure. Viking raiders burned it down and left it in abandonment. The Brothers came, the Benedictines, and constructed our Chapel above here using these walls as a foundation. And so this Abbey came to be.'

I could see a patch of lighter coloured stone in the outer wall. The monk followed my line of sight.

'This was a collapse, the void allowed earth and rain

to enter. When we began rebuilding, this undercroft was cleared and repaired. The villagers worked with us, they are our friends and neighbours. These altars were buried beneath the mud and we set them upright.' He shone the lantern toward the marble plinths. 'We honour all religions and all peoples. We are one under God.'

'Amen,' I whispered under my breath.

'What year did the Brothers come?' Swift asked in his policeman's manner.

Brother Paul gazed at him, no doubt with thoughts of reprimand, but he answered.

'In the year 1242 two men came. One a Christian Crusader, seeped in the blood of war, the other a converted Mahometan. They wished to wash away their sins in the Light of God and were ordained under the Rule of St Benedict. They came here to build the Abbey and Pharmacia. They built a hospital and offered succour and healing to the poor, they are our founding fathers.'

'Is there still a hospital here?' I asked, as Paul wasn't objecting to our questions.

'There is not, it is in York, where modern medicines are practiced. We retained our hospital during the Great War and we helped many injured. Then the authorities deemed it must close. The hospital is now the Refectory.' He turned abruptly and walked across to a raised platform behind the pool of dark water and stood next to it. 'This is the tomb of the Crusader, Michael de Montfort; our Brother founder and Knight Templar.'

It was a slab of sandstone, engraved with the effigy of a

knight and a Templar Cross with an inscription in Latin. I could make out the man's name and reached a hand to sweep fine dust away from the carved lettering.

'Where is the other?' Swift asked, looking around.

'The Mahometan was Iqbal Salim.' Brother Paul intoned. 'He is buried on the hill. It is Strangers Hill. He was not born a Christian.'

'But he died one?' I asked.

'He did.'

'They still didn't bury him here though?' Swift looked troubled.

'They lived according to their strictures, it is not for us to question what we cannot understand. Come.' Brother Paul turned and went back into the tunnel. He led us to a stone stairway and climbed the steps ahead. There was a heavy door at the top, set with iron bolts. He slid them open, they must have been oiled because they didn't make a sound. He passed through the door, we followed.

I'd expected to see the cloister but we'd arrived in another room. This was more modern. Well, medieval anyway. We didn't need to be told it was the Scriptorium. Monks in black cassocks were seated on high stools in front of beautifully constructed wooden desks. Each monk had his own nook, a mullion window at his side, a cushion at his back and a profusion of coloured inks and paints in ceramic pots arrayed on the top of each desk. All I could hear was the scratching of quills on parchment and vellum. I counted twelve nooks on each side of the room.

I paused to watch a young monk at work. He kept his head down, his tonsured pate showing downy growth. His eyes flicked sideways toward me and his lips quivered in a friendly smile. He had a very old book open to his left, it was mostly filled with tightly drawn calligraphy written in Latin. There were small paintings in the margins; peculiar and highly colourful. Birds were interwoven within leaves of green, a monkey grasped a frond, a mule with a fish's tail grinned with yellow teeth. Other beasts, half-man half-monster, cavorted down the side of the page. I had no idea as to their meaning.

I guessed the youngster was one of the novices Father Ambrose had talked about and he was a very skilled one. He was making an exact copy from the old book onto a blank parchment and it was very difficult to tell which was old and which was new.

Swift was gazing over the shoulder of another scribe. He was repairing a book which had suffered water damage. The binding had been removed and the pages cut away, one by one. They were stacked nearby under a heavy press. I joined Swift to watch the young monk at work, delicately applying vivid colour with a paintbrush, restoring the page back to the glory it had once been.

An old monk, tonsured and bent, walked slowly along the aisle, observing. He occasionally leaned in to whisper words of guidance to a youngster. I assumed he was the Master Tutor.

As Brother Paul paced slowly along through the Scriptorium, I noticed the scribes duck their heads closer to their work, although none stiffened or flinched. I suspect the man was respected rather than feared.

'Come,' Brother Paul ordered as he walked away.

I threw another look around the place, up at the tall ceiling and ranges of ancient books arrayed on shelves fixed to plain plastered walls. It was a huge library of precious manuscripts and I empathised with Father Ambrose's desire to preserve this place for all time.

'He's gone,' Swift said as we arrived back in the Refectory.

'What?'

'Brother Paul.'

I turned around and realised the monk had indeed vanished. We'd returned by a different tunnel and had entered the Refectory through a small door behind the lectern.

'Swift.'

He turned to me. 'What?'

'We need to talk.'

'I know.'

Foggy was the only occupant of the kitchen. He greeted us with a yip of delight and jumped up on hind legs for a ruffle of the ears and a treat from my pocket. I led the way upstairs to my room.

There were signs that Greggs had been busy, the bed was made and my clothes stashed away somewhere. A kettle, mugs and teapot had been left by the blazing fire.

'Fascinating history,' I remarked and lifted the kettle to hang it on a hook above the flames. 'I hadn't realised they'd nursed soldiers here throughout the war.'

'It would have been peaceful,' Swift rubbed Tubbs' ears until the little cat purred. 'What's Strangers Hill?'

I shrugged. 'It's where they buried outsiders back in medieval times. Many parishes have one. It was meant to prevent their souls disturbing the villagers.'

'Old superstitions.'

'It's an old country.' I stirred the tea. 'Greggs might have some biscuits squirrelled away somewhere.'

'Florence packed some Clootie Dumpling. I'll fetch it.'

I remembered the Scottish delicacy from my visit to Braeburn Castle. A few slices could sustain a small army for days.

He returned in quick time with a package wrapped in waxed paper. 'Here.'

I poured water into the pot and found milk in an enamel jug on the windowsill and we sat down to a small feast in front of the fire with dog and cat for company.

'Father Ambrose is impeding the investigation.' Swift was still simmering. 'If Danton knew Clarence's sin, why can't we?'

'He can't disclose the secret of the confessional, you know that,' I reminded him again. 'Let's stick to the facts.'

'Fine.' He took a deep breath. 'Danton demanded the Codex before the reading of the will. The Abbot told him Clarence had given it to him.'

'And that it's missing,' I added.

'Yes.' He frowned. 'Then Danton attempted blackmail.'

'The threat he used was Clarence's sin.' I bit into a thick slice of Clootie Dumpling.

'Which doesn't make sense.' Swift sat back in his chair, cake in hand.

'Clarence's sin compromises Father Ambrose…'

'So, Father Ambrose must be implicated in whatever Clarence was guilty of,' Swift concluded.

Perhaps someone murdered Danton to stop it being found out,' I suggested, which was an uncomfortable thought and it shut us both up.

Greggs entered, still humming some sort of tune. He carried a small pile of folded shirts.

'I have completed the pressing, sir. And I am preparing to go to the post office for supplies.' He was very spruce with his hair neatly parted. I could smell cologne.

'What for?'

'Anything you may want, sir.' He had a soppy smile fixed to his old phiz. 'I could make a list.'

'Wouldn't be in the chance of seeing a certain lady, would it?' I quizzed him.

His colour heightened. 'I do not know what you mean, sir.'

'The post mistress,' Swift put in.

Greggs bridled. 'It was not the post mistress. It was… ahem… I decline to answer, sir.' He turned pink.

'Oh, so that was it. It was the signorina! She came out just after you.' Swift laughed.

'Good Lord, not the Contessa!' I exclaimed.

Swift stifled his mirth. 'No, it was Marta! I saw her. You've got dangerous tastes, Greggs.'

'Nonsense, sir… I mean, I beg to disagree. The lady has

a classic air, exotic and… and cultured. Like an Opera singer, or a heroine of history…'

'Or Lady Macbeth,' Swift added.

'There's no point in lurking around the post office if she's the Contessa's lady's maid, old chap. You need Calderstone Hall and that's on the other side of the hill.'

'Very well, sir. I will take Mr Fogg for a walk.'

'No. He's coming with me.'

'You could take up bird watching,' Swift suggested.

'No, I could not, sir.'

'Of course you can.' Swift dug about in his trench coat. 'Here.' He pulled out a pair of field glasses.

Greggs held up a hand. 'No thank you, sir. I will take my journal and make notes on the local flora and fauna.' He left with a look of intent.

'We've got time to interview the local doctor.' Swift looked at his watch. 'Wexford, he was called.'

I finished my tea. 'Right behind you, Swift.'

We walked back outside into bright spring sunshine.

We didn't know where the Doctor's house was, but Swift once more entered the Calderstone Arms for enlightenment.

"Hark Away House' according to Betty. It's over yon hill.'

'Not the blasted hill again,' I swore, as we began the hike back up the track.

'Strangers Hill.' Swift panted as we reached the top, pausing next to the milestone.

We spotted Greggs in the distance, he was examining a hedgerow – book and pen in hand, bowler hat on head;

a very unlikely naturalist. We waved, he pretended not to see us.

'Love must have really struck this time.' I regarded my old butler.

'Lennox, on the subject of romance…' Swift began the steep descent.

'Don't worry, I'm not going to fall for the Contessa's abundant charms.'

'No, it's not that. We received a letter from Persi.'

'What?' I turned toward him as we kept up the pace. 'Why didn't you tell me?'

'We didn't want to interfere.' He sounded a bit sheepish.

'Well what did she say?'

'She was upset you hadn't replied to her. Apparently she hasn't heard a word from you since Damascus.'

'I didn't get her letter.' I ran fingers through my hair. 'Not the first one, assuming there was a first one. Then I got one with camels on…' I realised I was babbling. 'I mean, she sent another one and it only arrived yesterday.'

'You're still keen then?' He said between breaths.

'Of course I am! I wrote a reply, but… um the post is unreliable so…' I fudged a response.

'You could try Lady Maitland?' He suggested.

'What on earth for?'

'She practically runs the Foreign Office. She'll have access to the Diplomatic Bag.'

'Ah yes, good idea, old chap.' I'm pretty sure he must have heard the conversation with Tommy and drawn his own conclusions. Always a risk with detectives.

'Swift...' I began.

'What?'

'Talking of ladies... wives, um whatever, how are things on the domestic front?' I deflected the subject.

His face sharpened then he sighed. 'Florence and I couldn't be more content, but... I feel like a spare part, Lennox. I thought after that episode with the skeleton I'd develop some sort of role at Braeburn.' He was walking with his head down and shoulders hunched. 'I helped organise the rebuilding of the ruins, but we ran out of money towards the end. Since then I've been suggesting ideas to make the estate more commercial, like fishing or selling our whisky to outlets in London, but I can't convince the Laird.'

'What does Florence think?' I asked.

'She thinks I should do what I'm good at; detecting. Which is ridiculous because there isn't anything to detect in Braeburn.'

'You'll be a father soon, though.' I tried to jolly him along.

'Yes, and I'm thrilled, we both are. But I don't own my own home and I don't earn my own crust. I'm going to be the father of the next generation of Braeburns, but it's not a career, is it?' He ended on a dejected note.

'I doubt fishing is viable, you'd have to send them to a market somewhere and they'd go off too quickly.' I tried some positive suggestion. 'But there must be a market for the whisky.'

'Do you think so?' He replied, a glimmer of enthusiasm showing. 'Where would I sell it?'

'Try the gentlemen's clubs in London. My cousin Edgar is a member of the best of them, I'll drop him a line if you like.'

'Yes, that could be an opening.' He sounded more cheerful. 'And post that letter to Persi while you're at it.'

We'd descended the hill, passed the solicitor's house then carried on along the patched tarmac road until we reached the gateway to a short drive. A wooden name plate was painted with elegant lettering, 'Hark Away House.'

The house was modest in size, little more than a large cottage with an annex. It was stone built and homely, with low eaves and lattice windows under a slate roof. The door opened as we approached, a young lady in a nurses' uniform, a blue cape and starched white cap emerged. She came along the path as we stopped by the gate.

'Oh hello,' she smiled up at us. 'The Doctor's in, just tell the housekeeper to let you through.'

'Good day,' Swift bowed his head and held the gate for her.

She had chestnut hair tied in a bun, clear skin and pink cheeks. She glanced up at me with large eyes, they were the colour of cornflowers. My heart lurched and I stopped in my tracks. She waved a white-gloved hand then walked off along the road.

CHAPTER 9

'Chief Inspector Swift and Major Lennox for Doctor Wexford.' Swift made a polite introduction, for all the good it did. The housekeeper remained unimpressed. I didn't take much notice, my mind was filled with images of the woman we'd just met, her eyes were like... like...

'Sergeant Beamish was here last evening and again this morning. Doctor's got enough to do without having police bothering him day and night.'

A voice called out. 'Sarah, please show them in, I'm in the office.'

'Humph.' She stood back and reluctantly opened the door. 'You be going down there, 'tis just beyond the stairs and don't you be touching a thing.' She wore black with a starched white apron, like a matron, only one of the bossy types not the warm, plump ones, which I preferred.

I followed Swift across the threshold, she gave us a look that would freeze a cat. Foggy had been hiding behind me but he bravely came along in my footsteps.

'Oh, a doggie.' The lady melted. 'Now there's a little

sweetie. Come along with me to the kitchen and we'll find you a bite.'

He followed her of course, because he was quite aware what the word 'kitchen' meant.

A pleasant chap looked up from scribbling on a note pad; reddish-brown hair and lashes, green eyes and pale skin, he looked about the same age as me and Swift. He wore a starched white coat, which has become the habit of doctors nowadays.

We made the usual introductions.

'Do please sit down. Sorry about the housekeeper, she means well.' Doctor Wexford indicated two seats in front of his desk.

'Over protective?' I said.

'Like a bull terrier, but with a heart of gold.' He fiddled with his pen.

'We're investigating Danton's death,' Swift announced, although it wasn't exactly official.

Dr Wexford nodded. 'Sergeant Beamish told me there was a Scotland Yard man here. But he mentioned you were retired?' He fished politely for our credentials.

'I am, but I've been asked to intercede by the Foreign Office,' Swift lied.

I turned to stare, but he ignored me.

'Ah, well I'm afraid we haven't had the post mortem results yet.' Wexford smiled again. 'The Coroner isn't really used to cases of unexplained death.'

Swift withdrew his notebook and handed it to me. 'Take notes, Lennox.'

'What?'

'It would help.' He gave me a look that was part demand, part pleading.

'Oh, very well.' I withdrew my Montblanc fountain pen and gave it a shake, which was a mistake. A splatter of ink blots flew off the nib when I unscrewed the cap. Dr Wexford passed me some blotting paper and I cleaned up the pen and book. 'Right, ready.'

Swift turned to Wexford. 'Did you find any signs of trauma on Danton's body?'

'None.' He leaned back and put his own pen down on the desk, no doubt more comfortable discussing professional matters. 'I didn't undress the corpse but I made as thorough an examination as possible. There was no evidence of physical assault. I took swabs from under his finger nails, nose and eyes. The tongue had slipped back, preventing access to the throat, but the pathologist will examine all the cavities during the post mortem.'

Swift seemed impressed. 'Very good.'

'I didn't want any evidence lost before he thawed out.' Dr Wexford continued. 'By the state of the body, I thought he'd been in there most of the day. I knew once he warmed up there was a chance we'd risk missing any residues.'

'Did you scrape his eyebrows?' I asked.

'I didn't. What makes you think it was necessary?'

'There were crystals of ice on his eyebrows,' I replied.

'Hum.' Wexford leaned forward to place his elbows on the desk. 'That's interesting. I had ambitions to be a forensic pathologist when I started my training, but then

I met my wife and we moved to Calderstone after the war. She's the local midwife; she was raised here and doesn't want to leave,' he shrugged and smiled. 'So here we are.'

'I think we met her on the way in,' I mentioned, the blue of her eyes seared into my brain. I'd spent the last four years trying to block out the image of another girl, a girl with eyes the colour of cornflowers, and now...

'Do you think the crystals are relevant?' Swift's questioning brought me back to the present.

'I don't know.' Wexford considered. 'I didn't observe any when I examined him, but, by the time I arrived, the police had spent almost an hour in proximity to the body and you'd both been in there too, so...'

'What time do you think he died?' Swift asked.

'Sergeant Beamish said Danton had left Calderstone Hall at eleven o'clock in the morning to travel the two miles to Fenshaw's place. I'd say Danton died not long after eleven, although the cold inside the ice-house makes it difficult to be certain.'

I wrote down *Danton dead, 11am.*

'What were the weather conditions yesterday morning?' Swift continued rattling off questions.

'The same as this morning, cold but clear. Very pleasant actually, I took a walk about that time, I went over the hill to the village, met my wife and picked up a letter at the post office.'

'Did you see anyone?' Swift shot back.

'No,' Wexford shook his head. 'Not a soul until I reached the village.'

'Oh,' Swift slumped a tad.

'He could have just had a heart attack, you know,' Wexford suggested. 'He may have felt ill, pulled off the road and stumbled to the nearest shelter.'

'And hid his briefcase, then closed the door after him?' I remarked.

The Doctor regarded me with cool appraisal.

'You were at the Hall when Clarence Calderstone died?' Swift switched the subject.

'I was.' Wexford turned to reply.

'Please tell us what happened?' Swift sat back in his chair, trench coat undone, legs crossed and arms folded.

'Yes, of course. We were riding with the hunt, it was...' The Doctor stared at the ceiling for a moment. '...ten days ago. The weather had broken after a long cold spell and the Master announced a 'meet'. Clarence had only been back for a couple of days, but as soon as he heard, he declared the Hunt should gather at Calderstone Hall. So we did, and had the usual 'cup', then set off. The horses and hounds were fresh...'

I interrupted him. 'Did Clarence take the communal cup or did he have his own?'

'You are suspicious, aren't you, Major?' Wexford smiled and picked his pen back up. 'He had the same as the rest of us. There was only his old butler and housekeeper working at the Hall, so the pub did the honours.'

'Betty?' I asked.

'Yes, she brought a couple of men from the village to help her.' He turned the pen with long fingers. 'Anyway, the hounds picked up a scent and headed east, toward the moors. The riders spread out, Kitty, that's my wife, and I fell behind, our horses are more used to light hacks than cross-country gallops.' His smile rose and fell. 'The hounds lost the fox, but picked up a new scent and set off again going north. We were up in the high fields, the hounds went through a gap in the stone wall near the top of the hill. Some of the hunt headed down to the gate and others jumped the wall, including Clarence. I didn't see him fall but I saw the aftermath. He'd misjudged the jump, took it too late and his horse hit the coping. The poor animal was completely unbalanced, it stumbled on landing, threw Clarence off and then crashed on top of him.' He sighed. 'Broken pelvis, spine and ribs which punctured his lungs. Vital organs were crushed and he was bleeding internally; I knew he was finished and so did he.'

'What happened to the horse?' I asked.

'Bruised, but alive,' Wexford replied.

'Clarence was brought home?' Swift intervened.

Wexford nodded. 'My wife and I galloped back here. I picked up my medical case and drove to the Hall. The huntsmen had carried Clarence back on a gate, they arrived at the same moment I did. Clarence was still breathing, which surprised me, but he was a tough man, big boned and seemed fit for a sixty year old. We carried him upstairs, he was calling for the Abbot, insisting that he be fetched. The Master and a few others went off to the Abbey and I made Clarence as comfortable as I could. I offered him morphine but he refused.'

'Who else was in the room with you?'

'Clarence's old butler. He drew the curtains, got the fire blazing, that sort of thing, but he was very shocked, so I sent him down to the kitchens.'

'Did Clarence speak to you during this time?' Swift continued.

'He had a key around his neck on a gold chain, he said it was to the strongbox and I had to make sure it was given to Father Ambrose. He was very agitated and kept repeating himself. Then Father Ambrose arrived with Brother Paul and Brother Tobias.'

'Brother Tobias?' I exclaimed.

'Why was he there?' Swift asked.

Dr Wexford shrugged. 'I don't know, you'll have to ask him.'

'Lennox,' Swift turned to me.

'What?'

'Are you writing this down?'

I'd become distracted by the story. 'Yes, yes.' I scrawled *ask Tobias*.

Wexford carried on. 'There wasn't much more I could do. Brother Paul gave Clarence a sedative and...'

'What form did this sedative take?' Swift cut in.

'He held a sponge under Clarence's nose for him to inhale. It's called a soporific sponge – it's a very old form of sedation, I haven't seen it used before, but I've read about it in medical history books.'

That caught my interest and I recalled the jar of sponges in the Pharmacia. 'What was in it?'

'Herbal sedatives, its effect is mild but it ameliorated the pain.' Wexford put his pen back on his desk. 'Clarence was a great deal more comfortable afterwards.'

'Was he coherent, not dotty or drowsy?' I wanted to know.

'He was entirely lucid.'

'Did you hear the conversation between Clarence and the monks?' Swift switched the subject back to the death bed confession.

Wexford thought for a moment. 'Father Ambrose began the Last Rites and asked Clarence if he had sinned. He replied, 'yes, all the time,' and said he'd had his punishment.'

'What was it?' Swift continued.

'Ah, well that's when Brother Paul put a hand on my shoulder and escorted me out of the door.'

'So you heard nothing of the confession?' Swift grilled him.

'No, I waited outside the room,' he replied. 'By the time I was asked to return, Clarence was dead. I confirmed time of death and wrote the certificate.'

'Was there anyone else present?' I asked.

Wexford shook his head. 'No, as I said, I had sent the butler to the kitchens to recover his wits. The housekeeper is his wife. They left the same day and have gone to live in York. I heard that the Italian woman has moved into the Hall.'

I thought he was fishing for gossip, so I said nothing.

'Lennox, have you written all this down?' Swift demanded again.

'Yes.' I penned, *butler and wife gone to town.*

'Father Ambrose told us about a book.' I rejoined. 'What do you know about that?'

He picked up his pen again. 'Not much. Clarence had shown me the key around his neck, but I've told you that already. After it was all over, I went with the monks to the gun room. Brother Paul opened the strongbox and found the book, it was very old by the look of it. Father Ambrose was agitated, he's quite a nervous man. He didn't seem to want to touch it and declared he would leave it there.'

I wrote *Wexford saw the Codex,* closed Swift's notebook and handed it back to him. He opened it again, stared at the scrawl, ink spots and smears, frowned and put it in his pocket.

'I hope I was of help.' Wexford stood up.

'Yes, thank you, Doctor.' Swift shook the man's hand in formal manner and made for the door.

I gave him a wave, being wary of shaking doctor's hands on the principle that you never know where they'd been. I went off in search of my dog, he was in the hall being cooed over by the prickly housekeeper.

'He's had a bone.' Her face creased into what could have been a smile. 'He buried it in the garden. You should take him up yon hill, there's more up there.'

'Well, I don't want Foggy digging them up.'

She didn't reply, just shut the door behind us.

I had my hands in pockets as we strode back toward the hill, the Abbey and the village. 'What time is it?'

'Not long before lunch, or dinner, as they call it.' Swift's mind hadn't moved far from the killing. 'The murder was sophisticated. Danton wasn't just bashed on the head.'

'If it was poison then...'

'How many times do I have to say it, Lennox? It can't have been poison, you saw the mouse. Danton would have died in convulsions.'

'Do you have any better ideas?' We were treading the track towards the crest.

'Yes, we wait until the post mortem results and proceed from a basis of fact, not speculation.'

'We're becoming distracted by the murder, Swift.'

'I'm not distracted,' he retorted and stared into the distance before turning a sharp gaze back at me. 'Why not kill the Contessa? Why murder her lawyer?'

'I was thinking about that.' We were passing the milestone, a gust of wind caught us and we paused to catch our breath. 'They have to kill her claim, not her. If she is the legitimate heir to Clarence's estate, then whatever she owns would belong to her next of kin on the event of her death.'

'Ah, yes. I forgot you aristocrats know all about inheritance law,' Swift remarked. 'So, the killer sought to destroy her legal claim to prevent her inheriting the estate.'

'Probably, although any paper she had could be replicated and authorised by whoever issued them,' I told him. He was right, the law of inheritance in all its facets was a subject at many a dining table – although, it was mostly gossip about who'd died, what they'd left and who was going to get it.

'They couldn't replicate the will,' Swift replied. 'It has to be authenticated, signed by the testator and independently witnessed. It's a unique document.'

'True,' I agreed. 'Although even without a will she still has a chance if he's declared intestate. She only has to prove she's his wife and she'll be entitled to a portion of his estate under English law.'

'Hum. Father Ambrose said Clarence had been a Casanova, what if there's a child?' Swift deliberated as we crossed the village green.

'That would depend on legitimacy,' I replied. 'And I think it would be known if any were born within wedlock.'

He paused at the wicket gate into the Abbey. 'So, if any by-blows exist, they'd get nothing?'

'Not a bean,' I replied.

CHAPTER 10

Brother Tobias was seated at the kitchen table, the arms of his black cassock rolled up and an apron tied behind his ample waist. He was peeling potatoes into a white enamel basin. 'Dinner will be ready shortly, it's bean stew,' he indicated a large pot of beans in water beside an even larger heap of carrots and leaks.

'Beans?' I uttered.

'We have beef, beans or mutton, except Friday and then it's fish.' Brother Tobias grinned. "Tis the way it is and the way it's always been.'

'We'll have lunch at the Calderstone Arms,' I told him.

He laughed. 'I'd be comin' with you if I could.'

'Do you ever leave the monastery?' Swift sat down on the bench opposite the monk.

'Aye,' Brother Tobias nodded. 'I go to see the farmers for vittles and meat, it's the duty of the Kitchener to buy in provender and keep it fresh.'

'What about yesterday morning?' Swift asked.

'I was out and about, as I am most days.'

I noticed he was very adept at potato peeling, the pile in the basin was filling up quickly.

'Did you see anyone near the ice-house?' Swift continued rattling out questions.

'No.' Tobias answered sharply.

'I haven't seen a meat-store here?' I mentioned.

Brother Tobias stopped peeling and eyed me. 'There ain't one, I use the ice-house and I weren't in there yesterday, so don't go askin'.'

'Does anyone else use it?' Swift leaned forward. We'd wondered why the blocks of ice were fresh when the Hall was barely occupied.

'The pub keeps a few boxes in there.' Tobias picked up another potato and sliced the skin off.

'Betty?' I asked, just to be clear.

'And the folk who help her out,' he replied.

'Do many of the Brothers leave the Abbey?' I continued.

'Brother Paul attends to the sick, and delivers medicines. None other goes out.' His good humour seemed to be evaporating.

'You're local, aren't you?' I tried a lighter approach.

'Aye, well spotted lad; you should take up detecting with a mind as sharp as yours.' He dropped another potato into the basin.

'So you're Calderstone born and bred, where everybody knows everyone's business?' Swift was all policeman.

'Kick one and they all limp, just as always.' He finished the last potato and lifted the basin load of potatoes off the table.

'There was dead mouse in my room,' I remarked.

'Poisoned, no doubt,' he replied. 'Don't be afeared for the kitty. Cats won't touch carrion. Nor your little dog.'

'Did Brother Paul supply the poison?' I asked, feeling like a proper detective asking proper questions.

'Aye, he did.'

'You don't attend the services?' Swift remarked.

'I do my share of prayers and gospel.' The big monk's genial smile turned wry. 'But, I'm a lay brother, so I don't go to the services. As you can see, there's no servants here – chief cook an' bottle-washer, that's me.' He had poured the potatoes into the cauldron suspended over the fire and came back for the vegetables. 'Now, if you're not going to join us for the bean feast, I'd best be getting on.'

'Wait.' There was something we'd forgotten. 'Why did you go to Calderstone Hall when Clarence was dying?'

He stopped and looked at me.

'I was Sir Clarence's servant in my youth. I went to say goodbye to my old master and I'm saying no more on it.' He spoke with a note of finality.

'There's a man dead and Clarence's confession could be the reason,' Swift suddenly snapped.

'It's nowt to do with me, or you for that matter.' Brother Tobias put his hands on his hips. 'Now I'm not in the habit of repeating myself, so you'd best let me be gettin' on.'

Even Swift wasn't impervious to such a dismissal.

'Not very forthcoming was he.' We left the kitchen and headed for the village.

'No, I'd say he's got something to hide.' Swift was in a low mood.

It was a brisk walk, the wind had risen and clouds were sweeping across the sky. I paused at the pub doorway to read the name of the Licence holder posted above the door. It was one Elizabeth Sykes, I wondered if that was Betty herself.

'Aye, it is.' Betty handed us a pint of ale each. 'This pub's mine, lock, stock and barrel, and I'm the boss. But I'm soft with it.' She laughed good-naturedly. Her welcome was as warm as yesterday, but I noticed a few sideways glances coming in our direction from the locals.

'Seems they know who we are, Swift,' I remarked as we made our way to the same table in front of the fire.

He shrugged and raised his pint. 'Being unpopular is part of a policeman's lot, Lennox.'

I can't say I felt quite so sanguine about it.

Betty returned, holding two steaming plates piled high with deliciousness. 'Steak pie and mash today.'

We tucked in, all the hill climbing had sharpened the appetite.

'Shouldn't we have made statements to the police, or something?' I remarked between bites of succulent steak with crusty pastry.

'I did,' Swift replied. 'I debriefed Sergeant Beamish this morning when I saw him. We can sign them later at the station.'

'What are they doing?' I drained my beer and considered another.

'They're supposed to be making a fingertip search of the ice-house and woodland, then interviewing the Contessa, although I doubt she'll co-operate.'

'Lennox,' Swift began. 'Your questioning...'

'What about it?'

'There's a modern police method being talked of, it's called good copper, bad copper. One detective is friendly toward the suspect, the other is abrasive. It's thought to knock the suspect off balance.'

'Um.' I thought about it. 'It wasn't mentioned in Sherlock Holmes.'

'Sherlock Holmes is fiction, Lennox.'

'Right, fine,' I agreed, because he really did take things far too seriously. 'Actually, we do that anyway, Swift.'

'I know, but I'm drawing your attention to it.' He pushed back his cuff to check his watch. 'Ten to two. We'll have to look sharp.'

We tackled the hill in quick time and reached the other side to stride along the quiet stretch of tarmac toward the lawyers' place. A rumble behind caused us to turn about. The blue Lagonda swept around the corner, top down, the Contessa in the driving seat. She raised a black-gloved hand in salute as we leapt off the road.

'That's Danton's car!' Swift glared after it. 'That's downright theft.'

'Possession is nine tenths of the law, Swift, you know that.'

'Yes, and I imagine she tends to hold on to whatever she's got,' he retorted.

It was parked outside Fell House when we arrived, Swift gave it a close look as I went to rap on the door. We were shown straight in by the elderly butler.

Fenshaw was in charge, he wore the same brown suit and tie, with his hair carefully oiled. He'd had the dining room cleared out, put a table at one end and arranged chairs in rows to face him. It looked like a drab wedding venue which even the fitful sunshine coming through the solitary window couldn't enliven. The Contessa, draped and veiled in widows' black, was seated at the very front, almost within grabbing distance of Fenshaw. He was red in the face and fiddling with the files on the table in front of him. I had the impression there had been some sort of contretemps.

Father Ambrose was also seated on the front row, as far away from the lady as possible. He raised a hand as though in blessing and seemed to have cheered up. Brother Paul was with him, sharp angles defining his face and eyes. He was watchful but mute.

We gave nods all round on arrival; it seemed inappropriate to break the uneasy silence with words of greeting.

Sergeant Beamish was sitting at the back. He grinned when he saw us, then remembered where he was and pulled a straight face. Constable Burrows stood a little way behind him against the sombre wallpaper, a look of intent on his grizzled phiz.

Kitty Wexford sat next to Beamish on the back row. She had slipped off her cape and was dressed in a dark blue uniform with white collar and cuffs. I edged in close to her. Swift sat next to me and withdrew his notebook and pen. He leaned around me to glance at Kitty Wexford, no doubt wondering why she was present. Then he began to note down names and where they were sitting.

Fenshaw opened his mouth to speak, but closed it when the door opened again and Wexford himself entered. The doctor offered solemn smiles to the assembled then came to sit between me and his wife.

Fenshaw picked up a buff coloured file and pulled out papers to place on the table, ostentatiously making small stacks in a row.

'Ladies and…' he began.

The door opened again. A short man with a foreign hat put his head around the door. 'I can come in?'

Fenshaw frowned and waved his arm to indicate admission. A ripple of whispers ran around the room.

'Good Day to you all.' The stranger whipped off his felt hat, it had a red feather in it. 'I am named Herr Johan Roche.' He bowed.

'The Swiss,' Swift muttered under his breath.

Nobody replied so he walked into the room, manoeuvred politely around the two monks and sat close to the Contessa. He wore a dark green felted jacket with mustard yellow waistcoat and trousers. He formed a florid contrast between the monks' black cassocks and the Contessa's mourning garb. At least he was sporting proper trousers rather than embroidered leather breeches, which I'd once had the misfortune to witness.

'Ladies and Gentlemen,' Fenshaw began again. 'I have

asked you here…' he leaned forward and corrected himself. 'I have asked *some* of you here, to witness the legal proceedings required to settle the goods and chattels of Sir Clarence Fitzroy James Nimrod Calderstone, seventh Baron Calderstone of the domain of Calderstone and Monks Hood. It is my understanding that the Lady Mirabella, Contessa Ferranti of sestiere Castello in Venice, has lodged a formal challenge to this proceeding.'

'I have.' She rose in her seat and lifted back her veil. 'You must put an end to this theatre. My man of law has been murdered.' Her voice picked up an octave. *'Assasinato,'* she shouted for dramatic effect, 'and my papers have been stolen. A *malfattore* is trying to take my inheritance. Murderers and thieves!' She pointed a black-gloved finger at Fenshaw. 'You must stop now.'

'Madam… Lady Mirabella, I have tried to explain…' Fenshaw didn't get very far.

'I order you to do as I say,' she commanded, her dark eyes blazing.

'My dear lady, you cannot simply…' The little Swiss stood up, no doubt to offer reasoned logic to the widow. She whacked him round the ear with her black-beaded handbag.

'Idiote!'

That shut him up. He sank to his seat, rubbing his cheek then squeaked in annoyance because he'd sat on his felt hat. He picked it up, the red feather was bent and broken.

I sat back to enjoy the show.

'Lady Mirabella.' Fenshaw leaned forward, keeping the

table between him and the incensed Contessa. 'I have told you already, a note has been made of your objections. This proceeding is merely the necessary first step towards probate. If you would please allow the assembled to listen...'

She was still wielding the handbag. 'You were supposed to be of help to me. But now I see it, you work with these people.' She waved a hand towards the roomful of mesmerised onlookers. 'You want to give away all my things which were belonging to my husband. It is theft! You are here to steal from me. You murder my man, you steal my papers and now you are stealing...'

'Now just a minute...' Sergeant Beamish had remembered that he was the law and mention of murder and theft were his domain. 'Madam, if you do not desist...'

She turned and thwacked him round the head too, knocking his helmet flying. Two bright red spots appeared on his cheeks. He pointed a warning finger at her while trying to retrieve his helmet. 'That's an offence that is. You aren't allowed to hit a policeman, I can arrest you for that.'

Constable Burrows took out his whistle and give it a good blast.

'Lady Mirabella will you please listen...' Fenshaw bashed a gavel on the table, no-one took any notice.

The Swiss leapt to his feet. 'You are impeding proper process, Madam. You are incorrect in your actions.' He tried to shout over the racket.

The Contessa towered over him, splendidly incandescent, and raised her handbag again. He ducked behind a chair.

'Enough!' Brother Paul suddenly stood and raised his voice. It brought instant silence to the room. 'Sit down and be quiet.'

They all stopped, then duly sat down, muttering beneath their breath. I noticed Kitty Wexford hide a smile. Her husband reached out to place his arm around her shoulders.

Fenshaw took his chance. 'I, Stephen Fenshaw, of Fenshaw and Lawson, solicitors, do formally declare that there is no extant will of Sir Clarence Fitzroy James Nimrod Calderstone. I can therefore announce that he ...'

A gasp of surprise rippled around the room.

'Ha!' The Contessa's red lips suddenly broke into a wide smile and she purred. 'You should have told me, *tesoro*.'

'I tried,' Fenshaw hissed.

The door opened. 'Oh Hello! What a pleasant surprise.' An elderly man tottered in, a short Pickwickian type with crinkled grey hair, wire rim spectacles and an amiable smile. He wore an old-fashioned frock coat, a stiff collar and white shirt, a waistcoat with fob chain, black socks and gaiters. He appeared to have forgotten his trousers. 'I say, nephew, are we having a party?'

CHAPTER 11

'Uncle.' Fenshaw flew to his side. 'You should be in your room, what are you doing here...'

'Wait.' Brother Paul rose to his feet. 'I will assist.' He went to the elderly man's side and led him out.

'I... I apologise for my Uncle. He's not quite himself.' Fenshaw sounded rattled. 'Please let me proceed. So, as no will has been discovered...' He nodded toward the triumphant Contessa. '...I declare that Sir Clarence Calderstone died intestate. Given these findings, the law of intestacy prevails. Under this law, the entire estate will cede to his wife, the Contessa Mirabella Ferranti, *providing*,' he stressed this last word, 'she produces a properly notarised marriage certificate.' He picked up his papers with a satisfied smirk and shuffled them back into the file.

Silence fell for an instant, then murmurings of confused anger were heard. The Contessa pulled the veil back over her face and rose to leave. The little Swiss leaned away as she made her way past him.

The door opened once again and Brother Paul returned with a fully trousered Lawson. The Contessa stopped in her tracks and raised her veil with a flick of the hand.

'Nephew!' The old man waved a sheaf of yellowed papers. 'I've found it! I knew it was somewhere. Brother Paul helped me – it's Clarence's will!'

'No!' The Contessa shrieked.

'Haha,' I heard Constable Burrows laugh quietly.

'Ladies and gentlemen, if you would please be seated.' Lawson looked around, beaming behind his wire rimmed spectacles. 'Oh!' He regarded his nephew as though surprised to see him. 'Stephen, you still here? Jolly good show, young whippersnapper. I'll take the chair dear boy and I rather think I'd like a brandy.'

'Uncle, you mustn't...' Fenshaw wavered, no doubt trying to cudgel a reason to remove the old fellow. His shoulders drooped when he realised it wouldn't get him anywhere. He ceded the chair to his Uncle, then retrieved another, tugging it to the wall and sat down looking as sulky as a schoolboy.

'Now, where were we?' Lawson pulled out his fob watch and peered at it. It must have stopped as he banged it on the table twice, which can't have done it much good, to my mind.

He picked up the fold of papers he'd brought with him. I could see the frontispiece was written in curling calligraphy with a red wax seal fixed across its folds.

'Please observe the seal. It is intact.' He held it up, then carefully broke the wax seal. 'I will now formally read the document.' He adjusted his spectacles and began reading in a quavering voice.

'This is the last will and testament of Sir Clarence Fitzroy James Nimrod Calderstone made on this day eighteen hundred and ninety five. I revoke all previous wills...'

I calculated the age of the will while he burbled through the formalities. It would have been written twenty seven years ago, or thereabouts. I leaned over to see Swift had written the figures in his notebook.

Lawson continued. 'To the villagers of Calderstone, I bequeath the land upon which their cottages lie and the surrounding gardens, to each and every one of them.' A gasp ran around the room. 'To the Abbey of Monks Hood, I bequeath the land upon which the Abbey stands and all the remaining land I own, with the exception of that which lies within the curtilage of Calderstone Hall. The house can go to my creditors, or to hell, for all I care. Unless...'

The murmuring grew louder, mostly coming from the Contessa who had yanked her veil off entirely and was biting her red lips in fury.

'Now, now, do let me finish,' Lawson quibbled. 'Oh, and my brandy, nephew. Come along young man, you have forgotten.'

Fenshaw turned red in the face and stalked out.

'My sister's boy, you know.' He beamed at the room from behind his spectacles. 'He's coming along very well; nothing that a talented tutor and a few whacks on the posterior can't cure, eh!' He laughed genially, along with most of the room.

Fenshaw returned with a small glass of brandy before retaking his seat.

'Let me see, ah yes!' Lawson drained the liquor with obvious relish, adjusted his glasses and continued. 'Unless the child survives. If the child should reach majority, then the entire Calderstone estate and all it contains must accede to Calderstone blood.' He put down the paper and beamed. 'Thank you all for coming. I do enjoy a party!'

The room sat frozen in confusion for a moment. Swift and I looked at the Swiss when mention of 'the child' was made, but he didn't bat an eyelid. I turned to the Wexfords, the Doctor was looking decidedly cheerful, whereas his pretty wife's face was tense. I wondered what it all meant. The policemen moved forward, anticipating trouble, but everyone was flummoxed and for a moment nobody did anything. Then the Contessa swore loudly in Italian and stormed out, fury blazing in her eyes. Lawson stood up, fumbled with his papers, beamed once more at the assembled, and tottered off, his nephew at his heels. I watched Roche dart out after them, then I heard a door close in the distance. The elderly butler came and hovered as though to encourage us out.

'We need to speak to Roche,' Swift addressed the butler.

'Or Lawson,' I added.

'I'm afraid the gentleman are now in the office and the door is closed,' the old butler replied.

Swift looked inclined to argue.

'Too late, Swift. Come on,' I told him.

The policemen had led the way out, but had stopped to wait for us on the drive.

'What was all that about?' Swift demanded.

'No idea, sir, but I don't think that lady was happy,' Beamish replied. 'She should never have hit me, neither. I could arrest her for that.'

Constable Burrows was fixing bicycle clips to his legs. 'Told you to keep away from her,' he called out.

'She was rude this morning, all we was doing was trying to interview her,' Beamish carried on, patently aggrieved. 'Proper police procedure it is.'

'Right,' Swift sighed. 'I'll go with you next time. Go back to the station, we'll meet you there.'

'Yes sir,' Beamish saluted and went to retrieve his bicycle from next to the gateway. We watched them wobble off down the road.

Father Ambrose and Brother Paul had emerged as we were talking and passed us by. They were walking toward the road with their cowls up and heads down in quiet conversation.

'Why was Mrs Wexford there?' I raised the question. Even as I spoke, the Wexfords rushed past us and caught up with the monks. They stopped to form a close huddle. We moved to join them.

Brother Paul stepped forward as though to ward us off. 'Father Ambrose will see you later.'

We didn't seem to be getting very far and headed toward Strangers Hill.

'Interesting outcome,' I remarked as we began the climb.

'The Swiss isn't 'the child'.' Swift replied.

'No. It could be Kitty Wexford, she's the right age.'

'Yes.' Swift paused. 'And there may be others.'

'They would have been at the reading.'

'I suppose so.' His lips drew in a line. 'It doesn't make sense, if she was his daughter...'

'Someone in the village will know,' I suggested. 'We could stop at the pub for a pint?'

'We need to go to the Police Station, Lennox.'

'But the pub would be a good spot to observe local reaction.'

'Fine, but not until we've been to the station.'

We ambled across the hill in silence, both lost in our thoughts.

Mine were on Kitty Wexford, her blue eyes and memories of another time and another place. Early dawn in France, the sound of engines running in the distance, the sharp tang of aviation fuel in the air and a girl with cornflower blue eyes gazing up at me. I let the feelings flow, the love, the hope, the happiness, then shut the images out, trying to bury them as though they never existed.

We reached the village and Fogg chased the ducks again. I shouted in exasperation and called him to heel as we crossed the green to find the police station.

It looked much as the other houses, except for a blue lamp hanging above the gate with POLICE painted onto it in white letters. It was a sturdy stone cottage, where the downstairs was given over to official business. We entered a narrow hallway and turned into the parlour. A dark wooden counter ran the entire length of the far wall, there was a simple Lino floor, polished but showing signs of muddy bootprints, a printed portrait of the King on one wall and a green noticeboard on the other. I paused to read the solitary sheet of paper; two ginger and white kittens were available, free to good homes.

A couple of wooden chairs stood before a cast iron fireplace, the grate glowed with red flames over black coals. A large ginger cat snoozed on a rug in front of it. Fogg went to say hello and was hissed at for his effrontery – he came to hide behind my legs. I wondered if the cat was father to the kittens posted on the board.

The counter was fitted with a candlestick telephone, an ungainly black typewriter and a large open ledger with a pen fixed to a nail by a length of brown cord. There was a handbell next to it, Swift picked it up and gave it a sharp shake.

Beamish arrived from a door behind the counter.

'Inspector!' He stood to attention and saluted, then grinned. He was without his helmet; his sandy hair was neatly combed above his freckled face and his ears stuck out like wing-nuts.

'We'll sign those statements now, Beamish.' Swift was business like.

'Aye, sir.' He leafed back through the ledger and took two type-written statements from between the pages and handed them over. I read mine, it didn't say much other than where and when we'd found the body. We signed and duly gave them back.

'Coroner's office telephoned not five minutes since,' Beamish told us.

Swift's face sharpened. 'What did they say?'

Beamish flicked the pages back again. He leaned on his elbows to read his carefully formed handwriting.

'Asphyxiation,' he pronounced slowly. 'The deceased's tongue had collapsed back into the velopharynx and stopped him breathing.'

'He swallowed his tongue.' Swift sounded surprised.

'I reckon that's what he did.' Beamish nodded.

'That's unusual. Did they form any conclusions how it happened?' Swift questioned.

'Nope,' the Sergeant replied. 'Not got the blood results yet, but they didn't find anything in the stomach contents other than his breakfast. And there was no smell of poison about him, neither.'

'Was that it?' I asked, rather disappointed.

Swift whipped out his notebook and wrote it all down. I thought I should have brought mine because I'd have to remember all this now. Or ask Swift, which would make him tetchy.

'Right.' Swift leaned on the counter. 'What do you know about the Calderstones, Beamish?'

He moved a step back, a smile of apology on his young face. 'I'm not from round here, I'm from York. I only came two months back to take over from Constable Burrows. He can tell you, he's been here all his life.'

'Where is he?' Swift asked.

'Gone home for his tea and a listen to the wireless. He's fond of music and he likes an early night. You'd best be askin' him tomorrow.'

That took the wind out of Swift's sails. 'Well, what exactly happened this morning?'

'We went out just after I saw you, sir.' He turned to Swift. 'We searched for clues at the ice-house again but didn't find nothing. Then we went up to the Hall. The maid answered the door, she's right scary, she is. She looks at you like a cat at a mouse.'

'Marta,' I cut in and wondered how Greggs' romantic plans were going.

'Don't know her name, but she shouted at us in Italian. Then that Lady Mirabella came. She ordered us to go and find the murderer and stop askin' stupid questions, and she slammed the door shut in our faces.' He reddened at the memory. 'So we went and walked around, looking through windows, but they was grimed and murky. Even the Chapel where the family was buried looks ready to tumble down. The whole place is on its last legs. Burrows said it has been like that since he was a nipper, not got two farthings to rub together those Calderstones.' He leaned forward on the counter. 'I dunno why anyone would want to inherit the place.'

'Didn't happen to see my butler, did you?' I wondered how his attempt at romance had gone.

'No, we didn't. Sorry, sir.'

'Any fingerprints on the car?' Swift asked.

'Aye, the car had been moved but we found it in the old coach house behind the Hall.' He beamed. 'Got a lot of prints on it. I'll get me file.' He went back out of the wooden door and returned with a large buff file which looked to be almost new.

He opened it carefully. The ginger cat must have given up his place in front of the fire because he suddenly jumped up onto the counter and came to sit on the file.

'Now, William.' Beamish put the cat on the floor, then pulled out a number of papers and spread them on the counter. They were careful drawings of fingerprints showing loops, arches and whorls and labelled with neat notations; Steering wheel, Handle, Door, Seat driver, Seat passenger, Bonnet, Windscreen, Boot.

William jumped up again, Beamish caught him, gave his ears a rub and put him back down. 'Now give over,' he told him.

'You drew these?' I asked with brows raised.

'We haven't got a camera.' Beamish gave a shy grin. 'So, we did the best we could.'

'Very good police work, well done,' Swift commended him. The lad blushed.

'I need to take your prints now, Inspector. I've got all the ink and stuff.' He opened a drawer under the counter top and pulled out a box which announced, 'finger print identity kit'. It too, looked unused.

Swift and I duly went through the process of inking fingers and placing them onto blank sheets, then wiping them on a proffered damp cloth.

Beamish whipped out a magnifying glass and peered at our prints against his drawings.

'Look! Look! It's yours Major Lennox, it's a match!' He was thrilled.

'Lennox will you learn to wear gloves or stop touching evidence?' Swift was acerbic.

'And here's one of yours, Inspector.' Beamish peered at another print.

I laughed as Swift muttered under his breath.

Beamish carefully wrote our names under two of the drawings.

'I never done this before. I'm going to take everyone's prints in the village,' the young Sergeant declared.

'Good luck with that.' I told him as William jumped onto the counter once more.

We left him clutching his cat and walked alongside the green in the direction of the Calderstone Arms.

'The Codex is the only thing of real value in Clarence's whole estate,' I mused.

'What about the land?' Swift was striding along beside me.

'It's of more use to the locals,' I replied.

'You don't think it's worth much then?'

I shook my head. 'It's overgrazed and the soil is washed thin. Too many sheep for too many generations.'

'You mean the Calderstones squeezed the land *and* people dry.' Swift's socialist tendencies bubbled up. 'Typical toffs.'

I shrugged, and thought the sin of greed wasn't exclusive to the ruling classes – and they weren't the only ones prepared to kill for it either.

CHAPTER 12

There was laughter and loud chatter as we entered the Calderstone Arms, an atmosphere entirely different to our earlier visit.

Betty greeted us with a beaming smile. 'Welcome, lads. I'll be right with you.' She had two stoneware jugs in each fist and placed one on each crowded table, then went back to the bar for more. It seemed half the village was in the place.

We spotted Greggs in a corner, sipping ale.

'Rather lively,' I remarked as we joined him.

'Indeed, sir. A boy came in, said something to Betty, and within minutes it became quite festive.'

'Did you hear anything this boy said?' Swift asked.

'I do not eavesdrop on conversations, sir.' Greggs intoned.

I raised a brow because he and I both knew that wasn't true.

Betty put a jug of ale on our table. 'Busy today, you'll need mugs off the beam.' She smiled broadly.

Swift reached up, unhooked two pewter mugs from the beamed ceiling and handed one to me.

'What's the occasion?' I asked as another group of locals came in cheerfully calling for beer.

"Tis a grand day.' She laughed. 'Our homes belong to us now. We don't belong to the Calderstones no more.'

'Betty, wait...?' I tried, but she turned away as she was hailed by new arrivals.

'Jimmy you be giving me a hand,' she called to an elderly man who got up to help her out.

'Damn.' I sat down again.

'Does it mean they think there is no child, or ... they think the child will hand over the land?' Swift said almost to himself. 'And if Kitty Wexford is the child what is Roche here for?'

'Swift, we need facts, not conjecture,' I told him, because he was usually telling me that.

'Right, fine,' he muttered.

'How went your excursion, Greggs?' I changed the subject.

'I noted the spring flora, a hawk and a hare in a field.'

'Really and did you introduce yourself to Signorina Marta?'

He puffed up his chest. 'I did make a call on the lady, sir. I gathered some flowers from the hedgerow and presented them to her. She agreed to accompany me for a walk along the riverbank.'

'Did she now?' I grinned, because I had to admire Greggs' determined pursuit of the fair sex, although I never quite understood how he did it.

'Did she mention Sir Clarence?' Swift was still in detective mood.

'She said he was dead, sir.'

'Greggs, if you know anything...' I told him.

'Very well, sir. She said he had been largely absent from the Contessa's house in Venice during the last few years. She appeared to approve of the arrangement.'

'But he was the Contessa's legal husband?' Swift asked.

'Marta believes it to be the case. This is all I know.' He stood up, smoothed down his waistcoat and carefully straightened his dickie bow. 'If you would excuse me, I have duties to attend to. I bid you good day.' He made a dignified exit. I noticed Betty flashed him a beaming smile as he tipped his bowler hat to her on his way out.

'Swift, will you learn to relax?'

'Yes, right... um, sorry.' He reddened and sipped his pint.

I drained mine as it was excellent ale. Jimmy, the newly conscripted barman, came and filled it up again before darting off. The noise in the pub had risen to a happy racket.

'You could learn a few lessons in love from your butler, Lennox,' Swift remarked.

That wiped the smile off my face. 'Infra dig, Swift. Anyway, I've got Persi, so I don't need 'lessons'.'

'Are you sure?'

'What?'

He sighed. 'I noticed you were taken with Kitty Wexford.'

'She's married,' I retorted, as the image of another girl with cornflower blue eyes rose in my mind.

'Yes, I know.' He looked uncomfortable. 'But the thing is, I've only got eyes for Florence. I may notice a woman is attractive, but it's merely an observation. Whereas you turn into a gibbering fool.' He took a breath. 'It's just… well, we thought that you need to be sure in your own mind that you're marrying for the right reasons.'

'Who's "we"?' The conversation was sobering me up.

'Florence and I, and Miss Fairchild mentioned it too.' He held up a hand to stop my counter-blast. 'I know she's a bit strange but she's quite perceptive.'

'Look, Swift. I may not have much experience with women but I'm not an idiot. I've met any number of them.'

'When? You were an only child, you went to boarding school, then Oxford, then the war. So where did you meet them?'

'Around,' I retorted, then sighed. 'It's just that they don't play cricket, or rugger, so it's hard to know what to talk to them about. And then the war… well it was mostly us chaps.'

'That's what we thought.' He mellowed with the beer.

'What did you do in the war, Swift?' I turned the subject, because it was getting too close for comfort.

'I was a Detective-Sergeant in London when it started, so they sent me to join the military police. But I…' He stumbled for words. 'It didn't suit me. They sent me to the trenches and I was shot at for a year until a bomb landed next to our bunker and shredded us with shrapnel. I spent six months in hospital, then trained as a code-breaker. I speak Dutch from my childhood in South Africa so it was easy to pick up German. I ended up in Intelligence.'

'You mean you speak two foreign languages?' That opened my eyes. The English are terribly impressed by people who speak more than one language. We mostly shout at foreigners.

'Yes, but I'm better at reading German than speaking it. We recruited women into Intelligence too because they're just as capable as men.'

'Um.' I nodded agreement. Most of them were a lot more capable than men in my experience. 'So you met women in the war then?'

'I met women everywhere. After we left Africa, my mother and I lived in London, there's an awful lot of girls there.'

'Swift, are you saying I'm being too hasty about wanting to marry Persi?'

'I don't know. Are you?'

I paused again, trying to put my thoughts together. 'I'd been waiting for her reply, but when I read it, I suddenly...' I ran fingers through my hair. 'We don't know each other very well and I... well, I don't know what I'm doing, Swift.'

'You haven't sent the letter, have you?'

'No,' I admitted.

'She'll be on tenterhooks.'

I gazed at my empty beer mug. 'I know, I've felt that way all winter. When her letter didn't come, I thought I'd lost her. Now, it's suddenly real and that's...'

'Terrifying?' He finished my sentence.

I didn't want to tell him the truth so I merely nodded, then stood up.

'Let's go, Swift.'

We were a bit subdued as we entered the wicket gate into the Abbey.

'We said we would see Father Ambrose,' I reminded Swift.

He brightened. 'Oh, yes.' He paused to tighten the belt of his trench coat.

We found Brother Tobias kneading bread dough at the kitchen table and asked him for directions.

'He's in the Cloister garden at this time of day. Go out them doors, through the refectory and turn left down a corridor, then follow the sunlight. You'll find it.' He pointed a white-floured hand toward the big double doors we'd gone through earlier that morning.

Swift led the way.

'Good Lord,' I uttered as we both stopped to stare.

Budding roses laced a thorny lattice around slender pillars supporting the cloister roof. The square structure enclosed an enchanting garden, a fragrant haven of blossom and birdsong. In the centre, a fountain sprinkled droplets through rays of sunlight into a crystal-clear pool. Worn stone flags formed a square, fringed with arching shrubs and bushes, their delicate sprigs bursting with flowers in pastel shades. Pollen drifted across the flag-stones to swirl at the feet of a marble statue – a graceful Madonna cradling a baby, her soft smile a study of love. It was a scene of utter serenity at the very heart of the Abbey.

'Oh, dear boys,' Father Ambrose called from beneath a potted tree with trumpet-like flowers. 'Brother Paul said you would come and here you are.' He smiled, his eyes bright above rosy cheeks. 'Such a pleasure to share the cloister, I often sit here quite alone while the Brothers work.'

We swept aside fallen blossoms from stone benches and sat in the warm sunlight.

'Where are the Brothers?' I asked.

'Cleaning out the Dorter; it is the day for brushes and brooms.'

'Clarence's will.' Swift didn't beat about the bush. 'We need to understand what it means.'

'Yes,' Father Ambrose sighed. 'I suppose you do.' He rocked gently. 'Old sins cast long shadows,' he began, 'and the Calderstones have cast very long shadows indeed.'

Swift pulled out his notebook.

'Clarence had an older brother, Edmond,' Father Ambrose began. 'He died before I arrived at Monks Hood. Brother Tobias knows the story.'

'He was Clarence's servant.' I recalled.

'He was.' Father Ambrose nodded, his frizz of hair catching the sunlight. 'Edmond was the heir to the remaining Calderstone fortunes. He squandered it, of course, as they all did. The villagers toiled the fields, the Calderstones dissipated it in... well, in the ways of men. They travelled the Continent for their amusements; this rural backwater has little to offer in the way of debauchery. For which I daily thank the Good Lord.' He seemed to drift off.

'Edmond Calderstone,' I reminded him.

'Ah, yes.' Father Ambrose smiled. 'Edmond and Clarence spent their time in Italy, I believe they had a villa. I'm afraid I don't know the details, but they would return from time to time. The story, as I have heard, is that Edmond amused himself with a local girl during one of his trips back here. This was not as commonplace as you may think, there was said to be a dictum among the Calderstones, 'don't beget by-blows within the bounds.'

'An enlightened family motto.' My remark was laced with sarcasm.

Swift muttered something scathing as he made rapid notes.

'Indeed, and a child was born of this liaison – it was Kitty Wexford,' Father Ambrose replied. 'The mother was Katherine. You may have encountered her sister, Betty Sykes at the Calderstone Arms.'

'What? You mean...' I stuttered to a halt, realising we were right about Kitty, but the family connection was a revelation.

Swift wrote as he spoke. 'So, Betty is aunt to Kitty

Wexford. Kitty's mother was Katherine and her father was Edmond Calderstone.'

'Inspector.' Father Ambrose leaned forward.

'Yes?' He looked up.

'Would you mind awfully not taking notes while I'm talking, dear boy? It really is quite distracting.'

'Um, sorry.' Swift shut his book and shoved it in his pocket with his pen, looking like a sheepish schoolboy.

'When Katherine's condition became apparent, there were rumblings of discontent in the village. Calls were made to force Edmond to do the right thing and marry the girl. Rather than face his responsibilities, he ran away to Italy.' A shadow crossed the Abbot's face. 'I believe Katherine was a spirited young woman and she swore Edmond had offered love and marriage. She borrowed money and followed her lover to the Continent. When Clarence heard Katherine had gone, he decided to follow her and took Tobias with him. A month later he and Tobias returned saying Edmond was dead. Clarence was feverish, he'd suffered some sort of injuries. The baby, Kitty, was sickly, it must have been a difficult journey, it was twenty seven years ago, before we had motor cars, you know.'

'What happened to Edmond, how did he die?' I asked, thinking that the tale he'd just given was a good deal more coherent than his account of Clarence's confession.

'There was an accident, it affected both brothers,' Father Ambrose replied. 'Tobias cared for Clarence until he was fit and well again and Betty took in her sister's child.'

'Tobias works here now, so he didn't remain in Clarence's employ,' I stated

'He did not,' he replied. 'Clarence returned to Italy and Tobias felt the calling. He joined the few remaining Brothers here and did his best to help. This was before I arrived, and the Abbey was still in decay.'

'What happened to Katherine, Kitty's mother?' Swift's brows had drawn, no doubt his Galahad tendencies had been triggered.

'Tobias said she had died giving birth in a village near Verona. As I said, some sort of accident had befallen the Calderstone brothers. It had proved fatal to Edmond and almost killed Clarence. Neither Tobias nor Clarence would discuss it. It has remained a secret to this day.'

'Is this what Clarence confessed to you on his deathbed?' I'd heard worse scandals, I thought.

'Oh no, I cannot say. Please…' Father Ambrose became flustered.

'What was said in the village about the death of Edmond?' Swift cut in, picking up details in his thorough manner.

'I'm afraid I do not know.'

'The will that was read out today…' I was piecing the events together in my mind. 'Clarence must have written it when he and Tobias returned from Italy. Why call her 'the child'?'

'He couldn't have known if the baby would survive or not,' Swift must have been mulling it over too. 'The reference may have just been a custom.'

'It sounds as though he meant to make another will?' I was thinking out loud. 'You said he was feverish, he must have feared for his life.'

'It would seem so,' Father Ambrose agreed.

'Can Kitty Wexford prove who her parents were?' Swift was chasing facts.

'No.' Father Ambrose shook his head. 'She spoke to me today.' He sighed. 'Such a marvellous girl, and so very kind. But she does not have any documents and cannot prove her identity. And she said she does not wish to, she is content with the outcome. All the villagers will become legal owners of their homes, our land will be returned and Calderstone Hall can go to the creditors.'

'What of her husband, the Doctor?' I asked.

The Abbot's face fell. 'He believes she should have her inheritance.'

'He must be angry. Everyone benefits from the will except his wife,' I remarked.

'Now, now,' Father Ambrose gently chided. 'Robert Wexford is an excellent Doctor and as Kitty cannot claim her inheritance, he has no reason to be angry.'

I didn't agree with him, but kept my mouth shut.

Brother Paul arrived as silent as a cat.

'Ah, it is the hour.' The Abbot rose. 'Dear boys, may I remind you that your task is to recover the Codex? The Contessa was in a fury today and I am certain it will not be long before we hear from her.'

'We'd like to interview Brother Paul.' Swift eyed the silent monk.

'Of course,' Father Ambrose promised. 'You do agree, don't you, Brother Paul?'

'I do, but it must await the morrow, now is the hour of evening repast.' He bowed his head and led the Abbot away.

CHAPTER 13

Tobias was in the kitchen, stirring the stew pot. 'Ah, you found the Father then, and you'll have heard the news! A good day for the village and a good day for the Abbey.' He smiled broadly, his face flushed. The resemblance to Father Christmas was even more marked and I guessed he may have had a drink or two already.

'Yes and we were at the reading,' I told him.

'So, you saw the Contessa's fireworks, did you?' He laughed. 'I've kept you some supper. Thought you'd like something to line your stomachs.' Tobias ladled stew into plain white dishes. 'Your butler says to tell you he's gone to the pub. He's a cheerful soul, isn't he? Always with a smile and a song.'

I looked at the monk, wondering if we were talking about the same chap. 'Greggs?'

'He was in here earlier. He'd picked a bunch of flowers and was off to deliver them to the lucky lady!' He winked as he put a dishful of steaming stew down in front of us.

'I thought he'd already given her flowers?' I vaguely recalled.

'He had the flowers with him. Saw them myself.' Tobias seemed certain.

'Don't you mean he was going to Calderstone Hall?' Swift said while blowing steam from his food.

'No, I told you, he's gone to the pub.'

'You mean... Betty!' I exclaimed.

'Aye, that's it.' Tobias laughed.

That made us stare.

'Two women,' Swift arched his brows.

'Spring really has gone to his head,' I remarked.

Tobias deposited bread with a pat of butter on the table for us to dip into the thick gravy. He was singing under his breath as he bustled about.

'Father Ambrose told us about Kitty.' Swift tried a gambit between mouthfuls.

It didn't work, Brother Tobias was dismissive. 'Now, that's an old story. Everyone knows it, an' it don't rightly matter.'

'You were in Italy when it all happened though,' I added. 'Couldn't you prove Kitty's parentage?'

'No and she wouldn't want me to. You shouldn't go prying where it's not wanted. Don't you be saying nothing to her. Now then, me fine lads, this is liberation day! We're celebrating not chewing over old sins.' He went to the beer barrel in the corner and filled three pewter mugs. 'A pint apiece, you'll take a drink with me!'

'Liberation!' We all called out and drained our mugs.

'Ee, it's been a grand day.' Tobias laughed again.

I didn't want to put a dampener on the mood, but I didn't believe it was over as easily as that. The Contessa wasn't going to give up, it was obvious Fenshaw was helping her and the Swiss was supposed to have a claim.

We had a couple more pints, raising cheers of 'Liberation', then Tobias presented us with a glass of honey mead. Mead is a monkish speciality, it's sweet and deadly in equal measures and guaranteed to bring a smile to every imbiber. We shared a bottle amid much jollity and finally stumbled up the stairs in fine form. Swift was singing so I joined in...

'O ye'll take the high road, and I'll take the low road,
And I'll be in Scotland a'fore ye,
But me and my true love will never meet again,
On the bonnie, bonnie banks of Loch Lomond.'

'I'm going to write to Florence.' Swift sounded a bit slurred. 'I'll see you at breakfast.'

'Right-ho.' I rolled along to my own room and dropped into a chair in front of the fire to contemplate the day's events. That sent my eyes drooping, but, despite the fuzz of alcohol, I decided I'd better write something down before I forgot it all. I had a new notebook – smooth leather in dark green. It was very smart and I ran a hand over the pristine cover before opening it.

I noted the date, the time and place, just as Swift had done.

Confession? What is Father Ambrose hiding? How could Clarence's confessed sin implicate him?

I was aware we'd both shied away from upsetting the old chap any further, but we'd have to know sometime. I realised he was a weak man who leaned on the strengths of others – his formidable wife, Lady Maitland, Brother Paul and now us.

I sighed and put pen to paper again.

Clarence handed over the Codex in reparation. Was it a spur of the moment act? The Codex seems to have been the only object of value in Clarence's estate. What about his wife, or his niece, Kitty Wexford? Why hadn't he provided for them?

I didn't have any answers to that either. I went back over what we did know, writing slowly as I tried to untangle the jumble of events.

Danton dead. Killed to stop him handing over Clarence's alleged will leaving all to the Contessa. Which might be deserved, but was still a serious injustice to the lady.

List of people who were at Clarence's deathbed; Father Ambrose, Brother Paul, Brother Tobias and Doctor Wexford.

Brother Tobias knows more than he's saying. Italy?

I underlined the last word and stopped to think again. Wexford didn't hear the confession – and even with his ear to the door, he couldn't have heard the gasping words of a dying man.

Why? Then I scratched it out and wrote, *Motive –* because according to Sherlock Holmes – and Swift – that was the proper word. *Motive; to prevent the Calderstone estate falling into the hands of the Contessa. Dr Wexford presumably wants his wife to inherit it all – does that include the Codex? And what's the point if Kitty doesn't want it anyway?*

I paused, my mind drifting away. I watched yellow flames curl around the logs I'd thrown on the fire, Tubbs and Fogg quietly snoozing in front of it. I gave myself a shake and added a few more lines.

Danton was killed around 11am. Dr Wexford said he was walking across the hill to go to the post office but didn't see anyone. Was he telling the truth?

I returned to the mystery of how Danton was killed. He swallowed his tongue, something must have caused it to happen. It was a sophisticated murder, even Swift acknowledged that, and I was convinced it was poison. I thought back to the mouse and wrote; *How could poison be administered in such a way to avoid tell-tale convulsions?*

By someone who knew how to do it?

What about the villagers? They've just gained ownership of their homes. That's a very good motive.

I considered it. How many would have the knowledge? The monastery had been used as a hospital during the war and the villagers must have helped nurse the wounded.

Betty used the ice-house to store meat, she is Kitty's aunt.

I paused to think that if anyone was an unlikely murderer, it was Betty.

Fenshaw is a worm and in cahoots with Danton and the Contessa.

Perhaps he killed Danton in the hope of becoming the Contessa's new legal man? Actually, that seemed a little unlikely. I decided to add him to my list of suspects though, on the principle that he was a worm and bound to be guilty of something.

Codex? Danton threatened Father Ambrose. If the Contessa knows whatever Danton knew, will she try blackmail too? In which case, is she in danger? Or is she the danger?

I put my pen down, confused and fuddled by the alcohol. The sound of butler's boots wobbled past my door accompanied by loud humming.

'Greggs?'

A cough and then a hiccup sounded. 'Um, sir?'

I was about to open the door and remind him about the perils of drinking and imprudent romance, but then thought better of it. 'Goodnight, Greggs.'

'And to you, sir. Hic. Rain, sir… the car… open.' He called then started humming again. I heard his door close before I realised what he'd said.

I'd left the tonneau down on the car!

The chapel bell struck nine as I ran outside. Storm clouds had obscured the moon and it looked as though we were in for a drenching. I tugged the tonneau into place, cursing my stupidity.

'Guten Abend.'

'What?' I spun around.

'It is I, Herr Johan Roche,' the little Swiss informed me jocularly. He wore a coat of dense wool and his green hat on his head. He raised it. 'I wish you a good evening.'

I noticed the feather was missing.

'Good evening.' I buttoned the cover down and turned to face him.

'It is most noisy in the village. Quite a disturbance. I came to walk in peacefulness but now I believe there will be rain.'

'Yes well, it does that a lot in England.'

'You are aiding Father Ambrose?'

'In a way.'

He beamed with genuine delight. 'Excellent! Would you be kind to tell the Father that I have brought the rest of the money for the Codex. I will arrive in the morning at eleven of the clock to take my book away.' He bowed and disappeared into the darkness.

That took me aback.

'What... wait?' Damn it, I was too late.

His book? Money? What the devil did that mean?

'We have to find the Codex, Lennox,' Swift said for the third time the next morning. He'd said it twice already after I'd repeated Roche's words verbatim. Then he grilled me while Greggs cooked breakfast, not that I knew any more than he did. If it weren't for the excellent food I'd have gone to eat in my room.

'So you keep saying.' I pushed a piece of toast through my fried egg with a fork.

'And we'd better warn Father Ambrose that Roche is coming,' he carried on.

'No.'

'Why?' He looked put out.

'He'll only worry,' I told him between mouthfuls. 'As you said, we need to find the Codex – preferably before Roche arrives.'

'That's hardly likely, Lennox, it's only a few hours away.'

'Um,' I agreed while spearing a sausage.

'I'll search Calderstone Hall,' Swift continued. 'Beamish and Burrows can come. We should take the Contessa's fingerprints too and a statement.'

'You do that, old chap.'

The bacon was particularly good. Greggs had fried it to a crisp, and the black pudding was the best I'd ever tasted. I'd already mentioned to my old butler that he should acquire a stock of the stuff from the village shop.

'More tea, sir?' Greggs was poised with the pot.

'Please.' I held up my cup.

'We'll insist that the Contessa lets us in. She has no right to be there, so she can't demand a search warrant.' Swift had hardly touched his food.

'It rained last night, the trout will be rising,' I mentioned.

'I packed your fishing rod, sir.' Greggs bent to place a bowl of leftovers for Foggy and the same for Tubbs, although his had been minced first.

'Lennox, you can go and interview Fenshaw,' Swift told me.

'What? But...'

'And Greggs,' he addressed my butler. 'See if you can entice Marta out of Calderstone Hall. It'll be much easier to handle one woman rather than both of them.'

'Sir!' Greggs began a protest.

Swift cut him off. 'Needs must. It's all hands on deck, now. This Swiss has really thrown the...'

'Swift.' I leaned in to look him in the eye. 'We know. Eat your damn breakfast.'

He ate, although it didn't shut him up. 'Actually, perhaps you should go and interview Roche first, Lennox. Find out what he meant.'

'I won't have time to speak to Roche and Fenshaw, and I don't see the point in searching Calderstone Hall.'

'No.' He sighed in exasperation. 'But we have to start somewhere and if you can think of a better...'

I held up my hand. 'Pax, Swift. I'll see you back here at eleven.'

We left in different directions. I returned to my room to pick up my notebook. Swift had a point about Roche and I pondered rooting him out, but then I remembered that Fenshaw was probably the last person to speak to Danton. I decided the Swiss could wait and trotted back downstairs.

A silent figure stood in the kitchen, his cowl raised; a dark shadow in a dark corner.

'You wish to interview me,' Brother Paul intoned.

Fogg froze, the hackles rising on the back of his neck. Mine did too.

'Ah, yes.' Blast, I'd forgotten about that.

'Come,' he instructed and turned to lead the way through the gardens to the Pharmacia. I followed, thinking I really should have made an excuse.

We arrived at the door, he took a key from his cassock, unlocked it and went in.

'Sit.' He pushed the hood from his lean face, his bald head browned from the early spring sunshine.

I perched on a seat, breathing in the dusty scent of dried herbs and powders and opened my mouth to form a question. He beat me to it.

'The Brothers have tilled the soil for six hundred and eighty years. We have nurtured the land and garnered knowledge from the earth. We sow, we nourish, we reap. This is our way unto the Glory of God.'

'Right-ho,' I said, thinking he hadn't quite grasped the principles of interviews. 'Do you know who murdered Danton?'

He stared at me for a full five seconds.

I broke the silence. 'Or did you see anyone near the ice-house at eleven o'clock the day before yesterday?'

He continued to stare, then slowly shook his head.

'Is there a tunnel between here and the ice-house?' I was thinking of the underground tour he'd taken us on.

'No, we go there by river.'

'Ah.' That caught me off guard because it hadn't occurred to me. I switched tack. 'Do you know where the Codex is?'

'I do not,' he spoke slowly, 'but I know of it. It contains knowledge of medicine since time immemorial. It must not be lost again.'

'Good, um yes. Can you tell me what happened when Clarence gave it to Father Ambrose?'

'No.'

I stifled a sigh.

'What did the Codex look like?'

'The binding is similar in colour to our ledgers.' He

indicated the old record books on the shelf above. 'There is a lock, it has a hidden catch. A tree of knowledge is embossed in the leather.'

'Did you think it peculiar Father Ambrose refused to bring it back to the Abbey?' I tried another approach.

'He is our Master. I do not question.'

'Do you do his bidding? I mean, whatever he tells you to do?'

'Of course, I have taken an oath of obedience.'

I considered asking him if he'd been ordered to kill Danton, but thought better of it.

'Right. What was Father Ambrose's reaction when he saw the Codex?'

'He suffered a crisis of nerves and had to return to the Abbey. I requested permission to examine the manuscript for one hour and he granted my request.'

'Really, and what did you make of it?' I pulled out my notebook and pen.

'The Codex is a *Materia Medica,* it was begun in the twelfth century in Constantinople. The oldest section was copied from the *Juliana Anicia Codex* written in the year 515 after Christ. The Juliana Anicia Codex contained text from Galen of Pergamon. Galen is the father of medicine.' He paused to allow me to scrawl notes, then continued.

'Such copies were made for royalty and offered as gifts to allied realms.' His eyes fixed on a distant spot and he spoke as though far away. 'Each copy took a separate journey, they were added to by different hands in different countries and became unique Codices in their own right.

This particular Codex was taken from Constantinople to Spain where the Arabic speaking Moors were in the ascendant. It passed to a physician under the employ of Suleiman the Magnificent, the ruler of the Ottoman Empire. The physician was Jewish, he added his lore in Hebrew. An unknown hand added prescriptions and remedies in the Christian Syriac. More materials were included by the hand of the Jesuits from Egypt, Ethiopia, India and as far away as South America. This book is known as the Codex Corinthia, it is said to hold knowledge from the greatest civilisations.' He stopped abruptly.

'Extraordinary. And you discovered all this in just one hour?'

'I did not. It would not have been possible in so short a time. Before I entered Monks Hood Abbey, I was a scholar of ancient medicine.'

That was a surprise. 'You mean you've heard of the Codex?'

'It is a legend.' He continued, his voice deepening in intensity. 'It was believed lost to the world when the plague decimated the Ospedale Maggiore in Milan in the1600s. Now, I must leave, it is the time of Terce.'

'Wait, you mean the Codex is famous?'

'I thought I had made this plain.' He looked at me as if I were a dim-witted schoolboy.

'And valuable?'

'The medical knowledge it contains is beyond price.'

CHAPTER 14

I paused to wipe water off the tonneau of my car, my gaze drawn to the river, the Calder, as it was called. I recalled seeing it from the windows of Fell House when we'd first talked to Fenshaw and wondered if there was a boat to be had. It was a fine day for a spot of rowing and the fish would be rising. A muddy track skirted the fortress-like walls, so I followed it with Fogg, who raced about in spaniel fashion through the long grass.

There was an ancient picket gate in the rear wall of the Abbey, designed no doubt for easy access to the river and secret escapes should the need have ever arisen. The path led to the riverbank, and I walked down to stare into the crystal-clear water. Fat trout swam among submerged reeds, darting into the shadows as I neared the edge. I sighed because it was a perfect spot for fishing.

There was a short jetty and a rowboat; there was nobody about so I hopped in.

'Come on Fogg.' He raced over and joined me with a yip of excitement.

I had rowed for Oxford, and put my muscles to work against the flow. Within minutes I lost sight of the Abbey and rounded a bend to find myself in thick woodland, bounding the rear of the village. A slipway gave onto the water from a gap among the trees, four boats were tied to pegs and the same number were hauled out on the grassy shore.

A kingfisher flashed iridescent blue-green and orange ahead of me. Bright sunshine cut through the leafy canopy in fractured rays to flash from the water in diamond sparks. Bulrushes, lily pads and yellow iris clustered in the shallows and a swan glided by with cheeping cygnets, downy grey and gauche in their mother's wake.

Fenshaw's place had its own boathouse. It was a wooden building raised on stone foundations, a pitched roof of slate, blue painted planks and an air of tidy order. There was a long jetty reaching into the river, a boat was bobbing alongside it on a line. I hesitated, thinking to pull over and begin the tedious process of interviewing Fenshaw, but I was tempted to explore further toward the Wexford's house. I pulled on the oars and turned an outcrop of land planted with weeping willow to see Kitty on a dock, bare feet dangling over the lip.

'Greetings.' I coasted in.

'Hello, there,' she smiled. I noticed she had very white teeth – small and pretty. Her eyes were dazzling in the sunshine and I tried not to stare.

'May I?'

'Of course, throw me a line.' She rose to her feet. She wore a summer frock, white with floral print and trimmed with lace. A simple band held her chestnut hair to let it fall in curls about her shoulders.

'Here.' I gave her the rope and she tied it to a cleat with skilful ease. Fogg bounded out of the boat and snuffled among the reeds.

'You're a police Inspector?' She sat down again and I clambered next to her.

'Swift's the real detective.' I returned her smile and realised I hadn't actually babbled like an idiot yet. 'I'm more Watson really.'

'You're a doctor?'

'No, I mean I'm helping the police with their inquiries.'

That made her giggle.

'Why do people laugh when I say that?'

She looked up at me, blue eyes framed by thick black lashes. 'That's what the police say about a suspect when they're holding them for questioning.'

'Is it?' That raised my brows, then lowered them. Damn it, Swift had heard me repeat that any number of times and hadn't said a word. His idea of humour, I suppose.

'We haven't been properly introduced. I'm Kitty Wexford.' Her smile widened.

'Major Heathcliff Lennox.' I shook her proffered hand.

'Heathcliff?'

'Just Lennox.'

She nodded. 'I'm really Caterina.'

'Oh.'

'It's Italian for Katherine. My mother's name.' Her smile faded.

'Brother Tobias told us,' I said, before recalling I'd heard it described as an old sin. 'Erm… sorry, I probably…'

She looked up at me again. 'Don't worry, nobody talks about it now anyway. Or they didn't until Clarence died.'

'Do you know what happened?'

'In Italy?' Her focus returned to the water flowing below our feet.

'Yes.' I noticed she had long fingers, finely formed.

'My mother died giving birth to me. I thought it sad for her.' She watched the water. 'What about you?' She deflected the discussion. 'Do you have brothers and sisters?'

'No, I was the only one,' I replied, thinking of the quiet house that was still my home. 'As were you.'

'Oh, I wasn't alone, I grew up with my cousin.'

'A cousin?'

'Clara, Betty's daughter. She's a matron at the hospital in York.'

'There was a hospital at the Abbey during the war, wasn't there?' I said.

She smiled. 'Yes, most of the villagers worked there. It was terrific really, it helped everyone support each other. I wasn't here though, I was in Belgium.'

'Were you nursing?' I asked, watching as she turned her wedding ring round on her finger.

'There wasn't much call for midwives.' She laughed then changed the subject. 'I suppose you want to know if I'm going to claim the Calderstone estate.'

'Are you?'

'No,' she said sharply. 'Edmond Calderstone was an evil man. He cared for nothing but his own pleasure. He might have been my father, but I don't want anything that was ever his.'

'What about Clarence, were you close?' I asked.

'Not at all. He wanted nothing to do with me and I had nothing to do with him.' Which explained why she hadn't gone to see him on his deathbed; a niggle that had been bothering me since I'd learned who she was.

'Why?' I asked. 'Was he 'evil' too?'

She was dismissive. 'I have no idea.'

'What does your husband think about it?'

'Robert knows my feelings, but he thinks we should claim the house, Calderstone Hall, I mean.' Her pretty lips twisted. 'But I think it should rot.'

'Won't it go to his creditors?' I reminded her.

She shrugged. I wondered what she'd endured over the years, the child of a scandalous liaison, her mother unwed.

'Could you prove a legitimate claim?' I continued.

'Ha,' she laughed hollowly. 'My husband believes so, he's written to the Consulate in Verona. I didn't even know he'd done it. He only told me after the will was read yesterday.'

That raised my brows. 'When did he write?'

'A week, maybe more, I don't know.'

'Do you think they could find anything, a birth certificate, or whatever?'

'I don't know. I suppose they would keep records of births. Even if I were illegitimate, someone must have written it down.'

'You don't know if your parents married then?'

'No. Tobias told me once that my mother died in a convent somewhere in the countryside around Verona. The nuns saved me and kept me alive. They asked the local priest to find Edmond; he was in a bar. The priest forced Edmond to take me with him, if he hadn't I'd have been put into an orphanage.'

I pictured the scene in my mind, once more imagining a Victorian melodrama complete with fervent priest, dissolute father and a newborn babe. Actually, as it was twenty seven years ago, it was Victorian.

'Do you know anything about the accident?'

'No, nothing, except that Edmond died and Clarence was badly injured.'

My mind was turning. 'Your husband was at Clarence's bedside when he died, did he mention the book to you?'

She nodded. 'Yes, he said Brother Paul had called it a Codex something or other. He saw it in the strongbox.'

'Codex Corinthia,' I replied, distracted by her eyes. 'That's good.'

'Why 'good'?'

'I mean he told you, your husband, erm Robert...' I shut up. Damn it, I'd started babbling again.

'I truly don't want it, Calderstone Hall, or any of it. I hope you believe me.' She gazed into my eyes and for a moment the world stood still.

'Kitty?' A voice called.

'Robert?'

We twisted around to see Dr Wexford striding down the garden. 'I thought you must have gone to lie down, but I couldn't find you.'

I helped Kitty to her feet.

'I was watching the water. The swans have cygnets...' she told him.

'You must be tired, darling.' Wexford came to take his wife's hand and regarded me with a cool look. 'She's been out half the night with one of her ladies in labour.'

Kitty smiled. 'It was a little boy, he bawled the place down once we'd delivered him, but it was a difficult birth for his poor mother.'

Wexford was less forthcoming. 'Lennox, I bid you good day.'

'Wexford,' I replied, realising I was being dismissed.

He put his arm around his wife's slim waist and led her back toward the house.

Fogg ran back when I called him and jumped into the boat with me. I dropped the oars into the water, I wasn't in any hurry, my thoughts were on Kitty Wexford and the past. I gave myself a shake as we rounded the weeping willows and skimmed a blade to steer into the jetty beside the lawyer's boathouse.

I told Foggy to stay in the boat because he wasn't welcome in Fenshaw's office, and he didn't seem to want to come anyway. I clambered onto the jetty and strolled in unhurried fashion along the planking. Fenshaw's little boat was still bobbing on a long line and knocking against the decking. I walked over to have a look.

Fenshaw lay in its bottom. His head was resting on a plank seat in the bow. His pyjamas were neatly arranged on his cold body. His dead hands clutched a large and very old book.

It seems I'd found the Codex Corinthia.

CHAPTER 15

Should I alert the house, or search for clues? Or examine the body? I looked about, a cobbled pathway led through the trees to the garden and house beyond. All seemed quiet. I hesitated then stepped down into the boat. He was definitely dead, his staring eyes fixed upon the open sky between overhanging trees. He didn't look particularly perturbed, more mildly inconvenienced, actually he looked peeved, just as he'd done in life.

I scanned the body, there were no obvious marks of violence; no unpleasant stabbing, whacking over the head or bloody bullet holes. He was laid out in similar fashion to Danton, neat and tidy. Whoever killed him did so with a certain fastidiousness.

The red leather binding on the Codex was spattered with small rain drops, now drying in the morning sun. The book was as Brother Paul described it. A large lock fastening the front to the back with straps and a heavy clasp. Intricate embellishments of beasts with snarling faces were worked into the brass lock, as though warning of forbidden secrets. A stylised tree had been tooled into the leather; bits were rubbed off and it was peeling to show lighter layers beneath.

Why was it here?

I looked about again and decided action was required and Fenshaw could wait. I tugged the book from the corpse's stiff grasp, tucked it under my arm and returned to my borrowed boat.

My mind churned as I rowed back, the flow adding speed to my oars. I decided I'd better keep quiet about the Codex, and Fenshaw of course.

Cold shadows from the Abbey walls fell across the water as I neared the jetty. I tugged off my jacket and threw it over the Codex. It was a bit of a struggle to hide the damn thing because, even wrapped up, it still looked like a very large book.

Foggy hared around barking despite my efforts to quieten him. I tied up the boat and made my way with an air of feigned nonchalance through the front gate. Greggs was pootling around the kitchen as I entered. He sported an apron over his smartest butlering togs.

'Tea, sir?' He indicated a pot he'd obviously just brewed then stared at me. 'What would that…?'

'It's nothing, I won't be a minute.' I dashed upstairs with the book, looked about for a hiding place and then stuffed it under my pillow. Nobody would find it there.

Greggs was still humming some romantic aria. 'I have cake, sir.'

'Really? I didn't think monks usually ate cake.'

'I believe they may on special occasions, but this cake is a gift from Marta.'

'Ah, not Betty?'

His ears turned pink. 'She makes an excellent steak pie, sir.'

'Don't happen to have a slice of that do you?'

'No, sir.'

I eyed him as he poured tea through a strainer into my cup, then added milk. He had that look about him, the same sort of look he'd had about the lady in Flanders, and that one from Paris and the Belgian dancer. 'Greggs?'

'Sir?'

'Marta, what do you know about her?'

'She has dark eyes, a trim figure and is very fond of Opera, sir.'

'Thought you were more of a Gilbert and Sullivan man?'

'But Italians know how to enact Opera, sir. It is in their blood.'

Well, it had certainly warmed his blood. 'Where does she live and what does she do?'

'She is a lady's maid and dresser, sir. She comes from Garda and now lives in Venice in a house overlooking a canal. The house belongs to the Contessa.'

'Yes, I recall you saying the Contessa lives in Venice. Interesting that Marta comes from Garda, that's where the Calderstones had a villa.'

'I would not know, sir.' He placed a large slice of chocolate cake on the table next to my cup and saucer.

It was extraordinarily good cake! 'What sort is it?' I mumbled through a mouthful.

'*Torta Novecento*, sir!' he proclaimed. 'Chocolate cake with whipped *cioccolato* filling.'

'Hum. Well, it's jolly good.' I thoroughly enjoyed it. Perhaps Italy wasn't such a bad place, despite being abroad.

He began humming. I was still in sleuthing mood.

'Greggs, did Marta happen to mention anything useful about the Contessa and Clarence, like how long they'd been married?'

'They'd recently passed their twenty-fifth anniversary, sir. Marta thought that was quite enough.' He was cutting the cake into thinner slices, no doubt thinking to prevent my further incursions.

'You do realise that you'd have to move to Italy if something should come of this romance.'

'Anything is possible, sir.'

'Although if she finds out about Betty...'

He put down the large knife he was wielding and regarded me. 'Sir, I have desisted from commenting on your peculiar habit of discovering dead bodies.'

'Hum, well, speaking of which...'

'Lennox.' Swift walked in. 'Absolute bloody shambles, she threw things at us!' He unbuckled his trench coat and sat down.

'What sort of things?' I noticed his coat was wet.

'Vase of flowers, a bottle of wine, cushions, whatever she could lay her hands on until Beamish arrested her.

That caused even more tantrums. Constable Burrows took charge and read her the riot act.'

'Did you take her fingerprints?'

'Yes.' Swift was eyeing my crumb and chocolate covered plate. 'And we took a statement, but it doesn't amount to anything.'

'Would you care to take cake with your tea, sir?'

'Thank you, Greggs. Yes, I would!' He ran fingers through his hair. 'Complete waste of the morning and the lock was broken on the strongbox, Lennox.'

That made me look up. 'Someone had forced it?'

'No, it was just broken, it had rusted out. I used the key Father Ambrose had given me, unlocked the strongbox, searched it – there was nothing of interest – then locked it again. Sergeant Beamish decided to test it and lifted the lid straight up. The lock mechanism didn't engage.' He bit into his cake. 'Mmm, excellent, Greggs.'

'I'll have some more too,' I mentioned, 'and another cup of tea wouldn't go amiss.'

'Very well, sir.' He slid the thinnest slice of chocolate heaven onto my plate.

'We didn't find anything. Not a hint of where the book could have gone,' Swift said in exasperation. 'I've no idea how we're going to find it. I don't even know where to begin searching.'

'I found it,' I told him sotto voce.

'What?' He stared at me. So did Greggs.

'I found it. The Codex, it's upstairs under my pillow,' I whispered.

'You found it under your pillow?' Swift leaned forward.

'No, I hid it there. It was with Fenshaw.'

'What was he doing with it?' He sounded incredulous.

'Nothing, he was dead.'

'What?'

'In a boat. Found him and the book in a boat at the bottom of his garden. It's called the Codex Corinthia, actually.'

'Lennox!' he snapped. 'What the hell are you talking about?'

I repeated what Brother Paul had told me about the Codex and about my boat ride, and the dead Fenshaw. I decided not to mention my chat with Kitty Wexford, Swift had enough to excite him already.

'And I really think you should lower your voice, because we should keep quiet about it until we know more.'

'You just left Fenshaw there?' he hissed.

'Look, someone will discover him pretty quickly.' I'd been thinking about it. 'Fenshaw didn't die with the Codex in his hands, the murderer put it there. What if it isn't found with the body?'

'Yes... You think it might rattle him.'

'It's bound to and it may force him into the open – or make a mistake anyway.'

He stood up. 'Fine, show me the Codex.' He tightened the belt of his trench coat and marched off.

'Right.' I finished my cake and eyed the chocolate coated remainder on the plate. Greggs picked it up, put a lid over it and took a step backwards.

Swift arrived in my room ahead of me. I tossed more logs on the fire as he drew chairs around the hearth. Greggs arrived a moment later without the cake.

I pulled the Codex from its hiding place and we gathered around the low table. It was around six inches thick, fourteen inches long and twelve wide, the leather gleamed in the lamplight. I tested the clasp, it was locked.

'Brother Paul said it had a hidden catch or something.' I felt around the ornate brass lock but couldn't find it.

'Damn,' Swift swore. He tried the keys Father Ambrose had given him to the strongbox and Hall, but none fitted.

'Wait.' I had a set of skeleton keys in my possession which I'd confiscated from a petty thief on an earlier adventure. They were my favourite detecting tools. I fiddled about until we heard the internal levers release with a series of soft clicks.

We didn't say anything, just stared at the pages. It held the scent of centuries, a musty miasma from the hands of those who'd written it, studied it and revered it. The vellum was well fingered and grubby, but still thick and pliable. I recognised Greek, Latin and Arabic among the many different scripts. Their meaning was beyond my understanding, but the illustrations were astonishing; bright inked drawings of herbs with their roots, leaves and flowers in exquisite detail. Neat notations were written in the margins and around the plants. It was like viewing an Audubon version of botanicals.

'Some of it's in Hebrew,' Swift muttered, he was engrossed, gazing in wonder at the drawings.

I turned the pages over slowly; we each let out gasps of admiration as another elegantly executed flower or seed was depicted. There were many pages filled with neat calligraphy, most of it in black, some of it faded to sepia, the capitals were in red for the most part.

'Medical prescriptions?' Swift remarked.

'I suppose they must be,' I replied.

'Clarence told Father Ambrose it could save lives.' Swift hadn't lifted his eyes from the pages. 'Perhaps these medical formulas are unknown today?'

'Brother Paul said the same.' I was sceptical. 'But this is the modern age, how could our scientists know less than people born hundreds of years ago?'

'If you'd ever been to Africa, Lennox, you wouldn't ask that,' he replied dryly.

'Hum.' I wasn't sure. 'More to the point, what are we going to do with it?'

Tubbs had been asleep on my bed and decided to come and join us. He rubbed against our legs, gave a little mew and then jumped onto the table to sit on the Codex, as cats do.

'We should hide it,' Swift said.

'Where?'

'There's a loose board in the bottom of my wardrobe,' Greggs explained. 'I found a dead mouse in it, sir. It was skeletal.'

'You do realise two people have already been murdered over this book,' I warned him.

That gave him pause, but he was a stalwart old soldier. 'I will keep my wits and my service revolver about me, sir.'

Swift raised his brows because he didn't know Greggs as well as I did.

'Very well, Greggs,' I said.

He gently removed Tubbs and handed him to me, closed the Codex and carried it off.

'We should tell Father Ambrose,' Swift said, as Greggs shut the door behind him.

I stroked Tubbs until he settled to purr on my lap. 'I'm not sure. Danton threatened him with blackmail, but Mirabella may be behind it all.'

'So, you think Father Ambrose would hand it to her?' Swift suggested.

'If she knows about the sin, and however it implicates the Abbot, then yes.' I sighed, unhappy with the thought. 'She could blackmail him just as Danton tried to.'

'Look, Lennox, leave the conjecture for a moment, there's something more pressing.' He took a deep breath and let it out slowly. 'Once Fenshaw's body is discovered, Scotland Yard will be down here the next day. One murder might be left to the local police to investigate, but not two. And once the Yard starts investigating, they'll turn this place and all its secrets, inside out. The sin will be exposed and so will whatever Father Ambrose is hiding.'

'Damn, I hadn't thought of that.'

'I doubt the murderer did either.' He pulled his lip. 'We should tell Father Ambrose that we've found the Codex, then demand he asks Lady Maitland to hold off Scotland Yard.'

'He's more likely to agree if he knows the Codex is safe,' I agreed. 'But we won't tell him where it is.'

'Right, that might give us twenty-four hours to solve the murders.'

'Ask for forty-eight,' I said.

He frowned.

'Be realistic, Swift. We don't have Scotland Yard's resources to fall back on.'

'We've got Sergeant Beamish and Constable Burrows.'

I'm not sure why that should bring him any comfort.

'Right,' I said. 'Roche will be here soon. Come on.'

Brother Tobias arrived just as we reached the kitchen. We didn't say a word about the morning's events, although I thought I spotted a hint of expectation in the old monk's eyes.

'There's a note for you.' He withdrew an envelope from his cassock and handed it to Swift.

'We'd like to talk to Father Ambrose,' I said as Swift tore it open.

'Aye, well I'm sure he'll be willing. You'll be wanting me to go askin' him for you?'

'Please,' I replied.

He went off.

'It's from Fenshaw.' Swift scanned the letter.

'Written in blood?'

'Very amusing, Lennox.'

It was dated yesterday, he read it out.

For DCI Swift and associate,

As you appear to be aiding Father Ambrose in his current

difficulties, I am directing this to you. The Contessa Mira-
bella Ferranti has authorised me to let it be known that I am
her designated legal advisor. Forthwith, you will approach
me in all matters pertaining. As her legal representative, I
demand you cease your persecution of the Lady.

'That's a bit rich.' I was stung.

Swift shrugged, he had thicker skin and carried on reading.

I would like to remind you that Lady Mirabella is seeking
notarised copies of her marriage certificate and that her claim
is valid. We intend mounting a challenge in the courts to
overturn Sir Clarence Calderstone's will of 1895, unless an
agreement can be achieved that satisfies all parties.

I am authorised to negotiate this matter, and all the per-
tinent details, with Father Ambrose in person at his earliest
convenience.

Until that time, I suggest you remove yourselves from this
'investigation'. Indeed, I question the very legality of your
intervention and will be contacting York Constabulary in
this regard by the next post.

Sincerely etc…

'He stepped into Danton's shoes.'

'And paid the price,' Swift said, then scanned the letter,
reading it again more slowly.

Bother Tobias arrived out of breath. 'The Father says,
if you'll await him in the cloister he'll be down as soon as
he's finished his prayers. And Fenshaw's dead, you know.'

'We heard,' I lied.

'All over the village it is.' The monk shook his head.
'Dead in his boat wearing his pyjamas. And that's another

death – three now. Always comes in threes, so the saying goes.'

'Danton, Fenshaw and who's the third?' I asked.

'Sir Clarence, of course.' Tobias gave me a narrow look.

Swift folded the letter and pocketed it. 'Brother Tobias, who delivered Fenshaw's letter?'

'The little lad brought it with him from Fell House last evening. He's the boot boy, grandson of the butler, he didn't want to come up here in the dark so he left it with Betty at the pub. She gave it to Brother Paul this morning when he was delivering medicine for one of the Blacksmith's nippers.'

Judging by all the hands the letter had passed through, I thought Fenshaw should have just proclaimed the contents by the town crier.

'The Father will be waiting for you,' Tobias reminded us.

'Yes, we're going.' Swift tightened the belt of his trench coat. 'Come on, Lennox.'

CHAPTER 16

Father Ambrose wasn't waiting for us in the Cloister, the little Swiss was. He was standing by the potted tree Father Ambrose had been seated beneath only the previous afternoon. He'd picked up a fallen flower and was sniffing it.

'Brugmansia,' he said and turned to beam at us. 'A tropic! A challenge to keep in frosted places, but I believe this has been nurtured indoors and carried to this beautiful garden for the warmer months.'

'Greetings,' I called by way of answer.

'Ah, do excuse my enthusiasm, mein Herren.' He whipped off his hat and bowed. 'Grüezi.'

'Grüezi,' Swift replied, which made me stare, then I remembered he'd learned German.

'How did you get in here?' I asked Roche.

'I came through a gate and walked about. I did not find any person to ask.' Roche replied. 'Do you know about this wonderful tree?'

'No,' I admitted.

We went to have a look at the green-leafed specimen out of politeness.

'Brugmansia is also called the Angel's Trumpet tree. It is quite an excellent choice for a monastery, is it not?'

'Uhum,' I nodded.

Swift didn't even feign interest.

'Observe the flower.' Roche pointed to a large white flower hanging among the pale green leaves. 'It is an angel's trumpet! Haha.'

Actually, it did look like a trumpet and it was white, although I've no idea why he thought it should belong to an angel.

'It is quite deadly,' he added, then strolled over to poke his nose into another bush.

That pricked Swift's ears up. 'Do you mean it's poisonous?'

'Oh yes, all parts of it are highly toxic. Do not eat it my friend, it will not do you good. Many fine flowers are toxic, this is why they are so familiar, because nothing will eat them.' He turned to point at a late blooming daffodil. 'Narcissus. It is thought to be named from the Greek boy who fell in love with his image, but this is not so. It is from the Greek word for numbing, *narke*. Bluebells, foxgloves, larkspur, yew, even apple pips, all quite deadly. I tell you in English, so the Latin will not confuse you.' He smiled as if it was all a rare treat.

We weren't smiling at all.

'You mean they can all be used to kill?' Swift gave the Swiss his full attention.

'Even apple pips?' I asked.

'Ja, indeed. They contain cyanide. It would take the seeds of twenty apples to kill a man. They must be crushed and taste quite bitter. There are easier ways, you know, than crushing apple pips.'

'Like what?' I asked.

'A tisane of Hemlock or Monkshood would be sufficient. Both are lethal even in small quantity, but the taste is terrible and the effect on the body is very severe.' He shook his head, his smile extinguished.

'So, if you could disguise the taste you could use it to murder someone?' I asked with enthusiasm, thinking this might be a clue to the murders.

'It may be possible, Major Lennox but I am a botanist, not an executioner.' He looked up at us both, his eyes filling with suspicion, then stepped smartly away.

'Oh, Good Heavens! So many of you.' Father Ambrose entered from the shade of the cloister walkway.

Brother Paul followed him as a dark shadow looming in his wake.

'Grüezi!' Roche bowed again. 'My book, the Codex Corinthia. I am ecstatic to be receiving it at last.'

'What?' Father Ambrose's eyes flew open.

'The Codex Corinthia,' Roche repeated.

'Oh, oh my...' The Abbot sank onto the bench below the Angel's Trumpet tree, a hand to his pale cheek.

I felt a tinge of guilt, perhaps we should have warned him.

'Spell it out, would you Roche?' I said as we all took

seats, apart from Brother Paul, who remained standing sentinel behind Father Ambrose.

Roche reached inside his jacket pocket and extracted a folded document. It was of heavy manila paper, neatly typed bearing an impressed stamp. 'I have here my signed contract with Sir Clarence Calderstone for the purchase of the thirteenth century Codex Corinthia. You see, I have paid half already and now I come with a bank draft for the other half.' His beaming smile returned.

Father Ambrose's face was a picture of horror. 'You have a legal c...c...contract,' he stammered.

'Of course! It is all here,' the little Swiss held out the document.

Father Ambrose sagged. 'I... how much did you pay for it?'

'Ten thousand English pounds.' Roche announced as though he'd won the jackpot. 'Sir Clarence made an offer, and once we agreed, he pledged to remedy the damage to the binding.'

I thought the Abbot was about to fall off his seat, even Brother Paul leaned forward as though to catch him.

'I do not have your book.' Father Ambrose's voice shrank to a harsh whisper.

Roche's face fell. 'But Sir Clarence said he was bringing it to you, here to this Abbey.' He waved his document again. 'The Codex is mine, I am ready to pay the remaining five thousand English pounds.'

'We can't, we don't have it,' Father Ambrose whispered.

'It is the law, my dear Abbot, so I must have my book

or my money returned,' Roche insisted with polite Swiss exactness. 'I am sure all will be made correct. We can rely on the Church for honest endeavours, haha.' He stood up and bowed again. 'I bid you good day, gentlemen.'

'I'll show him out,' I offered, as the poor Abbot slumped in his seat. Even Brother Paul remained frozen.

'I'll let him know about the um... you know,' Swift called after me.

I was inclined to take the little Swiss by the scruff of the neck and toss him out. But I merely frog-marched him as fast as his legs would go.

'You can't have the Codex,' I told him, once we reached the kitchen.

Brother Tobias looked up as we entered.

'I have paid for it. Under any legal system it is mine, you cannot refuse the contract.' Roche was becoming red in the face. 'I spoke with Fenshaw, the legal man, he said the Abbey was responsible.'

'Well...' I cursed Fenshaw and realised Roche might be right; the legal owner would have to hand him the book or his money back. 'You'll have to wait.'

'I cannot wait, I must return to Switzerland.'

'Where are you staying?'

'At Calderstone Arms. I am to leave tomorrow morning.'

'If you leave tomorrow, you leave empty handed,' I snapped and left him to find his own damn way out.

I knew he didn't deserve my churlishness and he wasn't actually to blame for the chaos he'd just thrown our way, but it didn't lessen my temper.

'Brother Paul has gone to prepare a telegram to Lady Maitland about delaying Scotland Yard.' Swift told me as soon as I returned to the Cloister.

'Good, what about the...' I looked about, to check if anyone was listening.

'Once we were alone, I told Father Ambrose we'd found the Codex. It gave him some relief, although he's still very agitated.'

'So Brother Paul doesn't know about...'

'No, no-one does except the Abbot.' Swift was ahead of me. 'I'm not stupid, Lennox.'

'I didn't say... oh, come on.'

We headed for the pub, replaying what Roche had said about poison, the Codex and the legal connotations of his contract. We weren't any wiser by the time we reached the Calderstone Arms.

It was buzzing, no doubt with the news of Fenshaw's peculiar demise. The chatter stopped as we crossed the threshold, we were looked up and down, and then the talk took up again. I assumed they were either used to us, or we weren't considered culprits. We made our way to a quiet spot in the corner.

'Roast beef, Yorkshire pudding, mash and green beans, if you're after eating.' Betty greeted us with a pint apiece and an offer we couldn't refuse.

'Go easy on the beans.' I gave her a grin.

She laughed and returned to the bustling bar. I noticed a large bunch of flowers in a glass vase, but there was no sign of my gallant butler.

'What the hell was Clarence thinking?' I took a long draught of beer before making the comment.

'That he was dying,' Swift said, before downing most of his pint.

'He had a damn strange idea of atonement.'

'Perhaps he thought the monks would get Roche's money,' Swift replied. 'He said its worth would come to them.'

'How? And where's the down payment? It was five thousand pounds, that's a small fortune.'

'It's a large fortune, Lennox,' he rejoined, then sighed. 'The Contessa might have it.'

'I don't think so. She's fighting too hard, there's a desperation beneath the theatrics.' I put down my empty mug.

Betty brought refills and plates piled with slices of beef, creamy mash and Yorkshire puddings with everything swimming in gravy. It was heavenly and we ate in appreciative silence.

'We should have gone to examine the body.' Swift's brows were knit.

'We were busy, Swift.'

He reverted to detective mode.

'When you said Fenshaw was laid out the same way as Danton, did you mean it looked as though he had been killed in the same manner?'

'Yes, but I couldn't see any means of murder. It has to be poison.'

'Right, well, I agree.' He took another sip of ale.

'Really?'

'Yes, but I don't understand how. What did his eyes look like?'

'Um...' I tried to remember. 'Staring, glazed, with tiny pupils, like he was caught in headlights.'

'Colour of lips?'

'Pale, very pale, actually. So were his face and hands, they looked almost bloodless,' I replied and now I came to think of it, that was rather odd because you'd expect him to be grey, or blue or something.

'Syncope,' Swift announced.

'What?'

'It's a sudden drop in blood pressure, particularly to the brain. Usually it just results in fainting, but it sounds as though it was more pronounced, as though he were anaesthetised or paralysed.'

'Like the effects of curare?' I'd read about hunters in far flung lands using blowpipe darts to paralyse their prey. I'd always wanted to try it, actually.

'No, not curare.'

'Why not?'

'Where would they get it?'

'Hum. Not curare then,' I agreed. 'But from what Roche was saying there are any number of plants that could have been added to tea or whatever.'

'Monkshood for a start. It must grow around here, given the name.' Swift finished his drink.

'I haven't seen any, but it's too early in the year.' I suddenly remembered the square of waxed paper we'd found. 'It could have been put in a cigarette and he inhaled it.'

'What Fenshaw and Danton? There was no sign either of them smoked and they didn't look the sort to roll their own.' Swift was dubious.

'Perhaps it was a toffee or chocolate?' I wasn't ready to give in.

'The pathology report was clear, Danton didn't ingest anything unusual.'

The chatter fell for a second, causing me to look up. 'Roche has just come in.'

'He's staying here, isn't he?' Swift swivelled around in his seat.

We watched the little Swiss as he made his way to a solitary table, wearing his felt hat. He suddenly reached up and snatched it off his head to clutch in his hands. With his pale hair and skin and smooth plumpness, he looked like a stray dove among rugged moorland hawks.

'We'll interview him later. We should go and inspect the crime scene first,' Swift said.

'I was going to ask about pudding.'

'Lennox, will you concentrate on the job.' We placed coins on the table and left with a wave to Betty.

'What's wrong with pudding?' I continued.

'This is a murder enquiry and you need to be disciplined!' he continued the lecture as we headed for the hill. 'It's not a game, it's work and it's difficult. And sometimes it's bloody unpleasant.'

'Swift,' I snapped, stung by his words. 'How do you think I became a Major in the RAF? They didn't hand it to me because of my title.'

He muttered under his breath then said, 'Well how did you get it?'

'Because I was a damn good pilot,' I retorted. 'And I had an instinct for hunting. The men liked that, they trusted me and I ended up leading the squadron.' I was a bit sharp, but then sighed as the memories crowded in. 'You know what it was like, Swift.' I shut up abruptly because I didn't want to talk about it, I didn't want to think about it. I still saw the faces in the night's darkness; my friends, my foes, death in all its grotesque guises. I extended my stride to reach the top and paused beside the milestone.

'I apologise,' he said when he caught up with me.

'The war must have got to you, too.'

'Intelligence was mostly in London, away from the front line. But the trenches were something else.'

'Why did you leave the Military Police?' I asked.

He looked sideways at me, his lips tightening.

'You were thrown out, weren't you? You almost let it loose the other day.'

'I hit an officer,' he admitted.

'Ha!' I grinned. 'Very self-disciplined, Swift.'

'He was an arrogant bully. Typical toff, throwing his weight around. He'd never lifted a finger in his life.'

'We're not all like that.'

'I know.' He ran fingers through his hair. 'My father was a non-commissioned officer, he said the good ones could win you a battle, the bad ones could cost you your life.'

'I remember you telling me he died at the siege of Ladysmith.' We were heading down the steep track.

'It was one of the battles around it, he was badly injured at Talana Hill and died of septicaemia.' His voice faltered in the telling, he cleared his throat and returned to the fray. 'What did you mean by title?'

'Ah.' I realised I'd let that drop and he always was sharp. 'The reason I still use Major is because I'm actually a Sir and I'm damned if I'm going to go through life as Sir Heathcliff.'

He laughed. 'So, when your uncle dies, you'll be Lord Melrose. And you'll have the responsibility of running Melrose Court and the whole estate.'

'No, I'm not. I'm going to keep Uncle Charles alive as long as it takes,' I grinned. 'I'll have him stuffed, if necessary.'

We reached the tarmac and turned toward Fenshaw's house as Sergeant Beamish and Constable Burrows came around a bend on bicycles. They tinged their bells, drew to a halt beside us and dismounted.

Beamish stood ramrod straight and saluted. 'Doctor's just finished the examination on Fenshaw, sir. The victim died just like Danton. Two murders we got now, good an' proper.'

CHAPTER 17

'Swallowed his tongue?' Swift asked, just to be clear.

'He did, strange he should be out in the dead of night,' Beamish said.

'And dressed in his pyjamas,' I uttered.

'How do you know that?' Beamish pushed his helmet back from his freckled face.

'I was told,' I lied.

'The place is a hive of gossip,' Beamish conceded. 'Everyone will know it all before he's even cold. Not that he was much thought of, but his Uncle Lawson was born and bred here.'

'Lawson's one of us,' Burrows added. 'Even if he is a barmpot.'

'Who found the body?' Swift wanted facts.

'The gardener. He went to share his baggins with the ducks and saw the boat was out of the boathouse. It was supposed to be tied up under shelter,' Burrows explained.

Swift nodded. 'I assume Doctor Wexford has had the body sent to York?'

'Aye, he's along with the other one, now. Two lawyers that is.'

'Must be open season.' I remarked.

Burrows chuckled.

'Danton. Any news on him?' Swift asked.

Beamish replied. 'Blood results came through just as we got back from interviewing the Italian lady, sir. They said they couldn't find a thing, but it might be too late – something about molecules breaking down. I've got the report at the station.'

'Very good. Have you gone house to house?' Swift was in full police mode.

'There's only two houses up by Fenshaw, and one of them is the Doctor's.' Beamish shifted the satchel he was carrying over his shoulders. 'But we'll be asking in the village who's seen what.'

'We'll meet you at the station later,' Swift told them.

'Aye, sir.' Beamish saluted. Burrows gave a grin and a wave and they cycled off.

'What are baggins?' Swift asked.

'Whatever's in your bag,' I told him. 'Farm workers have their bags and baskets packed by their wives or mothers. Mid-morning snack is always baggins.'

'We have tea and Clootie in Braeburn.' He sighed quietly, no doubt missing his wife.

We arrived at Fell House and knocked on the door.

Lawson opened it, he was fully dressed in Victorian style, including trousers.

'Oh, how delightful to see you,' he beamed. 'Are we having another party?'

'Um, not quite,' I told him.

'We'd like to offer our condolences,' Swift gave the old man a bow as Foggy ran about yipping in excitement. I tried to shut him up.

'Come in, come in,' Lawson insisted and led the way to the parlour. 'I've got a good bottle of brandy somewhere.'

Swift and I exchanged glances and took seats on over-stuffed chairs in a room crammed with Victorian knick-knacks and thick velvet cloths over bulbous legged tables.

'A great shame.' Lawson beat the fire with a poker, before sitting on a low chair opposite us. 'I was quite fond of him, you know. He lived an exciting life, full of adventure, always off on his travels.'

'I thought he'd spent time in London?' I remarked, a bit confused.

'Oh no, he didn't like England at all. Italy, France, Spain, anywhere with sunshine and a good bottle of wine to be had.' He waved a hand about. 'Haven't seen the old fellow these last three years and he comes back and snap, gone in a trice.'

'Do you mean Sir Clarence?' Swift asked.

'Yes, of course! Dead, you know. Fell off his horse.' He tapped the side of his nose. 'And that Italian dazzler is chasing what's left!'

The ancient butler tottered in to serve brandy snifters on a silver tray. Swift declined, which was a mistake because it was really quite excellent.

'We're here about your nephew.' Swift attempted a delicate approach.

'Ah, young Stephen. He's not here. Gone off in the boat or some such escapade. The police were looking for him but I told them he left before breakfast. I can't imagine why, but he always was a bit of a sly stick. Chin, chin.' He raised his glass, downed it in one then held it up for another.

'You didn't hear him leave?' Swift persevered.

'No, quite deaf.' He declared loudly. 'Can't hear a dickie bird, can we Hodgson?'

The elderly butler shook his head mutely.

Lawson leaned in to whisper hoarsely, 'I think he has run away with a lady.'

'Who?' I asked.

'Stephen! My nephew and it's just what he needed! A bit of zip in his life. Haha! Don't you agree, Hodgson?'

'Certainly, sir.' The butler's attention was on the brandy bottle, probably trying to estimate how much old Lawson had drunk.

'You don't happen to know who Clarence's creditors were, do you?' I asked.

'Ah, you have a mind for business, young man.'

'No he doesn't,' Swift muttered.

Lawson chortled. 'Clarence had only one creditor. It was me!'

'You?' That opened our eyes.

'Indeed, and do you know what?' He leaned forward, brandy glass in hand. 'The day before he went and fell off his horse, Clarence came to call on me and repaid every penny. Said he'd had some good fortune, sold some book or other to a Swiss chap.' He laughed and raised his snifter for another tot from his butler, who dribbled the remains into the old man's glass.

'How much had he borrowed?' Swift asked.

'And what did he use it for?' I added.

'Now, that sort of information is confidential, don't you know. But as you're the police and Clarence has gone, I am prepared to make a disclosure.' He sat up, adopting a more lawyerly tone. 'He offered me the deeds to Calderstone Hall many years ago, twenty five, if I recall. He'd recovered from his injury. That brother of his, Edmond, had died and there wasn't a bean in the bank.' He shook his head. 'Dissolute lot, the Calderstones. Anyway, I agreed to loan Clarence three thousand pounds.'

'And he repaid that amount to you just before he died?' I asked.

'Oh, no. Good heavens.' Lawson shook his head. 'He'd been paying it off for years. He took up in business and every time he returned to Calderstone, he would come and repay some of the debt.'

'So how much was left when he made the final payment?' Swift asked.

'One thousand pounds. He brought it with him and counted it out in front of me. He said he'd be back to pick up the receipt the next afternoon and discuss some other business. But next morning he went off hunting and met his maker. Such a shame.' He sighed loudly. 'But, I think he would have wanted it that way, you know, up on the wild moors on a fine horse, the sound of the horn and the baying of the hounds in his ears.' His eyes slipped out of focus behind his glasses.

I opened my mouth to tell him Clarence had died in bed, but then thought better of it.

'Did he deposit anything else with you?' Swift was on form.

'He did. It was a carpetbag full of money. Four thousand pounds. He said I was to put it in my safe for something or other he wanted to do.'

'Did he say what he had in mind?' Swift asked.

'He did, but I can't recall what it was now.' He looked fuddled. 'My memory, you know. I can remember twenty or thirty years ago as if it were yesterday, but yesterday is all rather a fog.'

'Can you recall anything else?' Swift persevered.

'Clarence had something else he wanted to discuss. I think I mentioned that to you, didn't I?' He peered at us.

'Yes, you did,' I reassured him. 'Did your nephew know about any of this – about Clarence's money I mean?'

'No, no.' Lawson threw his hands up. 'He's too young to handle the funds. I let him do the filing and label envelopes. He's got a lot to learn; can't let him run before he can walk.'

Swift was ready to go. 'Could we take a look around your garden?'

'Of course, it's very well kept. Good gardener, had him years! Plenty of flowers, I've seen them. You can pick some if you like. Must be a lady in the village who'd go soft for a bunch, eh?' He winked.

'Right, well, thank you.' I offered a bow to the old man

and we extracted ourselves with more words of commiser-
ation, though it merely confused the old fellow.

'Clarence was in business?' Swift was musing as we
strode along the cobbled path running through the garden.

'And had been for years, by the sound of it,' I added.

'Doing what?'

'Someone will know. The Contessa probably.'

His brows drew together at mention of the lady.

Signs of police activity were evident including bamboo
sticks pushed into the lawn with labels tied to them. I
caught hold of one as it fluttered in the wind. *'Footprint'*,
it read. I leaned over to take a look, it seemed to have been
made by a large boot – the sort gardeners might wear, or
any countryman, actually.

'Lawson didn't have a clue what his nephew was up
to,' Swift said as we wove through the trees toward the
boathouse and dock.

'Shouldn't we search his office?'

'Beamish would have done that already, he'll have taken
any relevant paperwork back to the station.' He walked
along the jetty to peer down into the now empty boat.
There were lashings of fingerprint powder. It must have
been applied while Fenshaw was still in place because it
formed a neat body-shaped outline.

'Well at least we can see where he was.' I remarked as
we scrutinised the crime scene.

'Make a search would you, Lennox, they might have
missed something.'

'Right.' I could have argued, but I thought about his

dictate on learning police work and wandered about the planked jetty with my hands in pockets.

Swift rummaged about the boathouse, picking up this and that, there were a lot of empty wine bottles and some rope hanging in looped coils. A red and white lifebelt was propped in a corner, he moved it, saw it was meshed in cobwebs and gave up.

'What do you think happened?' He had come back to stare down at the boat again.

I'd been musing on that myself. 'Someone came during the night and attracted his attention – probably threw stones at the window. Fenshaw would have been the only one to hear them. He would have opened a window to talk to whoever it was.'

'He didn't put a dressing gown on.' Swift's brows were drawn in thought.

'No,' I agreed. 'What if the person said it was an emergency of some sort? Fenshaw might have been persuaded to rush down, then the killer would have led him along the path, away from the house.'

'Perhaps they said there was someone drowning in the river and wanted Fenshaw to row out and save them?' Swift mused.

'Yes and then what?'

He looked blank. 'I don't know. I can't... It doesn't make sense. It was dark, supposedly urgent. Why on earth would Fenshaw lie down in a boat?' He put his hand to his chin. 'Lennox would you get down, I mean the same way that you found Fenshaw.'

'It's covered in powder,' I objected.

'It'll brush off.'

I climbed down, muttering under my breath and lay with my head in the bow.

Swift sighed in exasperation. 'Damn it, it doesn't make sense.'

'Wait a minute.' I noticed something lodged in a gap between planks. It had a faint sheen to it, almost invisible among the fingerprint powder. 'Do you have your magnifying glass, Swift?'

He whipped it out almost before I'd finished the sentence. 'What is it?'

'Here look.' I wet my fingertip and carefully wiped the powder away.

Swift passed me a pair of tweezers. 'Careful,' he said.

I manoeuvred whatever it was and gently extracted it.

We both stared at my palm supporting a small conical piece of what looked like beeswax.

'What is it?' I asked.

'It's a clue,' Swift replied. He placed it in an envelope.

'You'll squash it,' I warned.

'I don't have any jars.'

I raised my brows at him, because he usually seemed to carry an entire detecting kit around with him. Satisfied that at least we'd found something, we set off to cross the damn hill again.

'It looks like an eraser off the end of a pencil,' I remarked.

'They don't make erasers out of wax,' he replied.

'I said it looked like one, not that it was one.'

He shoved his hands in his trench coat pockets. 'Would it be part of the boat? Caulking or something?'

'No, wax wouldn't last a minute, it's far too fragile.'

'Fishing tackle?'

'Same answer as the boat.' I tried to imagine someone pressing the wax into a hollow. 'It's a plug, I'm sure it's the end of something...'

'A glass phial perhaps?' Swift's brow had creased. 'Maybe it was a stopper?'

'That's a good idea,' I said, then had second thoughts. 'But it wouldn't work. It could only be removed by melting the wax or putting a pin in it to pull it out. Either method would have destroyed it.'

'Right,' he agreed. 'And the killer would have carried an oil lantern or a torch. So it can't be dripped from a candle...'

We were approaching the crest of the hill.

'It was made by something like a pipe, but smaller.' I stopped. 'A peashooter, Swift! That's it!'

He looked at me. 'A peashooter...'

'Well, a blowpipe anyway. The killer could have used poison on a small dart.' I grinned, being pretty sure I'd solved it.

'The pathologist would have seen any piercing of the skin.' Swift began walking again.

'A needle then.'

'Even a tiny pinprick leaves a mark, and it would never deliver enough poison to kill a grown man. The dose has to be large enough to kill but small enough to avoid showing up in analysis.'

'Oh.' That put a bit of a dent in my enthusiasm. 'How long does poison last in a body?'

That made him think. 'It varies, some toxins dissipate slowly, like arsenic. Others break down quickly and are undetectable within twenty-four hours or less.'

'The killer placed the bodies where they wouldn't be found immediately.'

He nodded. 'Yes, and the post-mortem would be delayed because of the distance between here and York. So it must be someone local.'

'Doctor Wexford,' I proposed.

'Or Kitty Wexford,' he countered.

'She's not the type.'

'Nonsense,' he retorted.

I let out a sigh. 'Damn it. It could be anyone, Swift.'

We reached the village, I called Fogg to heel as I could see he had his eye on the ducks. There were knots of people in the lanes, the largest knot contained the bean-pole figure of Sergeant Beamish and the much shorter Constable Burrows.

The crowd dispersed on our approach, casting dark glances back at us over their shoulders.

'What was all that about?' Swift asked, as we joined the two policemen.

'We were making house-to-house inquiries,' Beamish was despondent, 'and they all started coming out of their cottages to give us a piece of their minds.'

'Do they think we're interfering?' I asked.

'Aye, they do,' Burrows replied, his grizzled face unperturbed.

'Did you take any statements?' Swift demanded.

'Yes, but it was nothing you could print,' Sergeant Beamish muttered in miserable tones. 'I'll never get to be a detective at this rate.'

CHAPTER 18

We retired to the police station, a relative haven of peace. Both coppers took their helmets off and placed them on the counter next to William the ginger cat, who was asleep on the Records Book.

'I'll put the kettle on.' Burrows went into the kitchen, we could hear him clattering around as we sat on chairs about the fire. William woke up and jumped down to saunter over to join us. Fogg wriggled under my chair to hide.

'Do you have any evidence flasks?' Swift enquired.

'Yes sir.' Beamish went off and came back with half a dozen jars still stuck with handwritten labels for strawberry jam.

Swift extracted the wax plug from the envelope with tweezers and dropped it into a jam jar. Then he opened his wallet and took out the piece of crinkled paper and put that into another one.

He held them both up to show to Beamish. 'We found the wax in Fenshaw's boat and the paper by the ice-house. You missed them both.'

The lad turned red about the ears.

'So did you,' I reminded Swift.

He frowned at me and turned back to the young copper. 'Do either of these mean anything to you?'

Beamish regarded them solemnly then shook his head. 'No, it don't. The paper might be a sweetie wrapper.'

Burrows came in with a tray holding a blue and white teapot, four tin mugs and a plate of biscuits.

'Hold the paper up to the light,' he told Swift.

He took it back out of the jar to let the sunshine filter through.

'Powders. It's used to fold round powder. You can see the folds if you look hard enough.'

We all peered at it. He was right, six straight folds were visible among the random creases.

'What about this?' Swift showed him the plug of wax.

Burrows squinted from under wiry brows. 'It ain't from a gun cartridge.'

'We think it's from a peashooter,' I joined in.

'Blowpipe,' Swift corrected.

'You think they were shot to death with a blowpipe?' Burrows looked dubious.

'No… But the paper held some powder…' I began.

'Poisonous powder!' Swift exclaimed. 'The killer could have blown it into the victims face or mouth.'

'Ah, yes. That's it! Ha! Well done Swift.' I grinned.

'Have a cuppa, sounds like you've earned it.' Burrows handed round tin mugs and biscuits, they were chocolate with nuts and all the tastier for it.

'How would the blowpipe be made?' Swift asked the question.

'Hollowed out bamboo is the best,' I said, having manufactured any number as a boy.

'There's some bamboo sticks in the garden.' Burrows gave Foggy a piece of biscuit. 'Come on doggy, you come along of me and we'll fetch some.'

'I've got talcum powder,' Beamish offered. He went off to some distant bathroom and came back with an enamel tin bearing the name 'Johnson's baby's powder'.

'We need a candle,' Swift told him.

I ate another biscuit.

Burrows returned and arranged the table with one burning candle, four hollowed-out bamboo sticks, each six inches long, and a few heaps of talc on a piece of blotting paper.

I tried sucking up some talc and nearly choked when I got a mouthful.

'If that was poison, you're be dead already,' Swift remarked dryly.

'Well, I've never tried using talc before,' I spluttered, wiping it off my face.

Beamish tried to stuff the powder in his blowpipe a pinch at a time.

'You need a bit of paper,' Burrows told him and produced a cigarette paper. 'Look, you do it like this. Dip the end of the blowpipe into the wax first.' He stoppered the end by prodding it into the liquid wax around the rim of the burning candle. 'Then tip the powder in like this.' He folded the cigarette paper in half, scooped up some talc and dribbled it into his hollow bamboo stick. 'Then you tamp it.'

He tapped it on the table top, let it settle, then closed his lips around the end and blew into it. Nothing happened, so he puffed out his cheeks and blew harder. A blast of talc exploded from the blowpipe straight into Beamish's face.

We all burst out laughing.

Swift retrieved the plug of wax Burrows had blown out. It was very similar in size and shape to the plug we'd found in the boat. He held it in his palm for all to see.

'You could be right, Lennox,' he conceded.

'Maybe he's not as daft as he looks.' Burrows grinned.

'Pass me a cigarette paper,' Swift ordered.

He plugged one end of his blowpipe and poured talc into the other as Burrows had demonstrated. Then he shook it, sending plumes of talc back into the air.

We tried to waft the stuff away but it swirled about to settle on our hair and faces, despite our best efforts.

'Swift why did you do that?' I objected.

'Demonstration. Both ends would have to be stoppered or the killer would risk the powder flying out as he moved.'

'Let me have a go,' Beamish said. He dipped a blowpipe into the candle to stopper it, then filled it with talc. 'Do you have a Swan Vesta?' He asked the old policeman.

'Aye.' Burrows dug a box of matches from his top pocket of his blue uniform and passed it to him.

Beamish placed the end of the match into the soft candle to form a collar of melted wax around the flammable red head. Then he gingerly pushed it into the other end of the blowpipe.

'There.' He grinned and gave it a good shake, the match flew out sending more talc all over the rest of us.

A knock sounded at the door. A postman walked in, complete with black and red uniform, peaked hat, black boots, post sack and a bundle of brown envelopes tied in string. He stopped and looked at us, then he placed the post on the counter, shook his head and went out muttering. 'Daft beggars.'

'Use three matches,' Burrows told Swift, then he went to the kitchen and returned with a damp cloth. 'Best get yourselves wiped off, you can't walk about lookin' like ghosts.'

We cleaned up as best we could and Burrows tidied away the paraphernalia.

'Right, I'm going to write all this down.' Beamish took out a pristine notebook and carefully noted the date, time and location at the top of a blank page. 'So, this murderer made blowpipes and used them to blow poisoned powder into the victims' faces...'

'Yes,' Swift said with an air of confidence.

'Then what?' Beamish was poised over his page, pen in hand. He looked up when Swift didn't answer.

'I...' Swift began.

'Perhaps the poison was strong enough to kill them?' I suggested.

'Why did they both swallow their tongues then?' Beamish asked.

'And you said if it were poison it would show up in the blood,' Burrows added. 'And it didn't.'

'Well, we may not have the full story yet,' Swift admitted.

Doubt crossed their faces. I feared Swift's Scotland Yard kudos may have slipped a notch.

'Did you record Fenshaw's time of death?' I sought to divert attention.

'Doctor Wexford said it was probably around midnight,' Burrows replied.

'You need to establish everyone's whereabouts at the time,' Swift ordered him.

'Does that include all the villagers? Because I've tried that already.' Beamish's enthusiasm showed signs of wilting.

'I reckon it's a waste of time, they don't know the story do they,' the old policeman replied. 'About the book.'

'You heard about that?' That was a surprise.

'Aye, me and Beamish both, but we haven't let on to nobody,' he said.

'Who told you?' Swift demanded.

'Young Kitty. That husband of hers told her about it the day Sir Clarence died,' Burrows replied.

'But why would she tell you?' I asked.

'Because I'm her grandad.'

Swift looked at me, his face falling.

Well, that just added to the complications. *Kick one and they all limp,* the phrase came back to mind.

'The doctor lives on the other side of the hill,' Swift carried on, though I could hear he was shaken. 'I assume the monks provide the villagers' medical care?'

'Aye, it's the Benedictine way.'

'Like in the old days,' I said.

'And Wexford's patients are in York?' Swift was making notes as he spoke. Beamish was doing the same, I noticed he kept peering over Swift's shoulder to see what he'd written.

'That's right.' Burrows put down his empty mug. 'It's Kitty who works in Calderstone village, she looks after the women and babies.'

'Dr Wexford said he came over the hill to the village around eleven o'clock the morning Danton was killed,' I said.

'It was a bit after that,' Burrows replied. 'I saw him the same time as I saw Brother Paul on the river in that boat the monks use.'

'You mean coming from Calderstone Hall?' That made me sit up.

'It was that direction,' Burrows confirmed.

'Are you sure it was him?' Swift leaned in.

'Had his hood up, just like always. You can't mistake him, he looks like Death without his scythe.'

'Yes, he does, doesn't he,' I muttered.

We stood up and left the policemen with instructions to go through the papers they'd brought from Fenshaw's office and make note of anything interesting. Actually Swift told them to do it, I waved goodbye.

Swift was subdued as we made our way towards the pub.

'Burrows is Kitty's grandfather…'

'I don't see him as a murderer, Swift.'

'No, but… Hell.'

'Look, let's just get on with it,' I tried to bolster him up.

'What if the murders are about Kitty's inheritance, not the Codex, or saving the Abbey?' he said.

I didn't reply, just shoved my hands in my pockets.

'And there's a lot of cash sitting in Lawson's safe,' he reminded me. 'With a lot more to come.'

'But does anyone know about it?' I remarked.

'You keep saying everyone hears everything around here,' he reminded me. 'We need to establish the Wexfords whereabouts between eleven and twelve o'clock that day and at midnight last night.'

'Um… actually Kitty was in the village, baby being born or something.' I told him.

'What? How do you know?'

I admitted the conversation I'd had with her before I discovered Fenshaw and the Codex.

'Why didn't you tell me, Lennox?' he asked with a mixture of irritation and disappointment.

'Because I didn't know I was going to find a body!' I knew very well I should have told him, but I was troubled by Kitty, or rather memories of the past.

We arrived at the pub and a welcome dose of reality.

'We're out of food,' Betty called as we entered. 'But if you sit by the fire with your little dog, I'll fetch you both a pint.'

The place was much quieter with only a few elderly locals on a pew near the bar. I assumed everyone had heard about the latest murder, chewed over the details and returned to whatever kept them occupied during the day.

'Is Roche here?' Swift asked, as Betty placed a beer on the circular table.

'He's in his room. He was set fearful by the murder. Said he'd only been talking to Fenshaw yesterday. I'll tell him you're asking for him.' She flashed us a merry grin and went off.

We drank quietly, each with our own thoughts. A log from the fire cracked and split causing a waft of woodsmoke to rise from under the mantle.

'Good day.' Roche almost tiptoed in, clutching his hat.

'Roche,' Swift called to him. 'We want to talk to you.'

CHAPTER 19

'You are an expert in poisons,' Swift began.

'I am an expert in medicinal plants,' Roche corrected, his round face flushed. Betty put a pint in front of him and he sipped it hesitantly.

'But you know more than us, so you can help us in our enquiry.' Swift was in interrogative mood. 'What sort of powdered poison could kill a man?'

'Excuse me?' Roche replied.

Swift sounded exasperated and repeated. 'Powdered poison.'

'You mean the man they found today was poisoned?' Roche pushed his beer away. 'There was talk of a body, and then it was said to be the same man I had spoken to at the legal office. And another lawyer was found dead too.' He looked around then whispered, 'It is the Contessa. I think she will kill me next.'

'No, she won't,' I told him.

'How will you stop her?' he said

'She wants your money, there's no reason to kill you,' I assured him.

'You know this?'

'Yes,' I lied. 'Well, we're pretty certain anyway.'

He didn't look convinced. 'What form was this powder you speak of?'

Swift explained the principle of the blowpipe. He made it sound less dramatic and the little Swiss nodded as he listened.

'A sedative, but very quick.' Roche's pale brows drew together. 'There are very few, but blown into the mouth, you think? Ja, this could be done. The mouth and tongue is designed to absorb particles very quickly, the tongue has many blood vessels and membranes.'

'Where would it come from?' Swift asked.

Roche shrugged. 'Hemlock, Monkshood, Deadly night-shade, these plants grow wild here in the hedgerows. But you must realise they are not so easy to process. The plant must be picked at the right time, the toxin might only be found in the roots, seeds or flowers and some are in all parts.'

'The killer could have used seeds already stored away.' I recalled the saucer of tiny black seeds I'd seen on the windowsill in Brother Paul's pharmacy.

Roche nodded. 'This is quite usual, but you must understand it is not just any person can take a plant and produce a poison powder. They must have knowledge and experience.'

'Or they could access poison already prepared,' Swift interjected.

'This would be more easy,' Roche agreed. 'What was the appearance of the dead?'

'Fenshaw was very pale,' I began. 'His eyes were wide open and the pupils were tiny.'

'And the other death, was he the same?' Roche must have taken a liking to the beer because he began sipping it again.

'His pupils were constricted, but his skin colour was more grey than white,' Swift detailed.

'It could be Devil's Breath,' Roche announced,

'What?' I said.

'This plant in the Cloister, the Angel's Trumpet. It is known as an angel and a devil. Beautiful flowers, very fragrant and robust, but it has been used for thousands of years as a stupefaction. The powder is known as Devil's Breath. Many native Shaman took it to commune with their Gods and it was used to subdue slaves when they were to be buried alive with their dead masters.'

'So it's a sedative?' Swift asked.

Roche thought about it. 'It is more than this, it relaxes the muscles and slows the blood to the brain. Even small doses can produce a state in the sufferer, as if he is under hypnosis. He will be susceptible to suggestion, he will follow orders like a child and when he awakes from his unfortunate stupor, he will remember very little of his ordeal.'

'Good Lord.' I stopped mid-sip to stare at him. 'So the murderer would have blown the powder into the victim's mouth and then told them to go and lie down, and they'd have done it?'

'I have heard such reports of this, yes,' Roche replied. 'It is said in some parts of South America it is used to rob the unwary and they do not even recall they have been robbed, or by whom.'

'Would a shot of powder be enough to kill a victim,' Swift asked.

'I think not,' Roche mused. 'I believe it would take an additional agent to kill them.'

'They both choked on their tongue, lying flat on their back. You say this Devil's Breath is a muscle relaxant...' Swift was thinking.

'Perhaps more poison was used. It could have been dripped into the mouth, or down the victim's nose,' Roche suggested. 'It may have been enough to paralyse the throat and prevent the reflex action of the tongue. Monkshood, or Hemlock would suffice.'

'Would any of these poisons be found in the blood stream?' Swift asked.

Roche hesitated. 'I cannot know this. Many such poisons break down quickly and if there were only a small amount used, then it may not be possible to detect them.'

I thought of something. 'Those crystals, Swift, the ones on Danton's face. The murderer might have wiped the powder off with a wet cloth or handkerchief.'

'And the water droplets froze to ice,' Swift mused.

'Excellent,' Roche beamed, rosy cheeked from the ale he'd been drinking. 'Ha, you would make quite proficient murderers gentlemen. But, you must know where was the powder manufactured.'

'The monks have a pharmacy in the Abbey gardens,' I told him.

Roche brightened in enthusiasm. 'I would very much like to see this.'

'It's locked,' I mentioned because it had been bothering me. 'It was open the first time I went there, but this morning Brother Paul used a key to open it.'

'He must be worried someone might steal poison,' Swift suggested.

'Or he doesn't want us nosing around,' I replied.

Swift thought about it, then returned to questioning Roche. 'Does Devil's Breath have any use in normal medicine?'

'It can be helpful in the case of tremors,' Roche replied, seemingly enjoying himself, 'but it is most commonly used in child birth. The chemical is called scopolamine, which is combined with morphine for a remedy called the Twilight Sleep. In Europe, scopolamine is extracted from Nightshade, which is more available and is a similar in effect to Devil's Breath. Twilight Sleep is given to the mother to find relief from pain, she is not conscious and has no memory of her ordeal. It a very popular method in this modern age.'

'So mid-wives use it,' Swift glanced at me.

'This is so.' Roche nodded.

'How is it applied?' Swift continued.

'By injection, or spray into the mouth or nose. Liquid is most often used,' Roche replied with enthusiasm.

'Liquid would be too risky,' Swift's brow was creased in thought. 'If the victim moved a fraction when the killer blew it out, he could miss the mouth. But powder gets everywhere, it's harder to avoid.'

'Ja.' Roche leaned in and whispered. 'There was a lady in nurses' uniform, she was at the reading. It could be her.'

'Follow the money,' Swift said, almost under his breath.

'Swift, she doesn't want the house, or any part of it.' I put my drink down.

'Lennox, don't be misled by a pair of pretty eyes,' Swift told me.

'I'm not... look I'm going to take Foggy for a walk. I need some fresh air and... well, I need to think, Swift.' I tossed a few shillings on the table and left.

It was perhaps a bit precipitous, but my mind was as heavy as my heart. Fogg ran ahead of me up the hill, I followed with my hands in pockets and my head down, oblivious to where we were going. Dark clouds had massed on the horizon where the green hills gave way to rocky moorland.

I paused at the milestone at the top. Brother Paul's words came back to me about the Mahometan, Iqbal Salim who had been buried up here on Strangers Hill all those centuries ago. I walked around, there wasn't any sign of a grave. The back of the milestone was green with moss, but I could see shadows among the soft mounds. I pulled my penknife from my pocket and scraped the growth away from the stone. Beneath it lay a Latin inscription under a Crusader cross, it seems Iqbal Salim may have been a stranger, but he hadn't been forgotten.

A sudden rumble of thunder brought me back to the present.

Fogg barked and ran toward me, he didn't like storms any more than he liked dead bodies. I picked him up to tuck him under my arm when I noticed a movement on the road at the bottom of the hill. A cloaked figure was walking in the shade of the overhanging trees, I couldn't make out the face, but I recognised the white cap on chestnut locks, it was Kitty Wexford.

I hesitated, then lengthened my stride down the steep hillside. I was almost jogging when I reached the tarmac road and caught her up, only slightly out of breath.

'Oh!' She turned suddenly.

'Greetings.'

She smiled. 'Hello, Heathcliff. You again.'

'Not Heathcliff.' I returned her smile. A thunder clap suddenly broke above our heads, followed by a fork of lightning shooting from massing clouds. I pulled my coat around Fogg's eyes and ears so he wouldn't be frightened.

'We're in for a soaking.' She pulled her hood up.

'It won't last long,' I shouted as the heavens opened. 'But we should find shelter until it's over.'

'The ice-house is the only place around here,' she suddenly grabbed my hand and tugged me into a run.

We pushed the door open. The cold air hit us as we stepped inside the doorway and turned to watch the downpour. The confines of the brick-built space forced us to huddle together.

'We should be up on the moors,' she laughed.

'What on earth for?'

'Wuthering Heights!' She watched me, her face gazing up into mine.

'Good Lord, no.'

That made her giggle. 'And I thought you'd be such a romantic.'

'Well I'm not, that was my mother...' I began then gave it up and gazed back at her.

Her hood had fallen back and she tugged off her soggy cap, letting her hair fall around her shoulders. Her eyes were sparkling with surprise and delight and I suspect mine were too.

'Your poor little dog.' Kitty reached over and ruffled his head. I could feel the touch of her skin.

'He doesn't like storms, actually he's not very brave.' I hugged him closer.

'I would imagine you are brave, though. I heard you were a pilot in the war.'

'Everyone seems to know everything around here.'

Her smile widened. 'Aunty Betty runs the pub, she hears everything that's going on.'

'Does she know who the killer is?'

For some reason that made her laugh. 'If she did, she wouldn't hide it. She's God-fearing, just as most of them are in Calderstone.'

'Except the Calderstones themselves,' I remarked, then remembered she was actually one of them.

Her smile faded.

'We found Danton's body here,' I blurted and her smile vanished altogether. Damn it, I swore to myself, why do I always say the wrong thing. 'I mean... um, well he's been sent away now... to York for a post-mortem...' I stuttered to a halt.

'Yes, my husband had to come and examine the body,' she replied quietly.

'Sorry, I'm not very good at talking to pretty girls.'

That brought a smile back to her lips.

'Do you like being a detective?' she asked as another blast of thunder reverberated around the hilltop.

'I'm not a proper one, Swift's the expert.' I thought that sounded a bit tame. 'We've found quite a few murderers, actually.'

She looked back up at me again, I could see the pupils of her eyes widen, the black lashes forming a fringe, her face pale, her lips pink from the exertion of running. I stopped in confusion and for a few seconds neither of us moved.

She broke the silence. 'Am I a suspect?'

'No, no, not at all…' I lied.

'Since Clarence died, there's been so much gossip. It's a friendly place, and usually so peaceful. This disruption is awful, and… well two people have been murdered and I'm not sure if the villagers really mind very much. Which is a terrible thing to think, because…'

'It seems heartless?' I finished her sentence for her.

'But they're not, they're very kind. It's just, well, it's the first time they've had the chance to own their own homes. Do you understand what that means? To actually own your own home?'

I nodded. 'Yes, of course I understand.'

Her face fell and she looked away. 'If the Contessa, or any stranger got the estate, it could be worse than before.

People have worked for generations and everything is taken from them and squandered by...' She stopped because the Calderstones were actually her own family. 'Anyway, it's unfair. Why should the villagers work to keep rich people in luxury?'

'They're not all like that,' I replied. 'Many landowners work hard to keep their estates alive.' I saw the anger in her face and decided to switch tack. 'I suppose there's a lot of speculation about the culprit?'

'Ha.' Her laugh had a bitter ring. 'My husband's name is being mentioned. He's an outsider, so...'

'Could he have done it?' I asked the question outright.

'Don't be ridiculous. He'd never do such a thing, and he has no reason to.'

'I thought he believes you should claim your inheritance.'

'He believes it is mine by right.' Her brows drew together. My attempt at improving the mood hadn't achieved much.

'What would you do if you inherited Clarence's estate?' I tried a softer tone as rain dripped from the doorway.

'Robert would like to turn the Hall into a tuberculosis sanatorium, and I agree with him. It's a truly wonderful ambition. He's even discussed it with the Abbot, but he thought it should be somewhere near York.' She hesitated. 'Actually, I think he was right. I'm not sure I'm ready for that sort of change to our lives. We came back here to recover from the awfulness of the war, but now I think Robert is missing the buzz of hospital life.'

'You met in the war?'

'Yes we did. He was one of the doctors, I was a nurse. We'd both volunteered. And he was wonderful, I've never met a man so dedicated to helping other people. We fell in love among the blood and the bodies.'

'Can't he find work in a hospital in York, or wherever?' I asked. The rain wasn't quite as heavy as before and Foggy began fidgeting. I put him on the ground. He sat on my feet, leaning against my legs to watch out for squirrels among the dripping branches.

'It's too far away and the hospital in York is fully staffed. So he makes house calls on his patients, but it's mundane and... and so far beneath his abilities. It's such a waste.'

'So he's trying to prove your parentage?'

'Yes.' She sighed. 'Robert argued with Danton and Fenshaw. Neither of them would co-operate, and they wouldn't allow him to submit an objection to the probate proceedings. We can't afford lawyers to fight in court. It has caused terrible rows between us, I... I think he is becoming obsessed with this idea of the sanatorium and my inheritance.' She was clutching her hands together and had turned to gaze beyond the trees and presumably home. My heart sank.

I changed the subject because I wasn't sure if I wanted to hear any more. 'Do you know what Twilight Sleep is?'

That made her look up and smile. 'You're interested in obstetrics, Heathcliff?'

I think I may have reddened. 'No, no, I... I just heard about it, that's all. And I prefer Lennox, not... um.'

She smiled again at my babbling.

'I'm not keen on it,' she replied in a brisk tone. 'It places too much risk on the baby. Most mothers can manage without it.'

'But you have used those drugs? For Twilight Sleep,' I persevered. 'Morphine and scopolamine.'

'Yes, although my husband is the expert, he prescribes it for his dementia patients.'

'Would it have been used here, during the war when the Abbey had the hospital?' I asked.

'Yes, it was used in many places,' she replied. 'It still is.'

The rain had stopped and we paused, neither of us speaking.

'I should go,' Kitty offered a hesitant smile and raised a hand as if to wave or something. I caught it, held it, feeling the warmth of her fingers. For a moment I was back in war-torn France, back with Eloise, her hand in mine...

Foggy barked. I blinked, let Kitty's hand fall and straightened up.

'I... I think he wants his dinner...'

'Yes, poor little dog.' She stepped out of the doorway. 'Goodbye Heathcliff.'

'Goodbye Kitty,' I muttered.

She pulled her hood over her head, gazed back at me once more, then turned and walked quickly away.

CHAPTER 20

Dusk was gathering as I crossed the green. There wasn't a soul to be seen, the only signs of life coming from lamplit windows and the smell of woodsmoke in the air. I entered the Abbey in silence.

'Tobias left a bowl of stew in the oven for you,' Swift was seated at the kitchen table finishing his own meal. 'And there's minced steak for Fogg on the dresser.' He nodded in the direction.

I found the little dog's supper and placed it on the floor for him. 'I'm not hungry,' I said.

Swift gave me a hard stare. 'What happened?'

'Nothing,' I tried not to snap.

'I went back to the station and looked through Fenshaw's papers with Beamish and Burrows.' He withdrew a sheaf of folded pages from his jacket pocket to show me. 'Danton had offered to sell Calderstone Hall to Fenshaw at a knockdown price. There were letters to a building company in London, he was going to have it dismantled.'

That didn't surprise me. 'I heard there was a booming business in selling whole houses to the States nowadays.'

'Or just the stones and slates.'

I sighed, because the greed of man seemed insatiable. 'So, it's proof they were working together.'

'Like a pair of jackals.' he pulled a page from the sheaf. 'There was one proviso to Fenshaw's pay-off.'

'What?'

'He had to ensure all the contents of the Hall that existed on the day of Clarence's death would pass to the Contessa.'

'Including the Codex.' That didn't surprise me either.

'Exactly, and they thought no one could afford to fight a suit in the courts.' He gave a piece of ham to Tubbs, who was sitting on the table again. The little cat patted it with a soft paw until it fell off the table to the floor. He watched over the edge as Foggy ate it.

'They were probably right.' I sat down. 'There's no paperwork to prove Clarence gifted the Codex to the Abbey, nor any independent witnesses. The courts would be sympathetic to the monks, but that's not enough for a legal claim.'

'At least they won't have to worry about Roche,' he remarked wryly.

'Small comfort,' I ran my fingers through my hair and wondered how the Abbey would survive without funds.

'The Contessa sits in this like a spider in the web. Her lawyers were pulling legal strings to outflank other claimants and they were threatening blackmail,' Swift said, folding the papers together and slipping them back in his jacket. 'And now I have proof. We'll interview her tomorrow and confront her with it.' He gave a cool smile, then eyed me more closely. 'Are you all right, Lennox? You should have some food.'

I didn't respond.

'Kitty Wexford,' he guessed.

'No, but...'

'She's a suspect, Lennox, and a distraction.' He tried a mild tone, rather than the usual lecture. 'You need to think about Persi and make up your mind what your feelings are. You shouldn't leave her without an answer.'

'I haven't forgotten. I'm just... just. I can't explain, Swift.'

I got up and went to my bedroom. It was chilly and I chivied up the fire, raking the ashes and tossing a few logs on until it was blazing. Actually, I might have overdone it because I had to move my chair away to avoid being scorched. I felt for the letter in my pocket and pulled it out. The wax blobs had smeared and the impress I'd made with my ring had broken and cracked. Persi was on my mind. Kitty reminded me of Eloise and I was being a bloody fool. I had to forget the past, forget France... and yet... Was I trying to suffocate the loss with a love that was founded in loneliness? When we were in Damascus, Persi had confronted her past with that idiot ex-fiancé of hers – had she been doing the same as me? Were we both grasping at the chance of love, rather than loving each other? What would happen if we jumped into marriage on that basis?

I turned the envelope over in my hands, stared at it, then threw it into the fire. It burned in a flash, bright flames flickered yellow and turned the paper to ash.

Scratching sounded at the door, it was Fogg and Tubbs. They stood on the threshold looking up at me, then came in hesitantly. I picked them both up and held them on my lap as I sat down to stare into the flames.

Ten minutes later, a knock sounded followed by Greggs. He was carrying a tray, he walked in without saying a word and laid it on the desk. Then he took a white cloth off his arm, where he'd been wearing it like some French waiter, and spread it out. He carefully positioned a covered dish, a knife, fork and the usual whatnots, then went to the wardrobe, dug about behind my clothes and brought out a small basket. He extracted a bottle of red wine, a glass and a corkscrew.

'Dinner is served, sir,' he announced as he pulled the cork with a pop.

I sighed. 'Thank you, Greggs.'

It was excellent. There was even a large slice of Italian chocolate cake for pudding and he'd brought a bottle of brandy.

'How went your day, old chap?' I asked as I retired once again to the fireside, snifter in hand.

'Very agreeable, thank you, sir.' He was lighting the oil lamp on the desk and paused to blow out the match. 'I took Marta for an outing in a boat this morning. We went up river to the nearby town, it had a market, and we spent a pleasant hour strolling about the shops. Then we had lunch in a cafe overlooking the river.'

He began humming again as he turned down my bed.

'Don't you think they'd be in mourning, or something?' I mentioned. 'I mean, Clarence is dead and Marta may not have thought much of him, but he was the Contessa's husband.'

'Indeed, sir. It seems the relationship had become more business-like than the usual sort of marriage.'

'Really.' That pricked my attention. 'What sort of business?' I leaned forward and tossed another log on the fire. It flared with a crackle of sparks.

'I believe Lady Mirabella is a collector of antiquarian books, sir.'

'Is she.' That dropped a few pieces of the puzzle in place. 'A collector or a dealer?'

'I do not have that information, sir.' He coughed as though trying to ward off an indiscretion. 'But Marta let slip that the Contessa is angry with the late Sir Clarence.'

'Why?'

'She was not precise, but she said he'd entered a venture without the Contessa's knowledge.' He poured me another brandy.

'Is the book still in your wardrobe?' I lowered my voice, just in case.

'It is, sir.' He hissed in return and moved in the direction of the door, then paused. 'Your reply to the letter, to Miss Persi, sir – I could post it in the morning.'

'No need, Greggs. Really, old man. I'll deal with it.'

He regarded me with hangdog eyes. 'There was a young lady in the village, she had blue eyes, she reminded me of...'

'I know.' I looked away.

'Sir...'

'No,' I cut him off. 'I don't want to talk about it.'

He hovered, then nodded stiffly. 'Very well, sir. Good night.'

I finished my brandy and noticed the wine bottle was empty. Fogg gave a snore from his basket. I was tempted to stagger to bed, but my mind was still unsettled by the day's events and I decided that if I was going to take this detecting business seriously, I should jolly well get on with it. It was a distraction, too, which I felt in need of.

I moved to the desk in front of the curtained window and drew out my notebook, pen in hand. I wrote what I could recall of the day's events, then thought again about the poison powder. Surely the victim would cough and try to spit the stuff out. Would it really act so quickly? Perhaps some landed in their eyes and they staggered around, trying to find a handkerchief. I remembered our experiment at the station, Burrows had proved proficient with the blowdart. Actually, he had grasped the method very quickly.

Constable Burrows was Kitty's grandfather, Betty was his daughter.

Should I add their names to the list of suspects? They'd lost Kitty's mother to the appetites of Edmond Calderstone. They didn't even know where she was buried.

I sighed and added both of their names to my list, then paused – wasn't the object of an investigation to eliminate suspects? If it was, we were doing something wrong. Then I scratched a line through Fenshaw's name. That was one less suspect, although for all the wrong reasons.

Clarence had left the Contessa out of his venture with the Codex. The 'venture' was almost certainly the sale of it to Roche. But why had he paid off his debt to Lawson? He'd paid sums slowly over twenty five years, so why pay off the remainder now? Perhaps because he could afford to? Or was he settling his affairs?

That made me think, and I underlined the words.

I thought of Kitty in the ice-house, considering her words and actions in a more dispassionate manner. There was something missing? A bag, wouldn't she carry a medical bag?

Where was her bag? Did it have medicines in it? Including Twilight Sleep?

Then I thought about the ice-house. It was hidden away, Danton wouldn't know about it unless he'd been told.

Why was Danton in the ice-house? Had he been led there? But he'd driven his car off the road, almost as though to hide it. Was he meeting someone?

I yawned, the brandy fumes were causing my brain to fog. I screwed the lid carefully back on my pen, blotted my notebook, shoved it in the drawer and went to bed.

Mist clouded the windows next morning. Fogg pushed a wet nose in my face and I groaned as the hangover hit. I rolled out of bed and rummaged around for aspirin. I couldn't find any, so gave it up and decided a spot of fresh air would help. Tubbs remained firmly in the covers so I carried Fogg down to the kitchen to find it void of life. I didn't feel like talking anyway and headed for the gardens, intent on nosing around the Pharmacia. I didn't get very far. A procession of cassocked and cowled monks were waiting in a silent queue by the herb beds, the grey mist rendering their forms ghostly. As I watched, they were each handed a gardening tool – rakes, hoes and the like – by Brother Paul who pointed them toward various parts of the garden. He was holding a scythe.

I turned on my heel in the direction of the village. Despite the dismal murk, there were a few people around, greeting each other with a 'how do' and nods of the head. They were walking with intent and I guessed they were off to whatever work occupied their days. A pair of black shire horses attached to a brewery dray stood patiently outside the Calderstone Arms. Betty was paying a handful of coins to a chap who wore a cap and uniform matching the dark blue and gold colours of the dray.

'Right you are, lass,' the delivery driver said. 'I'll be seeing you next fortnight.' He climbed into the seat above the wooden beer barrels. I read the name painted along the side of the cart 'Theakston' and wondered if it would be a cure for a hangover.

'We're closed, my lovely,' Betty called over, then bent down to stroke Foggy. 'But I might rustle something up for you and this little dog of yours.'

I gave her my best grin and followed her into the pub.

Theakston's ale is actually a very good cure for a hangover, so I had two pints with a large plate of bacon, eggs, black pudding, fried bread and sausages. Betty served me at the bar where I perched on a stool.

'Is Roche still here?' I asked, as she wiped counters and whatnots.

'I took him breakfast at six, he said he liked to rise early.'

'He survived the night then.' I ate a large slice of pork sausage.

'Frighted of his own shadow, he is.' She laughed. 'He asked me if we had cheese, I said of course we have cheese, this is Yorkshire. Then he said he wanted it melted with toast so I made him Welsh rarebit. He didn't know what to make of it, but he cleared his plate.'

I laughed with her.

'Does Kitty still keep things here? Her medical bag, for instance?' I tried a nonchalant manner – it didn't fool her for a moment.

'I'll not let you go snooping in her rooms.' She warned. 'She'd not hurt a soul, so don't you be thinking it.'

'No, no, I don't want to snoop... or, or anything,' I replied, horrified at the thought.

'Aye, well she does keep her bag here, it saves carrying it back and forth across the hill,' she admitted.

'How long have you had this pub?' I tried to mollify her.

'Since I took Kitty in. She needed a home and I needed a job.'

'Clarence gave it to you?'

Her smile faded. 'He offered me the lease, it suited us both, what with my husband just passed away.'

'I'm sorry to hear that,' I offered, then changed tack. 'Did Clarence ever say what happened to his brother? Kitty's father, I mean, when they came home after the accident?'

She shook her head, chestnut locks bobbing. 'Clarence wasn't in much state to say anything.'

'What injuries did he have?' I tossed Fogg a piece of toast dipped in egg.

'Ah, now. That's not something I can rightly put into words, me being a clean-spoken woman.'

That raised my brows. 'You mean erm, it was... below the belt?'

'Aye, he was cut off in his prime.'

'Or rather his prime was...'

'The blow was to the nethers.' She was matter of fact. 'Nothing was cut off, but his vitals was badly injured. He recovered his health, though it put paid to his cavorting.'

'So did Clarence spread his favours locally before the injury?'

'No, that was Edmond's game.'

'Did he father any more children here?'

'Not on your nelly. We girls were careful. But my sister...' She sighed. 'She wanted adventure, to go off and see the world and Edmond played on her dreams.' She shook her head. 'He was an evil beggar, I saw him try to shoot a cat once. He missed but he kept on shooting even after it was gone.'

'He sounds like an absolute bounder.'

'He was, and worse.' Her lips compressed in a tight line.

'The accident the brothers had, was it a fight?'

'I wasn't there, so I don't know. Now, I'm telling you this because there's two men dead and I'll not stand by and say nothing. But 'tis in private. So I want your word that you'll keep it to yourself.'

'I promise,' I said. I thought I was doing rather well,

so pushed my luck. 'Your sister's death must have been a bitter blow...'

She leaned forward on the bar. 'My Pa said you was prying into our business. It wasn't me,' she told me firmly.

'He's not supposed to tell anyone,' I objected.

'We're family,' she reminded me. 'And if you weren't such a charmer, I'd be giving you a right flea in your ear.'

'I'm sorry, I'm supposed to be detecting,' I admitted, which made her smile, so I leaned over the counter and gave her a peck on the cheek. She giggled, I think I was a bit lightheaded from the ale, and no-one had called me a charmer before.

Greggs came in as I was leaving.

'Greetings, old chap,' I stopped, surprised to see him at the early hour.

'Good Morning, sir.'

'Plans?' I guessed.

'Miss Betty has agreed to accompany me for a boat ride.'

'Has she? And where is this boat ride off to?'

'I offered to take her to the town, for a stroll around the shops and a light lunch at a cafe overlooking the river.'

'Greggs, wasn't this the same outing you went on yesterday with M...'

'Ahem,' he cut in with a loud cough. 'Sir, discretion!' He hissed and passed me to cross the threshold, removing his bowler hat as he went.

I wandered back to the Abbey, musing that interviewing suspects was a lot nicer over a pint in the pub.

Swift was in the kitchen eating toast and marmalade.

There was a toasting fork by the hearth with crumbs stuck to it.

I raised my brows.

'I'm quite capable of making my own breakfast, Lennox.' He frowned. 'There was a message from Father Ambrose. We've got 48 hours.'

'Good,' I sat on a bench opposite.

'Starting yesterday. Scotland Yard arrive tomorrow morning.'

'Hell,' I ran my hand through my hair, which was a mistake because it brought back the hangover.

'You smell of the pub.'

'I've been investigating,' I lied, then regaled him with the news of Kitty's bag and Clarence's unfortunate impediment.

'Good God, so he lost his ...' He blanched. 'That must have put a spoke in the works.'

'I should think it rendered all spokes defunct.'

'What about his marriage?' Swift turned serious. 'Would he have been able to consummate it?'

'How the devil would I know?' I thought about it. 'If he hadn't been able to rise to the occasion, I suppose it might be grounds to have it nullified.'

'So, even if they were married, it wouldn't stand up in court.' He replied.

'Sounds like it wouldn't stand up anywhere.'

'Right.' He tightened the belt of his trench coat. 'Let's go and question the widow.'

CHAPTER 21

The Contessa was dressed in a proper frock, rather than silk and lace. It was pale blue in the finest wool, stylish, expensive and matched by a scarf holding her hair back from her striking face.

'Sit down,' she told us with ice in her voice.

We perched on the same rickety chairs we'd occupied on our first incursion. Fogg hid behind my feet. Someone had spruced the place up, the thick dust on the mantle and furniture had been swept away. The moth-eaten wolf skin had been replaced by a moth-eaten Aubusson rug.

'You want information,' she stated, the Italian accent subdued.

'We know what happened to Clarence.' Swift moved into the attack. 'His... um, misfortune.'

She was dismissive. 'My husband's misfortune is not news.'

'It would void your marriage,' he continued.

'Prove it,' she opened her handbag to pull out a gold case and slipped a slim cigarette between red lips. She lit it with a matching lighter and blew smoke into the air.

That shut Swift up. She was right, he'd have a hard time proving anything; she could claim Clarence had recovered and fulfilled his marital duties and no-one could refute it.

He tugged out the sheaf of papers the police had found at Fenshaw's. 'You offered Fenshaw this house if he ensured you received the contents on the day your husband died. It specifically names the Codex.'

'Danton drew up those papers, ex-Chief Inspector.' She spoke with smoke streaming from her lips. 'He was the lawyer.'

Swift wasn't backing down. 'Danton and Fenshaw broke their oaths to uphold the law, they weren't acting according to the bequest Clarence made in his last will and testament.'

'I had his last will and testament.' She suddenly blazed. 'I know what was in it. Danton was acting with this 'accordance' and he is dead. And now Fenshaw too. Is this your 'justice'? Both my legal men murdered and my papers stolen and you come here to talk to me about my husband and things you know nothing of.'

Swift wasn't deterred. 'You can't prove the will ever existed. We only have your word for it.'

Her mood changed in an instant. She laughed. 'Oh, *stupidità*. Do your job, policeman, find this murderer and my papers, then you will see how false are your accusations.'

'What did the will say?' I cut in because we weren't getting anywhere.

'It was as I said to you. He left all to me.'

'You can't have the Codex,' I rejoined. 'Roche has a contract.'

'Then he must pay me the monies,' she replied calmly.

'Clarence gifted it to the Abbot on his death bed,' Swift rebounded. 'There are witnesses. No court will overturn that.'

He was bluffing because we both knew it wasn't true.

She gave us an appraising look and stubbed out her cigarette into a crystal dish. 'What do you want, gentlemen?'

Swift reached for his notebook, I stayed him with a hand.

'We want to catch the killer, Mirabella,' I told her in quieter tone.

She regarded me, then gave the faintest nod. 'I hope you do. I want to go home to Italy. I do not like this house or this horrible cold.'

I went over to the fire, knocked out the ash and threw on more logs until it blazed. 'Would you like my coat?'

She smiled and shook her head. 'You are gallant, Major.'

Marta appeared from a curtained doorway. I assumed she must have been there all the time. Mirabella rattled something off in Italian, Marta gave a nod and a stony glance in our direction then went out.

'Contessa…' I prompted her as I leaned back against moulting cushions. 'Would you tell us your story?'

She hesitated, pushing hair away from her face then she shrugged. 'I was just a poor girl once. Does that surprise you?' A smiled curled her lips. 'I have elegance now, but...' She paused, a distant look in her eyes. 'I would run barefoot in the streets of Venice, and I was happy. I had no cares, I was a child playing with other children. There was enough to eat, not much hunger. I had brothers and sisters, six of us, my father was a bookseller. We had a canary in a cage to sing in the sunshine, we had books to read and we had all Venezia for our playground. To me it was riches, I did not think we were poor.'

I watched Mirabella, her movements, the switch from artifice to artless. A vivacious woman who had learned how to use her looks and was now beginning to lose them. I wondered if that was the cause of her desperation; fear of a lonely future, fear of a return to poverty.

Marta returned, she'd tied an apron around her black housekeeper's uniform. She carried a tray with small coffee cups and large slices of chocolate cake. She served us silently. The coffee was strong and bitter. Swift stared at his cake.

'It eez not poison, eez good Torta Pistocchi,' Marta spoke with a thick Italian accent and stood over us, thin arms folded.

'Um delicious, thank you.' I decided that if it were poisoned, chocolate cake was a jolly good way to go.

Swift cleared his plate before turning back to the Contessa. 'When did you meet Clarence?'

'When my husband died,' she said straight faced, then laughed when Swift frowned in confusion. 'My first husband was the Conte Ferranti. He was so mad in love with me,' she continued, her coffee and cake forgotten. 'I was running in the streets, a girl with a dirty face, my dress torn and no shoes to my feet, he spied me from his carriage. I could not see on the inside, but he passed by every day. I thought it would be magnificent to ride in so splendid a carriage, so I smiled and waved, dreaming it was my handsome prince and one day he would come to carry me away. Then, one day, he did. He called on my Papa and asked for my hand. My Papa was speechless with joy. When I saw this Conte was just an old man, I was speechless too, and then I cried.'

She leaned back in her chair, a dreamy look on her face as she relived the past. 'Of course I married him, how could I not? He was a Conte, rich beyond our imaginings, and...' She paused, her face showing tenderness. 'He was kind, he taught me how to be a lady, how to talk, how to dress, and how to understand the world. I fell in love with his library, then his gardens, and then I fell in love with him. He died when I was twenty six, we were married eight years.'

'But how did you meet Clarence?' Swift was keen to crack on, but I wanted to listen; she'd lived a life very different to mine and there was something entrancing about her.

She regarded Swift appraisingly from under black lashes. 'The Conte had children from his dead wife, they did not want me. I fled to our little villa in the countryside at Verona, I took my jewels and a book I had been given by my father. It was a Latin prayer book, you would call it a Book of Hours. It had suffered much damage, this was how he could afford the price of it. Water had entered in and made some pages rotted with mould and others had the colour washed away. It was without value like this. A friend told me Clarence had knowledge of such things, he had a villa in Garda, it is not far from Verona, so I sought out this Englishman. This was how we met. It was long ago, twenty five years. He was so funny, very big and loud. He said he would have my book mended like it should be, and he did.' She smiled in genuine delight.

'How?' Swift asked.

'The monks restored it,' she explained.

Swift glanced at me, more pieces of the puzzle fell into place.

'The monks here at Monks Hood Abbey?' I asked, just to be sure.

'Yes, and I was thankful. I sent what monies I could.' A tendril of long black hair had escaped her scarf, she coiled it around her finger.

'We were told Sir Clarence had brought the Codex here for the monks to mend.' I recalled the conversation with Roche. 'Was this your husband's business, having old manuscripts repaired?'

'Yes, it was to sell them at a good price,' she replied.

'So there was some sort of commercial agreement between Clarence and the Abbey,' Swift stated.

'I do not understand these words 'commercial agree-ment',' she replied with a flash of her eyes. 'Clarence made donations to the Abbey. He helped them, they helped him. Why does this excite you?'

'What did you do with your Book of Hours, Mirabella?' I tried to deflect her anger.

'Clarence said he would sell it for me. In Italy, wives and widows have no rights, I was left with nothing. The Conte's children allowed me to buy the villa in Verona, but I had to sell my jewels and my precious book to pay their price.'

'Where did Clarence sell your book?' Swift asked.

'In London, Danton sold it to a collector.'

'Danton?' I sat up. 'So they were working together.'

'Always,' she replied. 'He knew many rich people in London and Switzerland. They like to own these books, they are beautiful treasures from the past.'

'Were you involved in Clarence and Danton's book dealing?' I watched her, it was hard not to.

'Not when we first married, but I became fascinated by it. I told it to you already, my father had been a bookseller and through him I knew people who owned old manuscripts. When someone wanted to sell, I would discuss with them the price. Then Clarence would take it to the Abbey for making it good and Danton would sell it for profit.'

'You worked together as a team.' Swift was absorbing the details.

Previous conversations swirled through my mind. 'How close were you to James Danton?'

She glanced from below thick lashes, her eyes showed a

brittle glimmer of light. 'He helped me, he said he would always help me. And now he is dead too.'

'I'm sorry, you've lost your husband and now your friend.' I softened my voice. 'Danton must have cared for you.'

'He... he did, when Clarence went to live in Garda, Danton came to see me in Venice. He was... he was kind.' She looked away at Marta, whose face darkened and I swear she flashed a look of warning.

Mirabella and Danton had been lovers, I was certain of it.

'Clarence went to live in Garda.' Swift returned to the subject.

She hesitated, choosing her words carefully. 'After my papa died, we purchased his old house and moved to Venice. It brought me comfort to return to my child-hood home and I had beautiful things to make it ele-gant. Clarence liked it very much too, but then... then we grew apart and he returned to his old villa at Garda.' She looked into the fire. 'I stayed in Venice.'

'When was that?' Swift asked, ever the detective.

'Nearly three years ago,' she replied with a toss of the head.

'And yet you claim he left his estate to you?' I reminded her.

'He loved me. Why would he not?'

I wasn't sure about that, but the rest had a ring of truth to it.

'Why do you call yourself by your first husband's name?' I asked out of curiosity.

'It is an honoured name in Italy. This English title is not understood in my country.'

'Do you know what happened between Clarence and his brother?' Swift was still gathering facts.

'No, it was before I met him. Clarence would not speak of it.'

'The Codex, you found it?' I led her back to the book.

'I did. It is a legend, this book, and I uncovered it.' She became animated, pride in her voice. 'The person who had it was ignorant of history, but he knew it was worth money so he demanded gold. It was a man who had been a soldier, he had bought it, or stolen it, I do not know.' She shrugged. 'I did not have the gold so I sent a message to Clarence. He came immediately. He was willing to pay anything for it.' She lowered her eyes. 'I tried to argue the price with the soldier but Clarence gave him what he asked. It was more than I had ever seen and I think it was all Clarence had. I said it was too much, but he didn't care.' She hesitated. 'He was different, I had not seen him for a long time, he had lost weight, and was not so loud. He had the look of an old man about him.'

'The Codex wasn't badly damaged,' I veered off as something had been playing in the back of my mind.

Swift looked at me. 'Lennox. Why the devil did you...'

'You have seen it?' She broke straight in. 'The Codex?'

I nodded.

'So!' Her anger flared again 'It is not 'lost' as the Abbot told Danton. He has hidden it and you have all lied.'

'It was lost and we found it,' I retaliated. 'And Clarence gave it to Father Ambrose on his death bed, Mirabella.'

'Ha, more lies. All of it is lies. Clarence took the Codex from me and brought it here. I see it all now, he had it planned.'

'What do you mean?' Swift's voice sharpened.

'He came home to die. Did you not know of this?' she blazed. 'Ha! You have learned nothing, you detectives.' She heaped scorn into the word.

'Clarence was dying?' That was a revelation.

'Yes and he said the Codex needed repairs and he was coming here to mend it. But there was no need to mend it. He lied, he was always lying. It was not why he came back, he came back to save himself from God's wrath and he did it at my expense.'

'Did you know he had sold it to Roche?' I asked, calm in the face of her storm.

'No, but this money is mine. It must be given to me.'

Swift's blood was up and he accused her. 'You sent Danton to blackmail the Abbot, didn't you? You threatened to disclose what Clarence had led them into.'

'Swift,' I warned.

'What is this blackmail? How can you talk so? Danton was a legal man, how could he make the blackmail?' she raged. 'Get out.' She suddenly rose to her feet. 'You men, always lying and bullying women because we are weak. I want no more men. Never! Out! Get out,' she yelled at the top of her voice then picked up a vase and threw it at us. I was surprised there were any vases left in the house.

'Contessa!' Swift tried to stand his ground.

I picked Fogg up and grabbed Swift by the trench coat. 'Come on.'

We left. The slamming door reverberating behind us.

'Damn it, she's impossible.'

'No, she isn't, Swift,' I told him as we stalked back over the hill. 'She's frightened and she's reacting like a cornered cat.'

We walked in silence to the top of the hill. Swift spoke first.

'She and Danton had an affair.'

'Yes, although she'll never admit it.'

'Clarence borrowed money from Lawson to buy books and he used the monks to restore them,' Swift said.

'They did more than just restore them.' I recalled the monks working in the Scriptorium.

'Clever,' Swift was striding along with his hands deep in his pockets. 'And now we know the truth that Father Ambrose was so frightened would come to light.'

'Yes, 'ruination' indeed.'

CHAPTER 22

We debated all the way back to the Abbey, going over what the Contessa had told us and how the monks had been inveigled into fraud. The puzzle was clearer, but we couldn't agree on the motive for the murders.

'Lennox,' Swift changed the subject. 'The letter...'

'Swift, I will reply to Persi, there's no need...'

'I meant your cousin Edgar,' he interrupted.

Damn, I'd forgotten about that. 'Yes, sorry. Been a bit distracted. I'll do it as soon as Greggs returns.' We were approaching the pub. 'We could take an early lunch.'

'No.'

'What, why?'

'Lennox we only have until tomorrow morning. The killer could strike again at any time and we have to stop him,' Swift lectured.

'Starving's hardly going to help,' I argued.

'No, we need to see the Abbot.' He turned in the direction of the Abbey.

'And Tobias,' I insisted. 'He's going to tell us what happened in Italy even if I have to shake it out of him.'

He gave me a sideways look.

'Inspector!' A shout made us turn about. The call came from the gateway. 'Inspector.' It was Beamish, fully uniformed and holding his helmet in place as he ran toward us. 'You'd best come quick. That Swiss bloke – he's been attacked.'

We ran, following Beamish and calling out questions. 'Where?'

'Did he survive?'

He tried to answer between breaths. 'Under the trees… in his dressing gown. Look.' Beamish stopped on the edge of the village green under a huge chestnut tree, its branches drooping to the ground.

'What's he doing there?'

A group of people had gathered, Constable Burrows was standing in the centre of the crowd. A small boy held his helmet, the young chap appeared to be standing to attention and taking it very seriously.

'He ain't dead, he's just sleepin'.' Burrows called out when he saw us.

'Are you sure,' Swift replied as the crowd opened up for him.

'Aye, he's breathing. Look for yourself.'

We looked, he was. Roche was lying in the long grass, almost entirely hidden. I could see his chest puffing slowly in and out. He was wearing a dressing gown over his pyjamas, there was white powder on his face and in his brows.

'Roche,' Swift shouted, he knelt down beside the coma-tose Swiss and shook his arm.

'I tried that already,' Burrows told him.

'Have you searched him?' Swift continued.

'I did, there's nothing on him, not no-where,' Burrows replied.

'Roche,' Swift shouted and shook the Swiss again.

'Throw some water over him,' a man called out.

'No,' I shouted. 'We need the evidence.' I turned to Beamish, who was watching over Swift's shoulder. 'Beam-ish you need to scrape the powder off him. It's evidence!'

'Aye, sir! Good idea, sir!' He grinned. 'I'll get a jam jar.' He ran off toward the station.

'Well thought, Lennox,' Swift said.

'I've got some vinegar,' a lady with a shopping basket called out. 'We can put it under his nose.'

'Thank you madam,' Swift replied. 'But we'll wait for the Sergeant to return.' He stood up. 'Who found the body... um, victim, I mean?'

'Me, sir.' The small boy with Burrows' helmet came forward and gave a Boy Scout salute. 'I was walkin' under the trees, looking for duck eggs, sometimes they lay them here, because it's quiet and a good spot to hide out. I'm doin' a school project an' I was going to draw them. Miss Wilkins says I'm good at drawin'.' He gave a shy smile.

'Right,' Swift bent over to regard him. 'And you saw this man lying in the grass here. Was he alone?'

'Aye, he was. I thought he was dead, what with them other blokes being killed off, sir.'

The crowd shuffled closer to hear what was being said. We all looked again at the recumbent Roche. I could see a damp stain where dew had crept up the back of his green dressing gown. The rest of him was entirely dry.

'Betty told me he'd eaten breakfast this morning,' I informed Swift. 'So whatever happened to him was in daylight.'

Murmuring rippled through the crowd. 'Broad daylight' was mentioned a few times.

'Did anyone see anything?' Swift called out, gazing around.

They all looked at one another, but no-one came forward.

'Old Mrs Thomson might have done.' A lady with a head scarf tied under her chin spoke up. 'She can't get out much, her legs have gone, but she likes to sit by the window and watch what's what. Lives right there, she does.' She pointed a finger at a cottage overlooking the spot.

'I know her,' Burrows said. 'I'll go and have a chat.' He took his helmet from the small boy, gave him a penny, and headed off.

'Did anyone see any monks from the monastery this morning?' Swift eyed the crowd.

They shook their heads.

'The Doctor? His wife?'

This produced more chatter, but no information.

'The brewers dray was here,' someone called. '"Twas all I saw.'

'I saw it too,' a number of others said.

'That would have caused a distraction,' Swift said to me. 'But why did Roche leave his room?'

'The washrooms are out the back,' I told him.

'Ah, of course and it's a maze of old outbuildings out there. The killer could have been hiding in one of them.'

'Perhaps they were disturbed,' I speculated.

Beamish returned with a blunt knife and a jam jar and addressed Swift. 'I'll gather the evidence now, shall I, sir?'

'Go ahead, Sergeant,' Swift ordered.

Beamish beamed, his chance to shine had arrived. He knelt down and carefully scraped the white powder from Roche's plump cheeks, brows and chin. Then he shook it into the jam jar. The crowd leaned in, forming a circle, watching every movement.

Beamish stood up, proud as punch. 'Got it, sir.'

'Well done, Sergeant.' Swift nodded, playing his part. 'Prepare to move the body… um, patient.'

'She saw him,' Burrows returned, his grizzled cheeks pink from exertion. 'Said he walked in front of her house just as the church bell struck seven, it was like he was in a dream, then he went and lay down in the grass. Strangest thing she'd ever seen, but she didn't think to tell no-one on account of him being foreign.'

'He was alone then?' Swift checked.

'Aye, just him.'

Roche gave a loud snort and all eyes flew back to him. He gave another, rubbed his nose and opened his eyes.

'Ooh…' He let out a squeak.

'Can you speak?' Swift demanded.

'Oooh,' he repeated and coughed. Then sat up, his mouth opening and closing.

'I don't have it. No-one gave it to me.' Roche suddenly shouted.

'What?' I leaned over him just as Swift did.

'I don't have the Codex, I don't know where it is...' He sounded terrified. 'I don't...'

'Stop,' Swift ordered him. 'Who asked you?'

Roche focused on Swift. 'A voice. Ordering me to tell him where is the book, he said I will die if I do not speak the truth.'

'It was a man?' Swift demanded.

'No. It was not, I think, I... I don't know. Where am I? Aaah.' Roche's eyes widened as he realised he was lying in his nightclothes on the village green surrounded by a group of strangers. A veritable nightmare for the prim Swiss.

'Beamish, Burrows,' Swift ordered, 'take him back to his room. You can question him when he's recovered.'

The coppers took an arm each, hauled Roche to his feet and helped him stagger off. The crowd watched them enter the pub, then gathered into a tight ring to exchange theories on the latest act of melodrama.

Swift and I walked off.

'The killer must have thought someone had stolen the book from Fenshaw's body and sold it to Roche,' Swift concluded.

I didn't answer because I'd just caught sight of my little dog. He was caked in mud with a duck feather in his mouth. He wagged his tail as I cursed under my breath.

We returned to the Abbey, debating our candidate for the killer their motives and cause. We clammed up as we entered the Abbey and went to the kitchen, which was vacant.

'I'll bathe Fogg,' I told Swift.

'I'll find Tobias,' he replied.

It took some time and put us both in a lather, but I cleaned most of the stink off the dog. My mind turned over as I rubbed him down; Clarence's sin involved the Abbey, and we were certain we understood how. But there were other things that didn't make sense, and now the attack on Roche. Things were heating up and we needed to put a stop to it.

I wrapped Fogg in a blanket and carried him downstairs like a rolled sausage to dry before the fire.

Swift and Brother Tobias were already seated at the table. I greeted them and I sat down, opened my notebook and pulled out my pen. 'Fire away, Swift.'

He raised his brows but didn't comment.

'You were in Italy when Edmond died,' Swift began the subject he and I had debated.

'Now look you here. I've sworn to keep my mouth shut and shut it will stay. I've told you enough times and I'm fair sick of this.' There was anger in the big monk's voice and he made to rise from the bench.

Tubbs had been sitting on the table washing his whiskers, he stopped and stared at the monk.

'Don't happen to have anything for Tubbs, do you?' I tried a distraction. 'He hasn't eaten much today.' That was an outright lie.

Brother Tobias eyed me. 'Aye, well if it's for the little 'un. I might have, and a bit of beef for the doggie too.'

He bustled off to the store room and came back with dried beef strips in a bowl for Fogg and a saucer of cream for Tubbs. He bent over, puffing as he did, and placed the treats on the floor.

I closed my notebook and slipped it back into my pocket. I was going to be the 'good copper' this time.

'Was Clarence a hunter?' I asked, recalling the wolf skin from Calderstone Hall.

Tobias sat down on the bench again. 'In his youth, he did no different than the rest of them. Took themselves off on the Grand Tour, visiting foreign places. It was supposed to learn them about culture and history, but they went shooting and hunting instead.' He seemed to calm down. 'One day, when we were in Spain, Clarence shot a bear, but it wasn't a clean shot, he only injured the beast. I was a good tracker and we followed its trail through the forest. Frightening it was – searching for an injured bear. Tis is a dangerous beast and worse if it's been hurt. When we found it, we found two little ones at her side. Clarence said he should shoot the lot because the cubs would die without a mother. I argued with him and in the end he agreed we would bring food and give the mother a chance to recover.' His voice mellowed. 'Every other day we went into that forest with food and left it for her. Three weeks we did it, him and me. The bullet must have lodged somewhere outside her vitals because she got better and the babes survived with her. Clarence didn't shoot nothing else after that.'

'He wasn't all bad then,' Swift remarked in a warmer tone.

'No, he was a fair master.' Brother Tobias gazed into the distance. 'It was his brother, Edmond. He didn't have a good bone in his body. Lived up to the Calderstone name and worse.'

I shifted in my seat. 'He seduced Betty's sister, Katherine?'

'Aye.' Tobias nodded. '*Tighten your knicker-elastic, lass, there's a Calderstone comin' over the hill.* That was the call when we was youngsters. It was in jest, an' a warning too. But Katherine was ripe for adventure, she was a rare girl; head-strong, spirited and a real beauty, just like young Kitty.' He sighed. "Tis a blessing there's nothing of her father in her, because he was the very devil.'

'You and Clarence helped Katherine, just as you'd helped the bear,' I suggested.

Tobias's eyes misted and he wiped a tear away with his sleeve. 'Katherine was in a rare pickle. Edmond had promised her the earth, then run off to Italy after he'd got what he wanted. Clarence and me had just come back here for money. Anyway as soon as we arrived, we knew trouble was brewing. Katherine's belly was blooming, the village was buzzing with talk, the men were threatening to withhold labour in the fields. Clarence said he'd do what he could, but then we heard Katherine had set off on the train. We caught up with her in Paris, she'd already run out of money and was fretted and broke. She wasn't for giving up though, she insisted we carry on, so on we went. It took a week to reach Garda and then we had to take a horse and cart out to the villa – Villa Flora it were called. Poor Katherine was worn to the bone, but it didn't stop her, she was in a right fury. We'd no sooner helped her out of the carriage than she marched straight into the villa looking for Edmond. He ran out of the back door as soon as he set eyes on her.'

'Did she find him?' I asked, leading him along as gently as I could.

'No, it was Clarence who did that. He knew the taverns where Edmond drank. He brought him back and made Edmond get on one knee and propose to her.' He smiled grimly. 'She looked down at him and then slapped him round the face.'

Swift let out a low laugh. 'So they didn't marry?'

Tobias sighed. 'I don't know. Clarence said we should leave them to talk out their differences and we went into the town for supper and a drink. When we got back to the villa, they'd both gone.'

'Where?' I asked.

Tobias shrugged. 'We never saw Katherine again. We searched for them, and we heard that they'd passed through Verona and beyond, but we couldn't find them. So we stayed at the villa and waited for news, then one night Edmond came back. Almost a fortnight had passed, he had the baby wrapped in a cloth. Said we'd better take it home to Calderstone or it would have to go to an orphanage.'

'There was a fight,' I prompted.

He bowed his head. 'Aye, nor was that anything new; they'd fought before. Edmond was drunk, Clarence was raging, asking how he could carry a new born babe and souse himself with brandy at the same time.'

'We know about the injury,' Swift told him. 'Mirabella confirmed it.'

'So she must be his true wife then.' His lips twisted. 'Swords it was. There were a pair above the fireplace. Old-fashion kinds, thin blades, sharp even though they'd not been touched for years. Edmond started it, he pulled one down, the other fell with it, clattering on the tiles. Clarence snatched it up, they slashed at each other, both getting bloodied, flying around the room. It was like something from hell. Two brothers fighting, trying to kill each other, gouging and hacking, they smashed the furniture, the baby was crying. I tried to stop them.' He wiped away a tear. 'They were raging, boiling with fury and hatred, then Edmond ran Clarence through, shoved the sword down into his guts and yelled in triumph.' He stopped suddenly.

'And Clarence killed him.' I finished the sentence for him.

Tobias shook his head. 'I've said too much and I'll not say more.' He went to the fireplace to stir the stew pot bubbling over the flames.

'Brother Tobias.' Swift rose to his feet, ready to march the monk back to the table.

Just then, the large double doors opened and two monks entered. I recognised them as the young men from the Scriptorium. They paused on the threshold, surprise in their eyes, then they both clasped their hands as though in prayer and bowed silently.

'Greetings,' I called but they walked passed us to the blazing fireplace.

'Keep yerselves quiet now,' Brother Tobias told us as he reached into a corner of the hearth. 'You mustn't interrupt the serving of the meal.' He retrieved a long thick rod and handed it to the monks. I assumed this was their daily ritual. The monks placed the rod through the handle of the cauldron, and holding one end each, lifted it from its hook and carried it away through the doors. Tobias opened the bread oven and picked out brown loaves one at time to pile into a basket by the hearth. Then he hefted it and followed the monks out.

CHAPTER 23

We headed for the pub and lunch.

Swift drifted behind, his hands stuffed in his trench coat pockets.

Betty wasn't behind the bar and I remembered Greggs had taken her to town on a boat ride. Damn, I sighed.

'Looking for grub?' Burrows suddenly appeared from below the counter. 'I'll get you a pint apiece.'

'What?' Swift's brows raised.

'He's Betty's father,' I reminded him.

'He's a policeman, he's not supposed to have another job.' Swift turned tetchy.

'He's out of uniform,' I told him as we took our usual table by the fire.

'I only took me jacket off,' Burrows corrected me as he busied about.

'Humph,' Swift's brow suddenly cleared. 'Lennox, that's it! Whoever attacked Roche might have been in normal clothes, not a cassock, or doctor's coat or midwife's uniform. They'd have barely been noticed from a distance.'

'Yes, and it was misty first thing,' I agreed, thinking it feasible.

'Roche is awake.' Burrows deposited two pint pots on the table. 'He's a bit dopey, but he'll survive.'

'Did he tell you anything more?' I asked, noting the excellent head he'd put on the beer.

'Nothing new, he didn't even remember going out to the netty.'

'Netty?' Swift paused over his first sip.

'Toilet,' I told him.

'Ah.' Swift switched back to police mode. 'So he had no idea who attacked him?'

'Nope, all he could talk about was that book and he didn't have it. Then Sergeant Beamish told him to go back to bed and back to bed he went. It's like he's been hypnotised and does whatever he's bid. We left him sleeping like a baby.'

'You searched the area and his rooms?' Swift rattled off questions.

He nodded. 'Didn't find nothin', except in the netty. There was a spot of powder by the door. I reckon that's where he was ambushed. The Sarge has gathered it up and made a note in the records book. He'll be sending everythin' off to York.'

'Was anyone seen in the vicinity?' Swift continued.

'Not as was told to us. I was down in the cellar putting barrels away.' He eyed us. 'Now, are you having dinner? Because it's nice and hot and I can dish your plates up before the crowd comes in.'

'We'll eat now,' I told him.

'Right you are.' He tossed a tea towel across his shoulder and went off.

'You don't even know what it is,' Swift complained.

'Whatever it is, it'll be good,' I told him, and it was.

Liver, bacon, mash and onions piled high, served piping hot. Heaven on a plate.

'We should go and see the Wexfords,' Swift announced as he finished eating.

'About Roche?' I slipped my last morsel of liver to Foggy.

'Yes, but there's something Lennox… something Wexford is hiding. I can't put my finger on it.'

'Like, he might be the killer?'

'Yes, no…' He pushed his cleared plate aside. 'What was he doing while the monks were listening to Clarence's confession?'

'That's a good point,' I agreed. 'Everyone thought he was waiting outside the room, but he could have been anywhere.' I considered it.

'Exactly, and there's something else he hasn't told us.' He drained his beer, stood up and tightened the belt of his trench coat. 'Come on, Lennox.'

I glanced over at Burrows, he was placing pint mugs on the bar, ready for the incoming crowd. I left coins on the table and followed Swift out to hike back over the hill. We were breathless by the time we reached Hark Away House.

'Now you just sit there and wait for the Doctor.' The housekeeper warned us.

I flashed a grin in her direction. 'Promise.'

She simpered. 'And I'll be sure to find the doggie a little treat.'

Fogg's ears perked up and he followed her out, his tail wagging.

Wexford entered, wearing his white doctor's jacket.

'I assume this isn't a medical call.' He manoeuvred around us to take his seat behind the desk.

Swift launched into the attack. 'Were you in the village this morning?'

'No.'

That took the wind out of Swift's sails.

'Clarence came back to Calderstone because he was dying,' I stated.

Wexford kept his head. 'I wasn't his doctor.'

'Who was?' Swift cut in.

'I don't know, someone in Italy, I suppose.' Wexford shrugged.

'You don't seem surprised to hear about Clarence's condition.' I leaned back to watch him.

Swift and I had pushed our chairs away from the desk and Wexford had to turn his head to look at whichever one of us was speaking.

'He told you, didn't he?' Swift continued. 'Before Father Ambrose and the monks arrived.'

Wexford stiffened. 'He mentioned it.'

'He was dying,' I put in. 'He came back to pay his debts, he intended putting his affairs in order before he died but the fall from his horse threw his plans into chaos.'

'So?' Wexford folded his arms.

Swift turned the screw. 'He would have been preparing a new will. He hadn't been back in this country for three years, he hadn't had any other opportunity.'

Wexford paled. 'I...'

'But he didn't mention it to Father Ambrose. Why didn't he?' I cut in. 'It's the obvious thing to do.'

'Because he'd already told you where it was, hadn't he?' Swift accused Wexford. 'And you must have reassured Clarence you'd fetch it.'

Wexford's face gave him away, colour suddenly flushed into his cheeks.

'Where is it?' Swift demanded.

'Tell them, Robert,' Kitty spoke from behind us. I hadn't heard her enter.

We swung around as she walked into the room. Her expression tense, she kept her eyes fixed on her husband as she went to his side.

Wexford slumped in defeat. 'It was for you, my love.'

'It wasn't right, Robert. You know it wasn't,' she told him.

'It was just a letter, it wasn't signed.' Wexford's voice was barely above a whisper.

I felt a sudden surge of sympathy for him. I noticed the way he'd looked up at Kitty when she'd come in. He loved her, it was written all over his face.

'Was it in the strongbox?' Swift softened his tone, he must have seen Wexford's expression too.

'Yes,' Wexford nodded. 'When I arrived I did what I could for Clarence. While I was tending him, he told me he'd returned home to Calderstone to make everything right. I assumed he meant for Kitty. He said he'd written a letter and I should go and find it, it was in the strongbox with a book, he called it the Codex. The Codex had to go to the Abbey for safe keeping, the letter was for Lawson.'

I glanced at Kitty, but she didn't return my gaze. She had her hand on Wexford's shoulder, as though impelling him to the truth.

'You went to search for the letter when you were told to wait outside, didn't you?' Swift stated. 'Did you take the key?'

'No, I was supposed to inform the Abbot that it was there, but I had nothing else to do and was curious. I tried the strongbox lid, it lifted easily, the lock didn't work.' Wexford replied, then stood up, a mix of defiance and defeat in his face. 'I'll get it.'

Kitty followed him out, he came back alone.

'Here.' He handed it to Swift. 'It has no legal standing.'

'Sit down,' Swift ordered and read the contents, then passed it to me. I pushed it into my pocket, I just wanted to leave.

'Come on, Swift.' I turned and walked out.

'Lennox, what was all that about?' We were striding along the tarmac.

'Wexford was wrong in what he did, Swift, but...' I thought of Kitty, the fear and dismay on her face, and on his. 'It was unpleasant, that's all.'

'I told you, detecting can be unpleasant.' Swift had his hands in his pockets, he looked as downcast as I felt. 'You should read the letter, Lennox.'

I withdrew it without a word. It wasn't long. It had been written in a rush, dated a few days before he died.

'*By my hand, Sir Clarence Calderstone, etcetera.*

Lawson, you'd better draft my will, put it into legal lingo. Kitty can't prove anything, no-one can. I wasn't even there when she was born, or when Katherine died. Edmond was, and he was a lying b*stard till the end. But she's one of us, she's one of the blood, God help her. She deserves the Hall and I want you to make sure she gets it. It's a bloody mess, all but ruined, but she's young, she's got time to make something of it.'

'*Tell Mirabella I'm sorry. Tell her I loved her from the moment we met and she'll be the last thought on my mind when the day comes.*

And that day's coming soon, I feel it.

Roche will arrive sometime, he's the Swiss, that's where the money came from. He'll bring more of the same.

I need to make my peace with God, and F. Ambrose. I'm going to give the Codex to him, it will be safe in the Abbey until Roche comes.

If I go before that date, Mirabella will demand it. <u>She mustn't have it.</u> If she gets her hands on it, she'll run, and I know what will happen, Danton will steal it away from her. He can't be trusted and she'll end up broke as always. She has no idea how to handle money, or men come to that, despite what she thinks. Poor girl, I loved her for so long and Danton took her, too. Damn him to Hell.

Use those funds I gave you to set up an annuity, she's to get two hundred sterling a year for life. It doesn't sound much, but she can live comfortably on that.

I've done terrible things, Lawson. Too terrible to write down, may God forgive me.

When Roche turns up, tell him to give the rest of the money to F. Ambrose in exchange for the Codex. Five thousand. That'll see them square, although I doubt he'll ever forgive me.

You know the rest, the villagers get their land, the Brothers get theirs, just the Codex to deal with, then it's done. And so am I.'

I folded it and handed it to Swift.

'When Clarence said 'he will come' I think he meant Danton.' I was trying to make sense of the details.

Swift nodded. 'Yes, and he didn't want Mirabella to have the Codex because he thought Danton would swindle her.'

'We should have questioned Wexford further.' I was feeling very low, for reasons I couldn't determine.

'His motive was obvious.' Swift was more prosaic. 'He wanted to wait to hear if there were other wills and what they contained. And he's right, the letter has no standing.'

'It's the killer's motive we have to determine,' I returned to the subject we'd been debating earlier.

'Danton and Fenshaw were either killed to prevent the Contessa inheriting,' he repeated the discussion. 'Or to keep the Abbot's secret.'

'But the attack on Roche wasn't, was it?' I said.

'No, that was about the Codex.' He stopped to face me, we were on the crest of the hill. 'Lennox.'

'What?'

'I think I know who the killer is.'

'So do I,' I replied and we walked back discussing how and why.

CHAPTER 24

'Dear boys, this is most rash of you. Four o'clock? Here in the monastery? I... I'm not at all sure we should...'

We'd just told him we were going to assemble the suspects at the Abbey.

'Father Ambrose.' I was rattled and not too polite. 'We need somewhere away from prying eyes and ears.' I didn't mention that I wanted somewhere that was also difficult to escape from.

'But, you would like the Contessa to come, too. This is... it's most irregular. We do not encourage women within the walls.'

'The kitchen is secular, though, isn't it?' Swift knew it was because it was part of the guest quarters.

'Yes, but...' Father Ambrose was vainly trying to protest but we'd caught him off guard, having walked through the monastery and into his library unannounced.

We'd already called in at the police station and Swift had given Beamish precise instructions who to round up and where to bring them. The young Sergeant was busy carrying out those orders as we confronted the Abbot.

'We know what Clarence did,' I told him. 'We can discuss it now or at four o'clock.'

'Lennox,' Swift protested at my brutal ultimatum.

I didn't care. I was sick of being lied to, or kept in the dark, anyway.

Father Ambrose shrank in his chair. 'You know? How? How can you know? Oh, dear Lord.' His hand flew to his cheek. 'You won't tell them will you? The scandal would destroy us, it would be the end of everything we have built here.'

'We won't tell anyone,' Swift promised, frowning at me.

I moderated my tone. 'Would you like to tell us how it happened, Father Ambrose? The fraud you were drawn into.'

He struggled with himself for a moment and we waited quietly for him to begin.

'Clarence had brought with him an ancient book, it seems so long ago now, it was an illustrated manuscript in a rather poor state. He asked me if the Brothers could repair it. It was a medieval Book of Hours made by our Benedictine brethren in centuries past.' He gave a wan smile. 'I thought it a great honour to add our hands to theirs. *Ut in omnibus glorificetur Deus,*' he intoned under his breath.

'And he paid you for repairing this old manuscript?' Swift asked.

'It was a donation from the owner, or that's what he told me,' Father Ambrose nodded. 'This is how it began. Clarence would bring manuscripts from the Continent. Psalters, Breviaries, Prayer Books, Hymnals. The Brothers would make the repairs and Clarence said he would return them to their owners. We did not ask for recompense, but a donation was always given.' A look of anguish crossed his face. 'Forgive me, dear boys, this has been such a shock to me and even now...' He took a breath and continued. 'As Clarence brought more books, and money, we were able to rebuild the Abbey.'

'You didn't just repair them, did you?' Swift said.

'You constructed missing sections.' I put in.

The Abbot nodded mutely.

'So they were partly fake,' Swift uttered the damning word.

'And Clarence confessed that he hadn't returned them to their owners, he'd sold them for profit,' I pressed him.

'I didn't realise. It never occurred to me.' The Abbot began rocking slowly.

Poor fellow, I thought. The Abbey should have been a refuge from the sinful world outside and yet sin had still found its way in.

'And Danton knew what Clarence had done,' I concluded.

'We had no idea.' He wiped a tear from his eye. 'I should have told you, but do you know what it would mean to the Brothers? Everything we have achieved, rebuilding the Abbey, teaching our skills to the novices

– our collective work over all these years has been built on… on fraud. Clarence has made a mockery of us and we knew nothing of it. If it became known, we would be disbanded, and our names spoken of in shame. Even the Order would not escape opprobrium and it would be due to my foolishness.'

Silence dropped again as we waited for him to snuffle into a handkerchief. Swift and I had conjectured the truth, but seeing the impact on the old man brought it home to us.

I wondered how much Mirabella knew and thought it probably wasn't very much. This particular sin had been Clarence and Danton's. And I was sure Danton had told Fenshaw, because he wanted to keep him in his pocket.

I stood up. 'Come on, Swift. Father, please forgive my anger.' I gave a bow. 'We will see you at four o'clock.'

'We're sorry for your distress,' Swift added.

We went to Swift's room and debated the duplicity of the sin and other revelations to come. We discussed the evidence, or rather the lack of it, and what Scotland Yard would require for a conviction.

'There isn't an easy way out of this Lennox. We don't have enough to convict the killer.' Swift was in a chair in front of the fire. He'd banked it up and we were stretching our feet toward it. 'We're going to cause a lot of grief,' he warned. 'I'll handle the questioning if you like.'

'No, I…' I hesitated and ran fingers through my hair. 'I can't leave all the unpleasant work to you, Swift. I'll do it.'

'Well, I can step in at any time, just give the word.'

'Yes. Thanks, old man.'

'Four o'clock,' he called as I made for the door.

'Right-ho.' I left him writing something or other. I had wondered why Swift had never seemed keen to unveil the murderers we'd uncovered and realised he was actually quite nervous, the tetchiness a reaction stemming from anxiety.

'And you won't forget the letter will you?' he called.

I mumbled a reply and left.

Greggs was pottering about my room. 'Good afternoon, sir.' He had a soppy smile on his face. 'I trust you have had a pleasant morning.'

'No. Do we have any writing paper, Greggs?'

'Certainly, sir.' He opened a drawer in the desk and passed me a blotter with papers in it. 'I can take it to the post office, I'm sure they will be able to send International mail.'

'It's a telegram to my Cousin Edgar in London, not...' I shut up, sat down and scrawled a couple of lines.

'Edgar, Swift has caseloads of Scotch from Braeburn. It's single malt, first class stuff. Do you know a merchant outlet? Or any of your London clubs looking to buy? Yours etc. Lennox.'

I handed it over and he held it up to his nose to peruse, then folded it, placed in his pocket and left quietly. I remained lost in thought until I heard the chapel bell strike four slow tolls. I thought again of the girl with cornflower blue eyes, then got up and walked out.

CHAPTER 25

I could see the shock in Brother Tobias's face. Brother Paul was less expressive but his eyes darted from Father Ambrose to the crowd filling the kitchen.

A proper chair with arms had been found for the Abbot and he was already seated at the head of the table, facing the huge fireplace. The two monks were either side of him, one on each bench. Roche was awake, although still round-eyed with fear. He was nearest to Tobias. Wexford was next, holding Kitty's hand. She wore a summer frock, he wore a suit. Opposite her, the Contessa in blue, had been ordered to sit down by Constable Burrows, who stood behind her. Swift was scowling, he and Beamish had apparently been trying to keep order. Marta was standing some way from the Contessa, her hands tightly gripped around her handbag. Greggs was next to her, presumably in case of need. That case of need arrived when the door opened and Betty came in. She was the only one smiling and greeted the throng gaily.

'Hello my lovelies,' she called.

A few greetings echoed back as she made her way to stand beside Greggs, whose colour rose the closer she came. She slipped a hand into the crook of his arm, I stifled a grin as he turned puce and Marta leaned around his portly form to glare at her.

'Sit down please,' Swift commanded the room, which gradually fell to a hush. 'Lennox?'

'Sir Clarence Calderstone,' I began and paused as all eyes fixed upon me. I was standing in front of the hearth, not far from the end of the table where Swift and Beamish had placed the meagre collection of evidence.

'Clarence was the only surviving Calderstone and heir to all that remained of the estate.' I took a breath. 'As riches go, it was a modest inheritance weighed down by debt and neglect. There was a villa near Garda in Italy, was it owned or rented by the Calderstones?' I looked around for answers and was met by expressions of wariness, curiosity or just plain hostility.

'They owned it, but it wasn't worth a groat,' Brother Tobias offered a reply, he was sitting with arms crossed over his broad chest.

'Edmond died there,' I stated. 'The brothers fought, it wasn't the first time, but it was the last. Edmond died and Clarence suffered a life threatening injury, it almost killed him and it would have put paid to the Calderstone line if it weren't for Edmond's child.' I heard puzzled murmuring from a few of the assembled, but I wasn't prepared to offer more details. I turned to look at Kitty's pretty face. 'Your mother died giving birth to you in a convent somewhere near Verona. Your father, Edmond had been killed and you were an orphaned baby in a foreign land. Tobias brought you and Clarence home and you were raised by your Aunt, Elizabeth Sykes.' I regarded Betty, she smiled. 'You were given the pub, the Calderstone Arms, as recompense.'

'That I was, and a good job I've made of keeping it ever since,' she replied.

I gave her a quick grin in appreciation of the excellent food and ale. 'Constable Burrows here is your father.'

'Aye, as I told you so,' the policeman replied in an even tone.

'So we have the remaining Calderstone family. Kitty by blood, and her aunt, grandfather and...' I turned on my heel to observe Wexford, 'her husband.'

He raised his eyes. He appeared calm, but a tic flicked in his jaw.

'This is of no interest,' Mirabella's dark eyes flashed in anger. 'Why did you bring me here?'

'Clarence married you, so you are family,' I reminded her. 'You made a claim on his estate and you were involved in his business venture.'

'You know this already,' she retorted sharply.

'Clarence financed the venture, he used this monastery to restore old manuscripts. You had found them and Danton sold them. How much more did you know Mirabella?' I raised my voice in intimidation.

'It was as you said. I told you this, why do you shout?' Uncertainty quivered in her voice.

261

'You knew the books had been restored,' I repeated. 'You knew how it was done.' I was trying to browbeat her, it didn't work.

'I was not selling the books, I hunted them out.' She threw back a sharp retort. '*Stupido*, you ask the same questions when you have already the answers.'

I looked at Swift, he gave an almost imperceptible shake of the head.

'When was the last time you saw Clarence, Mirabella?' I modified my tone.

'When he came to Venice. I had written to him.'

'Because you found the Codex…' I led her along.

'I said so already.' She pulled at a long tress of black hair.

'He was dying,' I said bluntly. 'He knew he was, and he came home to settle his affairs.'

A murmur rose in the room, this was news to most of them.

'Quiet,' Swift called out.

'Mirabella.' I turned back to her. 'What happened after Clarence left you in Venice.'

She shifted in her seat, straightening the blue fabric of her dress. 'He said the book needed to go to the Abbey. It would fetch the best price if it was mended. It would only take a few weeks. I had to agree.' She gave a hollow laugh. 'He would do what he wanted anyway.'

'Why have you never been here before, lass?' Betty leaned in to ask. 'You could have come with him. 'Specially if you knew he was dying.'

'Aye, it's a strange thing to keep you hidden away,' Constable Burrows added.

Mirabella glanced at me, so did the Abbot, worried their secrets may be revealed. It was Tobias who stepped in.

'The master was a secretive man,' he said loudly. 'He always was.'

I paced beside the hearth, the scent of stew and bread in my nostrils, then turned on my heel. 'Clarence came here to settle his affairs,' I repeated, 'and make his peace, but he died on the hunting field leaving chaos behind him. He had already arranged the sale of the Codex to you, hadn't he Roche?'

He jumped as I addressed him. 'Yes,' he squeaked. 'I... I mean to say, he knew I would buy herbal books from him. I am a botanist, it is my life's work. He had been writing to me, he asked what I would pay for the Codex and we made an understanding.'

'Danton wasn't involved?'

'No.' He shook his head.

'You paid Clarence five thousand pounds immediately. When was the other half due?'

'It was to be paid in one month from the time we made the agreement. He said I should come here when the time arrived, but then I heard he died. It was shocking. I had to consult my legal advisor in Geneva and he informed me I should inform the lawyers of my claim. And then I thought I should come, so I did.'

'Mirabella, how did you hear Clarence had died?' I asked.

'Danton wrote to me, he had seen it in a newspaper.'

'It was an announcement in the London Times. I had arranged for it to be posted,' Father Ambrose told us. 'I thought it was the right thing to do.'

'And so the heirs began to gather and the killings with them.' I took a few paces before the fire. 'Everything was at stake, and everyone here had something to gain, or something to hide.' I looked them in the face, one after the other. 'Two men lie dead in a mortuary. One of you killed them.'

That caused a collective gasp, I don't know why, it was hardly a surprise.

'You must find this killer,' Mirabella spoke first. 'The thief who took my papers.'

'Your papers are lost. They would have been destroyed by the murderer,' Swift told her abruptly, then tried to soften the blow. 'I'm sorry.'

Her face fell for a moment before she raised her chin in defiance.

I picked up one of the blowpipes we'd fashioned from the bamboo sticks and showed it around.

'Danton was killed with something similar to this.' They stared at it. 'It was filled with poison powder, and stoppered with wax.' I held up the jam jar with the plug in it, followed by the jar with the paper in it. I didn't bother with the talcum powder, it rather lacked the drama of a dagger or revolver. 'It was used to blow powder in the victim's face.'

'Why use a pipe?' Brother Paul asked. 'Why did they not simply blow it from a paper?'

I hesitated. Had we considered that?

'It would be too risky,' Swift answered for me. 'A draught of air could have blown the powder away before it was used.'

'Right, um exactly,' I agreed. 'More poison was dripped into the victims' throats, the murderer knew how to use poison and how to find it.' I looked around. 'Dr Wexford, Mrs Wexford, Brother Paul,' you have expert knowledge of drugs of all kinds. Burrows, Betty,' I turned toward them. 'You had access to Kitty's medical bag, either of you could have taken the drugs.'

'I've never hurt a fly, my lovely, so don't you go wasting your breath on me.' Betty was unconcerned and appeared to be enjoying the show.

'Burrows,' I regarded him. 'You must have been bitterly angry at the way Katherine had been treated. Your daughter was seduced and discarded by Edmond. You don't know where she died or where she's buried. And now your granddaughter is deprived of her inheritance.'

'Aye,' he replied calmly, 'and if Edmond weren't already dead, I'd have done for him myself.'

A few jaws dropped at that comment, including Sergeant Beamish's.

I had Burrows in my sights. 'Did you kill Danton and Fenshaw to save Kitty's birthright?'

'No,' he replied gruffly. 'We know the way of the world, she was born a girl and out of wedlock. The law don't favour folk like us.'

'Nothing about Kitty's birth was ever proven.' I

watched him, then turned about. 'Brother Tobias said Edmond had proposed to Katherine, but then they disappeared. No-one knew what happened. Or did they, Marta?'

Her hooded eyes suddenly shot wide. 'Do not look to me.'

'You're from Garda. Did you work at the Villa Flora for Edmond and Clarence all those years ago?'

Marta's face froze. Mirabella turned to her and spoke something in Italian, then Tobias leaned forward.

'Marta?' Tobias said, puzzlement in his voice. 'I remember now, the couple who worked for the master had a daughter called Marta.'

'Speak,' Mirabella commanded her.

Marta's eyes glittered beneath hooded lids. 'Si, it is so. My family worked for the Englishmen, but not I. They would not let me go to their villa, not to those *seduttori.*'

I ignored the hum of muttering growing in the room. 'Did your parents know what happened?' I demanded.

She stared back, then gave a jerk of the head. 'Yes. They saw.'

'What did they see?' I stepped closer to her.

She wasn't intimidated, she was almost contemptuous. 'The woman, she was big with the baby, she screamed at Signore Edmond, my mother and father were frightened for her. Clarence left, so they went to help. It took time to make her calm, then Signore Edmond said they wanted to be married but he did not know how. My father knew a Priest in a village near Verona, he could make the arrangement for them, but they had to wait for the time it takes. The law says notices must be shown for two weeks.' She stopped suddenly and rattled a question off in Italian to Mirabella, who gave a sharp reply.

'The word is bans.' Marta carried on. 'The Signore and the woman had to stay in the village for two weeks until bans had been shown in the village square. This is the law, but it was not to happen, the lady had the baby before the two weeks was over.'

'Did the marriage take place?' I demanded as Kitty let out a gasp.

'No, she died as the bambina was born.'

CHAPTER 26

A babble of noise broke as they realised what had been said.

'He was going to marry her…' Kitty paled as she raised her hand to her mouth. Her husband put his arm around her, offering comfort.

'Aye, well, I suppose that was something.' Betty turned to Burrows and the room, then fixed on Marta. 'But you should have said something, 'stead of hiding it. Not nice that ain't, nor is sneaking about behind people's backs.' The simmering tension suddenly broke.

'I? Sneaking? Ha! And you come in this room to put a hand on my man!' Marta's eyes suddenly blazed with fire.

I glanced at Greggs who took a hasty step backwards as the two inamoratas squared up to each other.

'Your man? I'll have you know we've been steppin' out right and proper. Took me to the town, he did, and treated me to lunch.'

'And he did with me.' Marta leaned in and the two ladies faced each other with fingers pointing.

Mirabella rose to Marta's defence and Burrows sat down and took his helmet off. Brother Paul looked on in bemusement, and the ladies let the sparks fly in loud and furious fashion.

Greggs sidled over. 'A drink, sir?'

'Please, Greggs and you'd better have one yourself,' I said above the racket.

He went to the beer barrel and poured a mug of ale. 'Um, may I be excused, sir?'

'No, you may not, Greggs. You reap what you sow and I need you here.'

He sighed, helped himself to a beer and retired to a distant corner.

'Stop. That's enough.' Swift was on his feet. 'Sit down, now!'

Sergeant Beamish was right behind him, whistle at the ready. He blew it, loud and shrill.

'Sit,' Swift yelled again and they did, albeit reluctantly.

Wexford took his chance. He was seething, I could see it in his face. 'My wife has suffered injustice all her life. She's a Calderstone and her rights should be recognised,' he shouted.

Burrows seemed more sorrowful than angry and took out his handkerchief to blow into it. 'All those years, lass, you've lived with that mark against you and your poor mother. Just knowing Edmond was willing to make an honest woman of her would have counted for something.'

Betty wiped away a tear and put her arm around her

father. Kitty watched in silence, her face a picture of shock and confusion.

Mirabella was still wrathful and turned on me. 'You do nothing but attack us. You have given no names, nothing but talk of powder and old stories.'

Brother Paul cut in. 'Madam, we are not finished. There is an accusation of murder to answer.'

'Yes, and it is you,' Mirabella threw the charge at him. 'I saw you on the river that day Danton was killed. You in your black, with hood over your head.'

'I was collecting plants in the shallows,' he defended himself calmly. 'I did not leave the boat.'

'I do not believe you, you are under your Abbot's rule. He told you to kill to save your precious monastery and you did,' Mirabella suddenly blazed at him. 'You killed Danton.' She looked ready to attack.

He didn't flinch. 'I am a man of God, I do not take life.'

Father Ambrose intervened. 'Madam, please desist. We have sworn oaths to protect life and help the suffering, we would never seek to destroy what the Lord has created.'

A rare act of courage from the Abbot almost shut her up. A glare from Betty silenced her altogether.

'Tobias is guilty.' Wexford suddenly spoke, his anger still evident. 'When I was alone with Clarence, he kept saying I must tell Tobias that he hasn't forgotten what he did. You've been hiding something.' He threw the accusation at the monk.

'Why didn't you tell us earlier?' Swift shot back at Wexford. 'Why leave it till now?'

'I didn't want to stir anything up. There's enough bad blood already,' Wexford retorted.

Tobias had shrunk back in his seat, but attention turned to him.

'I'm saying nothing,' he growled.

I stepped forward. 'Brother Tobias, there was something Clarence didn't confess, wasn't there?'

He looked down at his folded arms, his face taut with fury.

I waited but he didn't reply.

'You left Clarence's service after you'd nursed him back to health and joined the monastery to seek redemption. Redemption for what?' I asked.

Still no answer.

'Clarence didn't confess to killing his brother did he?' I continued. 'He was dying, he'd have admitted such a damning sin.'

He returned my gaze with belligerence, but then he sagged. He knew he'd given himself away when he'd told us half the story.

'Father, forgive me,' he turned to the Abbot. 'I killed Edmond. I am guilty of taking a life.' He paused as tears sprang to his eyes. 'I killed him because he was about to kill Clarence. The master had dropped his sword when he was struck and I picked it up. I stabbed Edmond right through his heart, he died straight off.'

The Abbot didn't seem shocked by the admission and I suspect he'd already guessed it too.

'Oh, Tobias, my son. What suffering you have endured.' Father Ambrose took the monk's hand. 'I have always admired your devotion and we know your kindly nature. We would not abandon you, my son.'

'I'm damned, Father,' Tobias wept.

'Misereátur tui omnípotens Deus, et dimíssis peccátis tuis, perdúcat te ad vitam ætérnam.' He put his hand on the old monks shoulder. 'We will endure.'

'Lennox.' Swift came over to me and spoke quietly. 'You need to bring this to an end.'

My shoulders dropped. I'd volunteered to do this, yet I'd been avoiding the final act, dreading it actually.

I glanced at our small collection of evidence on the table, it had helped us understand the method of murder, but not the motive. That had been obscured by secrets and lies.

I watched Wexford. Kitty had taken his hand and was holding it so tightly her knuckles were white. The whole room was rippling with tension.

'Kitty,' I began. 'Where were you this morning at eight o'clock?'

She stared back at me with cornflower blue eyes and my heart lurched, but I had to finish it.

Wexford went into attack. 'Don't involve my wife in this,' he yelled. 'She's spent her life under a cloud. Now the truth has come out and I'm not going to stand by and watch anyone abuse her any longer. Do you hear me? We've had enough.' He stood up, tugging at Kitty's hand, intent on leaving.

'Sit down,' I ordered him.

He glowered at me, then sat back down.

'Kitty, please tell me where you were this morning?' I tried again.

'If you are going to accuse me, then just do it.' Her anger flashed.

'I accuse you,' I said with steel in my voice.

Shock showed in the faces. Wexford again made to rise, Swift stepped forward and put his hand firmly on the doctor's shoulder.

Kitty's face crumpled, she held out a hand as though fending me off. 'It isn't true, why would I kill anyone?'

'For your husband's ambitions,' I replied coldly. 'Your determination to stay here in the village was putting a strain on your marriage. You knew how much he wanted Calderstone Hall, his desire to turn it into a sanatorium. Even if he had been able to prove your birth, the Hall wasn't enough; he needed the funds to turn it into a hospital. You both wanted the money from the Codex.'

'Why the hell shouldn't she?' Wexford couldn't stop himself. 'She's the only Calderstone left, all of it is hers by right.'

I cut him off. 'It was a terrible injustice, wasn't it Kitty? You have paid for your parents' sins your whole life and yet, when recompense finally seemed possible, Danton and Mirabella arrived to snatch it away from you. You stole the Codex then tried to make a deal with Danton and killed him when he refused. You killed Fenshaw because he was working with Danton. You returned the Codex after the will revealed Clarence's estate was to be left to you. You attacked Roche because the Codex had gone missing – you thought someone had stolen it to sell to him.'

'I didn't, I didn't do any of it.' She was crying, tears streaming down her face.

Burrows was growling and ready for a fight. Betty stepped forward, but Swift stopped them both.

Wexford shouted. 'She didn't do anything.'

'She had the chance. She was in the vicinity of both murders,' I shouted back, then at Kitty. 'Were you in the village when Roche was attacked? Were you?'

'Yes, but... but I was with one of my patients... it was...' She stuttered, her eyes wide with fear.

'Kitty.' I moved forward.

She turned to her husband, reaching out to him. 'Robert?'

'Don't say anything, darling. They don't have any evidence,' he warned her.

'Evidence of what?' I turned on him.

'Nothing. There's nothing...' Wexford stood up, kicking against the bench. 'We're leaving, you can't keep us here.'

Beamish stepped in front of him. 'You have to answer the Major's questions, sir.'

'Kitty?' Betty spoke quietly. 'Don't tell me you've done something bad, lass?'

'I didn't. I haven't... Robert.' She turned to him again.

'You had to save your marriage,' I stepped forward, towering over her. 'You knew about the Codex, the letter, you knew it all and you had the means.'

'No,' she shook her head, hands to her face, tears coursing down her cheeks.

'Swift, arrest her.' I ordered.

He moved forward as the room rose to their feet almost as one.

'Robert,' she cried again.

'Are you going to let your wife hang?' I turned on Wexford, he twisted his head this way and that, as though looking for a way out.

'Don't. Stop it.' He held out a hand to ward Swift off.

'It was you, Wexford.' I stated clearly. 'You killed them and you attacked Roche. You were the only one to hear Clarence say he'd come home to die, you stole the letter and you wanted Kitty's inheritance to fund your ambitions. You didn't need the land, but you did need the Codex. You would have your sanatorium and your grand career, even if you had to murder two men for it.'

'No. It wasn't me. I wasn't there! Tell them, Kitty.'

She looked on in desperation. 'Robert... I can't, I can't lie for you.'

I moved in. 'It was you, Wexford. You murdered Danton and Fenshaw and you attacked Roche.'

He blanched; his face gave him away.

Swift reached forward. 'Robert Wexford. I'm arresting you for the murder of James Danton and Stephen Fenshaw.' He turned toward the Sergeant.

Beamish was standing with his mouth open. 'Sir?'

'Handcuffs,' Swift said.

'Aye, sir.' Beamish withdrew a pair of cuffs. 'You'd best come with me, Doctor Wexford.'

Wexford looked stunned, unable to believe what was happening.

Burrows remained frozen. Betty took hold of Kitty who'd buried her head in her arms, sobbing. I could see chaos was about to erupt and walked over to Greggs, hiding in the corner.

'That was rather unpleasant, sir,' he remarked.

'I know, Greggs. Detecting can sometimes be unpleasant.' It was the strategy Swift and I had agreed to force Wexford into the open. I had volunteered to accuse Kitty, but it left me feeling utterly desolate.

'Can we go home now, sir?' he asked.

'Yes, Greggs, we can.'

EPILOGUE

Scotland Yard arrived the next day to take over and we dropped Swift off at York railway station after making statements and other tedious formalities. Greggs and I waved as he disappeared in a hiss of steam and a long blast of the station master's whistle.

Every day for a week I'd written to Persi. I wrote and rewrote the letter until I'd used all the sheets of writing paper and had to send Tommy Jenkins back to the post office for more.

He returned in the late afternoon with a pack of fresh stationery, brandishing an envelope. 'It's a letter for you, sir.' He bounded into my library as I sat at my desk, a glass of whisky at my elbow.

'Is it foreign?' I asked.

'No, sir. It's from London. I reckon it's from Mister Edgar.' He handed the items over, leaving sticky smudges behind.

'Did you take Sally Hastings for an ice-cream?' I'd guessed he had by the residue.

'I did, sir. We had vanilla and chocolate. She said she'd take a bike ride with me if I wanted. So I said I would and we're going to ride all round the lake.' He grinned from ear to ear.

'Homework first,' I reminded him.

'Already done it, sir.' He fidgeted. 'Is there owt else, 'cause she's waitin' outside.'

'No, off you go,' I told him, as I slit open the envelope.

It was brief, written in Edgar's elegant hand.

'Lennox, regarding the Braeburn Scotch. The London clubs are well supplied, but I mentioned it to Montague Morgan, he's big in the liquor trade. He said he'll take whatever Swift can spare.

It's destined for the American market, apparently demand is rocketing. I gave the Braeburns' address to Morgan and he was straight onto it. He's arranging shipping, bonding and all the licensed nonsense. There's a small commission in it for me, so it's a benefit all round.

I recall Swift used to be with the Old Bill, so keep the destination on the QT, there's a good chap. See you at Melrose. Yours etc, Edgar.'

I read it through. It seemed strange that demand in America was rocketing because only last year they'd passed a law prohibiting liquor in all forms. It had seemed an act of collective insanity to me. Perhaps they'd changed their minds.

'Sir,' Greggs entered. 'May I take the evening off? I have received a request from The Players to join them for a gathering at the playhouse. A new production has been decided upon, it is Pygmalion by George Bernard Shaw. I am to play Professor Henry Higgins.' The soppy smile had reappeared on his old phiz.

'I assume you're forgiven then?' I replied dryly.

'It was merely a misunderstanding, sir. As I have explained.'

'Well it's a good bit of casting, old chap,' I congratulated him. 'And would you mention to Cook that I'd like custard with pudding tonight.'

'Yes, sir, and I wish you a very good evening.' He went off with a spring in his step.

I opened the package of writing paper Tommy had handed me and placed the small stack of blank pages on my desk. A light breeze blew in from the open window carrying the scent of cut grass and fragrant roses, I heard a lark sing in the nearby meadow. Tomorrow would be the first of May – the village would hold a parade and dance around the Maypole, then there would be a fete on the green.

My mind caught on the memory of another Mayday. It was in France, the war pounding in the distance, but I was lying on a riverbank with a girl in a cotton dress, her eyes were the colour of cornflowers. I let the memories drift through my mind, the scent of warm grass, the sound of birdsong, the ripple of water and Eloise laughing.

Tubbs jumped up onto the desk, he padded over and rubbed his nose against mine. He was purring, a loud purr for such a small cat. I stared again at the blank sheet of paper, then reached a hand for the bell.

'Sir?' Greggs arrived a little flustered. 'I was about to…'

'Yes. But before you go, Greggs, packing required.'

'Really sir?' He raised his brows. 'Where to?'

'France, Greggs. I'm going to France.'

He insisted on coming, which was a noble act considering the hell we'd been through last time we were there. We left early next morning bound for Croydon airfield. We carried a carpetbag apiece and Fogg, but Tubbs had to stay home. I decided foreign fields were not suitable places for small cats and Tommy had volunteered to take care of him.

'You won't be long, will you, sir?' Tommy called out as Greggs clambered stiffly aboard the Bentley.

I couldn't give him a clear answer. 'As long as it takes,' I told him and swung the car around.

'Hey, wait up,' a voice shouted. It was a uniformed postman, he was waving a letter. 'From Scotland it is. You're gettin' a lot of foreign post, ain't you.'

I took it from him, noting Swift's careful script on the front. 'Scotland's part of the Union,' I remarked.

'You try telling them that,' he replied with a grin.

I forced a smile, then let the engine go and we roared off.

I read Swift's missive on the noisy aeroplane, flying across the channel. It was written in Swift's usual abrupt manner although there was joy in his words.

Lennox, it's a boy! Angus. Seven pounds and four ounces. Mother and son doing well. It was very sudden and earlier than expected, almost as I returned actually. But Angus seems in fine health and has a good pair of lungs on him. I'm a very proud father and husband!

Will you be God parent? We are going to ask Persi too.

We hope you have made your decision one way or the other and contacted her. (Florence has asked me to include her good wishes in this and had more to say on it, but I'm not including that here).

Montague Morgan wrote to us, he wants to buy our whisky – as much as we can supply! Even the Laird is impressed and we're already discussing plans to extend the distillery. It could mean more jobs for our people on the mainland. I am deeply appreciative of this, Lennox, and we want to extend our thanks to you and your cousin Edgar.

I paused reading at that point, wondering if I should mention where the whisky was headed. Then decided Swift's over-developed sensibilities shouldn't be an obstacle to commerce.

Lady M extends her compliments, it seems the outcome of our investigation was to her satisfaction. Scotland Yard have extracted a confession from Wexford. He'd stolen the Codex and arranged to meet Danton in the ice-house. He was proposing a deal, but that was merely a ruse. He murdered him there in much the same way as we deduced. He blew powdered Twilight Sleep into the mouth, using a medical instrument of some sort. Once the tongue had slipped back, he dripped a liquid extract of monkshood through the nostrils to cause paralysis. Fenshaw was despatched the same way.

Wexford exhibited pride in the method, he thought it a perfect murder and pure chance that we stumbled upon it.

The Abbot's secret remains safe. Kitty's birth certificate arrived from Verona, she received it the day after we left. She is free to inherit but has chosen to take only the Hall, the rest is to be distributed as Clarence had planned. The villagers and monks will have their land. Half the funds from the Codex will pass to the Abbey, the remainder will be used to purchase an annuity for Mirabella. She and Marta have returned to Venice. Kitty has promised the Hall will be turned into a Sanatorium, just as Wexford had devised. A Charitable Trust will be established in conjunction with the Abbey, who will act as advisors and have offered financial support.

If only Wexford had sought compromise, although I doubt Danton would have ever agreed. Nor Fenshaw come to that.

Roche works with a pharmaceutical company in Switzerland, that's where he's taken the Codex. Lady M says they'll trawl it for medical recipes and patent the best for commercial use. I can't say I agree with their methods, but at least the knowledge will be returned to the world.

Lennox, I am not adept with words, but Florence and I hope you can find the happiness we have been so blessed with.

Swift & family.

I tucked the letter into my pocket as the aeroplane landed with a bump at Le Bourget.

Greggs clutched Fogg all the way through winding tracks and roads to the airfield where we'd spent the spring of 1918. I'd hired a car, it would have been quicker on a donkey cart, but it got us there. There were signs of progress since the war, homes and churches were in varying states of restoration and some roads showed fresh tarmac. Ruination lay in other areas where death and destruction had run deep. We'd passed farms surrounded by tidy fields and thickly planted crops, then would crest a hill to find abandoned artillery, bunkers, trenches and rusting barbwire.

I didn't stop at our old airfield. It was already a forlorn relic falling to decay. We motored on to the hamlet in the nearby valley then stopped.

We climbed out to hear birds singing from rooftops, cattle in the meadows and the steady hammering of men at work. Greggs put Foggy down, he must have caught our mood as he remained subdued and close to my heels.

'Would some flowers be appropriate, sir?' Greggs crossed the single cart track that led through the straggle of houses.

'Yes, that's an idea.' I spotted cornflowers among the poppies massed along the verge.

We collected a large bunch between us and I held them tightly in my grasp. It wasn't far to the Church and we passed through the gate. Gravestones were set in crooked rows on either side of a grassy track, we walked between them to the furthest section of the graveyard. Heaps of soil the length and breadth of a body lay in tidy rows with wooden crosses at their heads. It took some time to find her name, Eloise LeFranc. The girl with eyes the colour of cornflowers, the girl I had loved with all my heart.

We lay the flowers on her grave, bowed our heads and whispered our prayers. Then we said Goodbye and walked away.

Author's notes

Please don't read or listen to this until you have completed the book.

I wanted to set the Monks Hood Murders in an ancient landscape and where better than Yorkshire? For centuries English rural society consisted of the triumvirate of the Lord of the Manor, the Church and the people. This has been breaking down for centuries, begun by Henry the Eighth in what has become known as the Dissolution of the Monasteries. The landowning lords took much longer to evict, although the process was well under way in the 1920s. Some of the aristocracy were exemplary, making huge sacrifices to hold their estates and communities together. Others, like the Calderstones, were part of the reason the system crumbled.

The old ways have largely gone now, but echoes still exist in quiet corners of England and many of those communities are the better for it.

Many parishes in England have their own Strangers Hill. They were used to bury unknowns who had staggered into the parish and expired. Given the multitude of disease and plague that affected people of the time, it was entirely understandable. Those whose religion was unknown, or could not be buried within the pale, often joined them.

As for methods of murder...

Twilight Sleep was indeed a popular combination drug offered to mothers from the early 1900's until the 1960s. The European version used scopolamine extracted from Deadly Nightshade mixed with Morphine. The drug was primarily prescribed to relieve anxiety and pain and to produce short term amnesia. The mother 'slept' through the birth with no memory of the experience on awakening. There are extensive articles and books on the practise and its effects. It fell out of favour as the desire for natural childbirth gained the ascendant.

Devil's Breath is indeed extracted from Brugmansia, or the Angel's Trumpet Tree. There are apocryphal stories in many newspapers about its abuse in various countries, where it is said to be used as a stupefaction by criminals intend on robbery (or worse). The powder is blown into the victim's mouth to render them docile, in sufficient quantities it will sedate the victim entirely. It is known colloquially as the Zombie drug.

Monkshood, Hemlock, Nightshade and even apple pips are indeed deadly. As are larkspur, foxglove, Daffodil bulbs and many others. Some plant molecules break down quickly in the blood stream and these would have been difficult to detect in the 1920s, if the quantities were sufficiently small. Not so nowadays, methods of modern detection are highly sophisticated. But, as I carried out my research, I have been quite amazed to find how many lethal poisons lurk in our hedgerows.

The tale of the Codex is based on a true story and was related by a Swiss friend. During the Second World War an ancient medical manuscript, much like the Codex, went missing from a renowned monastery in Switzerland. Sometime after the war ended, it mysteriously reappeared in its usual spot in the monastic library. It was shortly followed by a very large donation by a national drug company, a company that went on to release many new medical patents over the following years.

It has been said, by one or two readers, that lawyers strike high in my most murdered victims. I'm not too sure if I agree, and as we have a few in the family, I certainly don't hold them in any aversion.

However, some lawyers enter the business because they seek to use the sword of justice as their own personal sword of attack. And those that live by the sword risk to die by the sword, in a metaphorical sense anyway.

So, what next for Lennox and Swift, Greggs and Tommy, Foggy and Tubbs? And what of Persi – did Lennox go to Egypt?

Of course he did! Good Lord, how could he not. But not before he'd said goodbye to the past; lost loves in war-ravaged times aren't easy to recover from and Lennox had been carrying the grief for far too long.

And however much he'd wanted to hide away in The Manor at Ashton Steeple, he couldn't escape the world forever. So, he's about to take the next step in romance – along with a few mysterious murders along the way.

I do hope you enjoyed this book. If you would like to keep up to date with this series, you can do so on the Karen Menuhin readers page here…

https://karenmenuhin.com/

By signing up you will be updated about latest releases, stories, pics and news, including Mr Fogg, Tubbs and more. It would be great to see you there!

***

Murder at Melrose Court is the first book
in the Heathcliff Lennox series.

The Black Cat Murders is the second book.

The Curse of Braeburn Castle is the third book.

Death in Damascus is the fourth book.

The Monks Hood Murders is the fifth book.

If you like this book, please leave a nice review!!
It really helps.

If you feel there is something amiss, please do get in touch with me at karen@littledogpublishing.com and I'll do all I can to help.

A little about Karen Baugh Menuhin

1920s, Cozy crime, Traditional Detectives, Downton Abbey – I love them!

Along with my family, my dog and my cat.

At 60 I decided to write, I don't know why but suddenly the stories came pouring out, along with the characters. Eccentric Uncles, stalwart butlers, idiosyncratic servants, machinating Countesses, and the hapless Major Heathcliff Lennox.

A whole world built itself upon the page and I just followed along...

An itinerate traveller all my life. I grew up in the military, often on RAF bases but preferring to be in the countryside when we could. I adore whodunnits.

I have two amazing sons – Jonathan and Sam Baugh and their wives, Laura and Wendy, and five grandchildren, Charlie, Joshua, Isabella-Rose, Scarlett and Hugo.

I am married to Krov, my wonderful husband, who is a retired film maker and eldest son of the violinist, Yehudi Menuhin. We live in the Cotswolds.

For more information my address is:
karen@littledogpublishing.com